The Sea Change of Angela Lewes

CYNTHIA PROPPER SETON

The Sea Change
of Angela Lewes

A NOVEL

W · W · NORTON & COMPANY · INC ·

NEW  YORK

for Julia

He could see plainly that she was not herself. That is, he could not see that she was becoming herself and daily casting aside that fictitious self which we assume like a garment with which to appear before the world.

The Awakening, by Kate Chopin

The Sea Change of Angela Lewes

CHAPTER ONE

O_N the still-green grass between the farmhouse and the cottage in the early summer of 1939 there were gathered into a partial circle sufficient lawn chairs for everybody who wanted one, the grandmother sitting in the honored center. It was a women's circle. There were two of her daughters, a daughter-in-law, an unfamiliar cousin, much-removed—and Angela; all grownups but for Angela, wearing their good summer dresses and silk stockings, the aunts in brown-and-white spectator pumps, all but Johanna—and Angela, whose legs were bare and whose feet had sneakers. She stretched those legs boldly beyond the ladylike circumference of her territory, avoided the correcting flick of her mother's eye, and contributed what she regarded as a balanced commentary on the contemporary scene for the assembled relatives so that they might marvel over her advanced state of maturity. They marveled patiently for a while, then returned to their own topics, and the talk crossed back and forth before the grandmother, gently out of respect for her presence, first picked of burrs that would nettle Caroline or might cause Margaret to "start up." Indeed, they were all alert to burrs, all sensitive, except for the much-removed cousin, who, being the outsider, could be philosophical; from inside what was put to the cousin's credit was that she was sweet but not bright.

Angela, once out of focus, became bored immediately, but she did not jump up and go off to root out something livelier, because by staying on she gained points in proof of her maturity. And in her later life when she was drawn backward in time to search out the person of her grandmother, her mind rested upon what was probably a composite memory, or a screened memory, of that composed elderly woman in a Liberty print, sitting on the lawn, superintending by her silent presence the extreme civility of the women.

To Angela her grandmother was old but had not grown older and was never younger. This is a usual way with grandmothers. She had the very shape of the old: vaguely conical, shortish, roundish; and was fortified by a carapace of corset under which it would have been shocking to surmise a live, warm woman's body. Her head was the kind of head, now extinct, that grandmothers must then have had for a hundred years—oval, broad-browed, shiny, lined, with dark hair parted in the middle and drawn back to a soft thick bun—a head painted by Vuillard of his mother, by Degas before a table with flowers, by Cézanne of Mme Cézanne. In fact it is wrong to suggest that Mme Cézanne seriously resembled Angela's view of her grandmother, other than the dark dress (the winter dress) and that air of being removed, unjoined to those who were younger, who were growing older, who did move through time. Mme. Cézanne's eyes looked inward to an unpainted private world in which her soul moved, and nowhere was there a sign of that in this grandmother; and Mme Cézanne had a fine waist, and nowhere was there a sign of that either.

The grandmother's old face wore a glaze of repose with

no clue that she thought thoughts not attributed to her by her granddaughter, and under that head, attached by a white linen collar or a white lace collar, was the solid cone-shape of a nicely trimmed yew, but deciduous, changing with the seasons from dark woolen to navy-blue polka-dot silk to pastel-flowered lawn.

"Tell me about the first time you ever saw Grandma," she had asked her grandfather again and again through all the years of her growing up. "Well, your grandmother was such a beautiful girl," he would answer reliably, "and she had such thick brown wavy hair, such a slim waist, you can't imagine!" No, that was right, Angela could not imagine. To her eyes, the permanent *willing* oldness marked her grandmother apart from all other women, from woman herself. Nonetheless, the image imprinted on her mind this summer day of the oval face and the ample Liberty print coming to lisle-stockinged ankles and white, tied oxford shoes daily polished to a flat grainy whiteness, and the shiny wrinkled hands folded in peace on her lap, the thick gold wedding band, the inlaid locket on the chain because it was a holiday—was the image of a woman of only fifty-nine. One had to remember that she was only fifty-nine to begin to account for the unexpected turn she took. Before the summer ended she disappeared and was never seen by any of them again.

Angela had her grandmother's name, but the old woman had never in her memory been called by it. "Mama" and "Grandma" and "Auntie" and "Mrs. Porter" were what was said when she was wanted. And she had her grandmother's dark hair but was stalky, angular, and concerned whether she was still growing. She would enter Smith in the fall. It was unanticipated that exquisite little Margaret would have borne such a great girl, and Margaret, aristocrat among the Bohemians, would have preferred, had she been able to manage the thing (but it was just, *just* beyond the reach of her authority) to have an exquisite little daughter. Margaret was the daughter-in-law who kept the crushable beige Irish linen uncrushed, Charles's elegant rust-colored wife, the rust running from the palest tinting of the white skin to dark shades of russet on a groomed head. Margaret was forty on that day, which was the Fourth of July, and also, but by inadvertence, it was the holiday sanctified by the scattered Porter family for its annual pilgrimage to Moriches. There it found itself helplessly celebrating the birthday not of the country but of an in-law, or an out-law, which was of course not Margaret's fault. But it was an example of the metaphysical quality of Margaret's authority. Two other things set her above the Porter women: the one was that she had graduated from Barnard with a Phi Beta Kappa key which she was never known to mention, but there was no need, and the other that she used a black onyx cigarette holder with an ease that could have come only from lifelong experience in a previous incarnation. The Porter women, who were literally Bohemian by parentage, and actually Bohemian by airs and graces, were never subdued by Margaret, never recognized their lesserness, never found their places somewhat beneath her.

"I think, Mother," said Margaret to her mother-in-law, "that two of the saplings are not taking and we ought to have the nursery watch them." Somebody else didn't have to "start up" Margaret. Margaret regularly started herself up. The last large thing Father Porter had perpetrated before he'd died that spring was the planting of a double row of maples, fifty-six in all, along the two sides of his two-acre property bordering the road, and having the bill sent to Charles, his older son, Margaret's husband. The hurricane the year before had torn the old trees out of his property with a vicious wrench. Everybody agreed it was heartbreaking, but to spend so much money to put the new trees in when he was already seventy and could not expect to see them grow, and it wasn't his money, and why only maples ("On Elm Street for God sakes. He has no ear," said Theo, the second son, the son with the ear)—all his children found these saplings agitating. But Margaret, the daughter-in-law, who was extremely responsible, and for the whole world and not just the parts she superintended, an intuitive ecologist way before ecology, saw there was no question but that the trees must be replaced. Charles ought not to bear the cost of it alone, but his brother Theodore *would* not contribute, for reasons of principle nobody else honored, or even could make out, and Fanny was in Southern Rhodesia, and Caroline's husband would but *could* not because she wouldn't let him, and Johanna, by her policy of not marrying, thereby relieved the man with whom she lived of the necessity of considering these familial obligations in the first place. That left Charles. That always left Charles.

Margaret let her blue eyes graze along the outlines of Caroline, bulging like the coast of West Africa, a contour in profile turned toward her mother and thus turned away from her sister-in-law. Margaret let her blue eyes skim beyond the green grass between the two houses, grass that was destined to be burnt out for the month of August. "Why don't we sprinkle it, Papa, through August? It looks so ravaged," somebody or other would say, one summer or another. "Nonsense!" was the probable response of this laconic man. This summer, although the grass was still green, it was the carpet of a scene too ravaged to mock. Beneath all those uprooted trees of which no two, it seemed now, might have been the same—was there one maple? Had there been *one* maple?—lay Papa's flat stretch of "property," no longer graced and gentled by the dappled shade, its two houses separated by a hundred yards of frequently burnt lawn, with nothing to be said architecturally or historically for the houses, except that the cottage was weather-beaten shingle, circa 1910. Well, now all of this was laid bare, and pity alone would have you put in the saplings even if you sold up tomorrow. Margaret was for the moment touched with pity for Papa's undraped property. The continent of Africa swelled, shifted, and became Caroline once more, and Margaret's pity faded by Caroline's order.

Caroline's order was to Angela. "It wouldn't be beneath your age and station, Angie, to pitch in and help my boys shuck the corn?" asked her aunt in her hearty strain of strain. But the corn was done and Angela stayed on. Her mother and her aunt Caroline were two antipathetical women.

The two women were linked by marriage and antipathy. They did not recognize the same value system, kept their accounts altogether differently. For Caroline, as an example, Margaret's Angela was the single entry on the credit side; while Margaret recorded Caroline's Bobby, Willie, Annie, Teddy in the little black book of her mind as appalling evidence of irresponsible barnyard fertility. Lovely Margaret, fair and rust and blue-eyed and New Deal Margaret, who accepted as her province the care of the earth, and the oppressed, and English, French, and Russian literature and liberal philosophy, believed that the popularity of copulation was just that, a populist activity of the lower classes, residual. Elevate the lower classes, put them on their feet, stand them upright, advance their *position*, so to speak—that was something, a mission to which one could aspire as an egalitarian in a mobile society.

There was no accounting for Caroline's having impressed Bill Drinkwater into marriage. Bill, that half-elusive, half-bemused, great lumbering walrus of a man, must, alas, have temporarily lost his innate balance at the crucial moment, being overly bemused by the snatching Caroline, thus failing to elude her. They had been married shortly before Margaret was introduced to the family, and the first thing she wondered when she met him was why did he stick it, which is what she wondered the more, the longer she knew him. That he went on to father four children was inconceivable, but they were not inconceivable. That those two giant-sized people would pack themselves into one too-small bed in a too-small room of a peach-flesh decor faintly smelling of the marriage of bleach and Apple Blossom toilet water sent a shudder of revulsion through her for the fate of poor Bill. Why did he stick it? She suffered a moment's knowing, a moment's visualization of that great male body mounting that woman regularly on Saturday night, a necessary functional exercise of the male which Margaret believed to be class-based, and she retreated hastily from the carnal vision. It was entirely distasteful to her, this evidence of the animal appetites, nearly entirely. She brought herself back to the present moment, found Caroline's damp face directly in front of her wearing its hearty expression left over from a story she had told, which Margaret had missed, but which generally depended for its punch upon her eighteen-year-old Bobby's triumph over a predatory, guileful, and all-bad-things female in the junior class.

"Where could they have got Caroline from?" Margaret wondered again and inwardly only (she hoped), winced and shifted.

" 'It's not my place to tell you, Ellie,' I said to her when she called for the *fourth time*," bellowed Caroline into Margaret's now listening ears, " 'but you can't get a man that way. I may be old-fashioned, but there's something in playing hard-to-get.' " She then laughed at her own great way with modern jargon, and Margaret thought the tremor that shot through her own body must have been visible.

Now Bill was moving along her line of vision, loping casually toward them in white ducks and a tennis shirt with little Teddy making a wriggling mantle for his left shoulder, those long skinny little legs no testimony, Margaret thought, to the arch-mother Caroline made herself out to be. Why did Bill stick it? She put her reflections in sociological order and said to herself that Bill, coming as he did from working-class people, *nonverbal* working-class people, had not had deposited in him the *expectation* that marriage must be justified on some kind of esthetic level. So in the early years as Caroline gave herself over ever more fiercely to motherhood and found in Bill's reserve, his noninvolvement, his inviolate autonomy, his *silence*, an increasing source of her own bitterness and dissatisfaction, Bill was no doubt grieved by the way things had turned out, but he wasn't *disillusioned*, since he hadn't been led by romantic, middle-class sanguinity to suppose that deep, mutual caring was what characterized the average marriage. He wasn't disillusioned. Nobody had betrayed him. Roughly speaking, he stood by the social contract, played paterfamilias, accepted philosophically the broad outlines of his fate designed by Caroline, but the elusive self was always *not there*. He eluded Caroline, and it infuriated her. She tried to reduce him to an obedient child, one of her brood, and this infuriated him. But the gears that kept them meshed were not only mechanical, as you could see by the gentle way he stooped over her to let Teddy slide into her lap.

"You like to come to Grandma?" asked Mrs. Porter in a quiet, beckoning voice, reaching her ringed hand across to pat his bottom. But Teddy burrowed his head into his mother's lap, and his mother's fingers ruffled his hair, and his father's hand rested on his mother's head for a moment, and his father said it was probably time to put the corn on.

Margaret watched this brother-in-law who was so dear to her and thought, no, it is not all negative. Statistically speaking, you would have to record theirs under Happy

Marriage. Margaret believed in the Science of Social Improvement and the statistics that recorded its progress, although her confidence in statistics had been shaken several times of late. And perhaps, in an effort to shore up the truth of statistics, the impartial weighing implied by statistics, the right conclusions they proved—in this case, evidence of a Happy Marriage—she turned her mind against dear Bill, to even things up a bit, and said to herself, yes, outside the reach of Caroline's domain he is a loved man, loved by men, and very attractive to women, and seeming to be infinitely kind: but he has not been this to his wife. He has not been kind to her.

And she said out loud, "Come Bill, I'll do the corn with you," and knew Caroline's jaw clenched, and then, courteously, "Mother, do you think we'll need that big blue enamel pot from the farmhouse?"

"I think you'll need that. Oh, surely I think you'll need that." And the old lady pursed her lips, and she nodded her head slowly and wisely up and down, and her hands remained folded and quiet, and it was as if she were eighty-nine and not fifty-nine and her judgment about the blue enamel pot were drawn from her priceless store of traditional wisdom.

The seventeen-year-old Angela never knew more of her grandmother than that, that she was the household god or the resident ancestor or an ancient urn of earthenware set by the hearth, her very figure being urnish, and you went to her to draw out the right thing about corn-pots and roasting duck and making bread and jam sandwiches; and you found all these things out before she died, and the secrets died with her. Around and around this Victorian head went talk about the League of Women Voters, or the Arms Embargo, or experiments in surgical grafting of tissues (Bill was a professor of anatomy), or the interpretation of the Clear and Present Danger ruling (the Charles Porters were in the law), and always elegant references to Broadway theater people, and it all seemed to form a nimbus to that nineteenth-century oval head. Impassive, pleasant, holding her pose for Degas or Vuillard, she would occasionally cut through the surgical details, bypass international agreements, with an observation like, "Margaret, don't you think Charles had better go over for the pastry? Mrs. Swanson runs out on the holidays very early."

"He's already got it, Mother." Smiling and nodding on both sides, Margaret's nod making a notch on the log she kept in her head, which proved that, invariably, and she meant invariably, when something had to be done *and* paid for, Charles was asked to do it.

The high-flown references to the theater, always a family subject, were really a tribute to the star of the Porter repertory, to Johanna, or Jo, that last unanticipated child, coming twelve years after the others, now twenty-six, who mostly entitled the Porters to the Bohemian label. Who bore her, who honed her, shaped her, reared her, this very tall angular beauty who was Angela's idol, and not Angela's alone? There she sat very quiet, very kind, folded by two bends of the body into the wooden deck chair, seeming to Angela like a young Renaissance prince because of the long black-brown bob, and the bangs swept crossways over a very high brow, and because the end of her nose turned up to form a little plateau, a modified version of Lorenzo de' Medici's nose, which gave her beauty uncommon interest. Her very pale blue eyes were often half-lidded. Her mouth was a generous mouth as her soul was a generous soul. She had been an actress who was regularly employed in small supporting parts on Broadway but had now turned to play-writing and was working and living with yet another celebrated somebody associated with the theater world. The nonconformity of Jo's style of living had never been registered or acknowledged by her father or her mother, her remote parentage. They registered her legitimacy as an actress, her little successes, and were several times taken by her brother Theo to see her in a play when the part was long enough to warrant the excursion.

There was Jo, having got up now, and walked off to where Angela's mother and her Uncle Bill were by the open fire, Jo bending her head and neck to form a lovely crooked arch and looking with attention at whoever was saying something; Jo, listening and rarely talking and never standing up straight, a most ungirdled woman in a most girdled era, over whose long limbs rich silks rested, swayed, shifted. Angela longed to be listened to by Jo and prepared very deep monologues through the daydreaming parts of her life, for delivery on the next occasion when they might meet.

And then there they would be, Jo greeting her, Angela, so warmly, sliding her long arm around her shoulders, pulling her towards her with a hug, and saying, "How are you, honey?" really interested. "Now, I want you to tell me you're really all right, Ange, is that true?" and Angela, all the wires disconnected, all the plugs pulled out, throwing her immense stored-up passion into, "Fine!" (long pause) "I'm fine, Jo!" (Fine! What a travesty, what a travesty.)

Caroline regularly registered her opinion of this youngest sister, namely: "How can she expect to be a success on the stage when she doesn't stand up straight?" Caroline, even Caroline, liked Jo and wished vaguely she would stand up straight and succeed. But she wouldn't and she didn't in Caroline's view. For almost everybody else, in the family and out, Jo emanated success and riches of intellectual and esthetic quality, even though it was difficult to trace the cause of this success to much that Jo actually ever did.

Angela broke her restraint, having to be where Jo was, popped out of her chair, kissed her grandmother on the forehead, took a short quick tour beneath the enfilade of unimpressive saplings, loving them wildly, loving the memory of her grandfather for his stubbornness (plenty of material there), loving her mother for championing the trees, her father for paying for them, her Uncle Bill for wanting to. She let her head swivel and her eyes caress all her large family, the little ones by the open fire, Aunt Caroline and the odd cousin and Grandma, left alone in their chairs, every one of them she loved, root and branch. It was probable, her mother had once explained to her, that she had these bursts of love for her relatives because she had to be with them so rarely.

↗↗↗↗↗↗↗↗↗ CHAPTER TWO *↗↗↗↗↗↗↗↗↗*

*T*HEO, the second son, was thirty-nine
that summer before the '39 war, and when he died in 1960
at Angela's home in Massachusetts, he was as unknowable to
her as he was issueless. She might try to know him through
his two unpublished novels and a scattering of short stories.
She tried, but she never could. He had not married, had not
even been known to be interested in a woman (or, it seems
one would have to say today, a man), and had eked out the
sparse income from writing by newspaper work. He had
lived in many parts of the country, kept in touch with the
family, and, when the effort to live began to peter out in
him, he came back to the family, to Angela's branch, to die.
Of what did he die? Of cancer. But it sometimes seems that
the body will be host to this cancer when the soul has had
enough of mortality. Sometimes people fail to live. When the
elder William James lost his wife that is what he seems to
have done. It may be a quite common thing. Angela, for the
weeks that Theo was expiring in an upstairs bedroom, was on
the very verge of a conscious new awareness of herself that
made her look back upon her uncle's slipping off in her own

house, through her own hands, in astonishment that she did not detain him long enough to ask, "What was your mother like? I want to know what kind of person my grandmother was. And my grandfather?" But she had been on the unaware side of the very verge of awareness. It didn't occur to her to stay for a moment his intention to die.

The grandfather she remembered was among the dwindling band of elderly autocrats who still retained some arbitrary power over a family constituency, but it was a breed that did not survive World War II. In the actual case of old Adam Porter, he really had no power, arbitrary or otherwise, over anybody, but he had the gestures and language of a Victorian patiarch, the freedom from self-doubt of a character drawn by Dickens, like Mr. Dombey; and he ordered people about in a peremptory way, and people obeyed his orders, possibly often because they were amused to indulge him, or, in the case of his children, they kept out of earshot, ignored him, but paid his bills. He was arbitrary, righteous, self-important, intrusive in the grand manner. He was a beguilingly engaging man, and Angela had adored him.

"Your father is so charming!" people would exclaim to any one of his five children, but his children assured these people that they were not charmed.

The farmhouse was a royal, earthy preserve for the child Angela, but she could see, as she grew older, that living there in some role other than the fairy princess, which was hers, would cultivate all the instincts to flee and be freed. All five of the Porter children seemed to have taken a running jump through their adolescence and leapt to their freedom prematurely, before they'd finished school or before they were married; each landed on his feet. A miracle, Angela thought, even if you measured their chances of survival by the physical obstacles alone in that house. Her grandfather was patriarch *and* patriot. Early on the morning of every national holiday he had lugged a long flagpole from the dark part of the hall by the stairs and raised it on the front lawn and run the flag up. All the other days of the year the pole stuck out no more than perhaps three inches into what constituted a heavily-trafficked route to the second floor. It is true that only transients could be certain to stub the toe, buckle at the knee, catch onto the newel post so as not to sprawl on the face. (Although they were warned, "You've got to watch for the flagpole sticking out on the floor by the stairs." They remembered the first time.) This accident never happened to the residents. The will to live propels children past many of the obstacles to survival set up by the mother and the father—this in any family, the obstacles usually being only psychological and not physical, but in the Porter family, both. So the children must have skirted the physical in the Pavlovian manner, but in fact on that day that Theo did *not* skirt the tip of the flagpole, on the summer day in his nineteenth year that Theo tripped over it, hooked himself onto the stair rail, cracking his forehead against the polished dark wood ball of the post, on that day, as the legend had it, he pulled himself slowly upright, slowly together, wits and all, proceeded to mount the stairs, packed up, and left for good. Mama cried for days. Papa growled good riddance. One thing that did not happen as a consequence was the removal of the flagpole. Angela fell over it regularly through her childhood, came home to her own mother and father having had a wonderful holiday and with just a scab on her knee, nothing at all.

Theo had left his job in Denver, not merely to attend his father's funeral that May of '39 but to take up his old room in the farmhouse, lay out his writing things, and thereby be the solution to what to do about Mama, who shouldn't be left alone. There they lived together along two parallel lines for the few months until Mama decamped. Upstairs Theo was at work on his second novel. He was then a wiry man approaching forty with a somewhat yellow cast to his face, a suggestion taking color from the sight of him with a wet-ended cigarette stuck from a corner of his mouth, the smoke traveling along the side of his lean cheek, rounding his ear, and blending with his sandy hair. His fingers were stained by the nicotine. Night and day he was at his big worktable in his white shirt with the neck open and the sleeves rolled, breaking to sleep and eat according to his own cyclical needs, and, when his mother would call upstairs to ask about supper, he would tell her in his gentle drawl not to worry about him, that he'd come down to get something when he was hungry. Upstairs, he was, and downstairs, meanwhile, she was thought to be living out an expected mourning period, Theo providing her with security and with necessary little tasks, like airing out his smoky room and changing his linens and cooking their meals; but she wasn't doing any of this. The mother and the son lived on two levels, literally two levels, with, as far as was ever known, amiable absence of interest and attention the one in the other, and the barest minimum of mutual needs was attended to by the one as by the other. Irregularly Theo drove down to the post office and stopped at the grocery store and the butcher's. His mother, it was later surmised, did cook. ("Yes, she cooked! We didn't eat raw meat!" was the evidence Theo offered.)

The Drinkwaters with all the children drove out every Sunday during this late spring and found Mama tidy, trim, composed. Theo would descend to greet them, amble off to the empty cottage with Bill for a couple of drinks; and Bill never had a clue that Theo was concerned about his mother. Theo wasn't concerned about his mother.

And in the farmhouse—it was predictable—Caroline would be cheering this mother with an unending plot-free tale of her succeeding children and her defaulting husband.

The only question about that spring that later came to trouble Caroline's mind was that food was moulding in the refrigerator. Caroline would have brought the lunch, and, when she was putting the leftovers away, she'd find bowls with peas or pudding that evidently remained untouched from week to week. It was not like her mother to let such a thing happen. But to the extent that doors weren't opened —and Caroline was not one to open other people's doors— the outside of things seemed in the usual order, and her mother, in actual fact, looked very well.

The Drinkwaters would leave, and Theo and his mother would stand on the lawn by the kitchen stoop and wave them off, and then the two would go back into the farm-house, and the son would return to his stratum above, the mother to hers below, each absorbed in an exclusionary fantasy that kept their interests as effectively unconnected one from the other as if they had been fossils deposited by different geological ages. A few years later Johanna wrote a play set on two floors of a farmhouse with the son in the room above, the mother beneath, the stage set like Ibsen's *John Gabriel Borkman;* but it failed, for, while Borkman and his wife each seemed to be haunted by the proximity of the other, Theo and his mother seemed not. Jo laid out the two lives as she laid out her two hands before her—on the one hand, on the other hand—but she couldn't bring them to clasp.

Angela could recall very little of the stir that arose from her grandmother's defection. It was thought, at the time, un-seemly for the subject to be aired in front of the young, and, meanwhile, the dust rising from her preparation for college mixed with the other dust; the event was cloudy, unspecific, indistinct. She did not notice the transition of the Porter family profile from the pyramidal, with the old father and mother at the top—the whole resting on two unremarkable acres of East Moriches, Long Island—to a latitudinal line of peers, loosely strung out, and tending, as regards the pull of the Old Homestead and Kinship Ties, to be centrifugal. Only after she herself was married and had her own children did bits and pieces of that summer begin to fall into place. Twenty years after that summer, on the death of her uncle Theodore, the letter her grandmother left on the white enamel kitchen table for him fell into her possession:

> East Moriches
> Aug. 29/39

My dear Son;

Over and over I have tried to think what is right to say to You, but have failed to do so, and have destroied many letters before the where finished. Even now I don't know how to go on because I Know you and the other Children will be greatly astonished at my decision that I will take this trip of an uncertain Destination. However I will most assuredly write to you when I have an address. I will not be alone.

It will be strange to you if I say that during the years that you were finding your Way in life, underneath in my Soul I was finding my way also.

I have thought that to expres myself in writing English is so hard for me that I will wait hoping that some day we will all be together when we can talk in Understanding.

With Gods Blessing and much
Love to all of you
Mother

For Theodore Porter
It is my will that you have the property.

> Angelina Porter

Three days passed between the writing of this letter and Theo's move to bring its existence to the attention of somebody else. Theo had failed to be alarmed. Jo, who later became one of Angela's dearest women friends, was very like her brother Theo in this: that is, they were alarmed daily by *political* decisions; they were emotionally torn and clawed by the choices of senators, presidents, generals. They were unalarmed by private choices. Jo saw the three days from Theo's point of view.

"Well now, the first day, Theo's 'unalarm' passed by inadvertence because he went right by that table on his way off to somewhere and didn't notice the letter, and when he came back it was dark, and he assumed Mama was asleep. So you could say that plain chance intervened, you know, to cause a stasis of action-reaction for twenty-four hours, and, by the time he read the letter, he knew that she was a full day on her way. It made a difference."

"But he would have said, 'So be it,' anyway?" Angela wondered. Theo's reaction time on this occasion had so shocked her own father and mother for its being both unreasonable and irresponsible that his name for years after stood as an irritating reminder to Margaret—especially—of the persistence of widespread unreason quite regardless of education and the improvement of the social environment. For Margaret, at the time, Theo was a living rebuke to the Belief in Progress, a rebuke she was related to by marriage, and her bitterness about him only slowly dissolved.

"Why yes, he would have said, 'So be it,'" Jo agreed, paused, reconstructed the next scene. "Why, he'd read the letter again and shuffle around and go back up to his typewriter and work some. Then he'd pull the letter out again. And all the time his mind was settling what to do next. He wouldn't have wanted to call your father."

"If he had called my father, they might have reached her before the boat sailed and stopped the metamorphosis at the very beginning," said Angela, pleased that her dear father's embracing competence had not been mobilized to this end.

"Well now, you don't know about Mama," Jo said. "She had been coming to this for a long time; you have to assume it. By the time I was born she was already a layer removed from mothering. There was a film between her and the children. Caroline and Fanny, those two, were assigned to see to me. And while Mama was always around, you know, always in the house, it was another part of the house—when we moved to Moriches year round, it was the little sewing room off their bedroom, or upstairs in Theo's room because he was gone, where she had that radio and the couch; but wherever she was, the door was closed. Not tight closed. It was closed against your wanting to come in but kept that bit ajar as though to say she had not left me. She only needed to be private."

"So you weren't really surprised, you mean, that she took off?"

"Oh, I was surprised to death! But you know, the next second, it was like I'd heard the spring on a lock. *Ping*. And I thought, 'she's released.' And she confirmed me: it was if she confirmed my release."

Then Angela felt one small, distant reverberation of the *ping* and registered it privately and then prodded, "So he worked upstairs for a while until he was settled what to do next. Go on."

"He said himself it wasn't that he was inclined to do *nothing*. He was inclined not to stop her, was all. She wrote in that letter she wasn't alone, and he took that to be the truth. But he began on the basis that she didn't *know* anybody, and then he saw it had to be a false basis. I mean you'd have to discount her running off to the neighbors, or their running off *with* her—the Hudsons or the Schankenfelts, or those weird ones, I forget their name, who were in the grey shingle across from the garage. She never had much to do with the neighbors, but then she never had *anything* to do with anybody else. Outside the family. I mean she didn't have *friends*. You know that."

"So there's Theo upstairs, inappropriately unstirred by his mother's extraordinary behavior," said Angela firmly. She had caught Jo's eyes in a sweep around the room, and she wanted to head off a digression. "We're on a hunt, Jo. We are looking for antecedent behavior. We are deliberately, in this age when the young deny the relevance of history, pursuing our lineage backward in time, because we deny that I am Non Sequitur, or that you are Non Sequitur. Isn't that what we're busy denying? So there's Theo, and he calmly discards the assumption that his mother didn't know anybody."

She must have known somebody. She must have had some private contact with another person through which her subsequent decisions could be tracked. Once his mind accepted the logic of this, Theo had said, the tracking was easy enough.

A few hundred yards down the main road from the farmhouse was a small, neat white house with blue shutters and a small, neat sign in front identifying itself as Swanson's Bakery. For the three months of the summer season Mr. and Mrs. Swanson baked Danish pastry and spent the rest of the year some place in Florida ("on their yacht," said Papa), and the reason they were so successful was warm and simple: the pastry was delicious.

The Swansons could take nine months off every year because their trade was with people to whom it would not otherwise occur to stop for avoidable cause along the stretch of fifteen miles running from Center Moriches to the Hamptons. In those days, there seemed to be The Very Rich, and then a gap, and then people one knew, and then everybody else. The Very Rich had summer estates and enclaves stretching out forty miles toward Montauk Point, and the only way they could get to them, besides taking the express train called The Cannonball, was by the road that passed Swanson's (and the farmhouse), and the liveried chauffeurs of these very rich people could be seen following their employers down the steps of the bakery carrying stacks of pastry boxes to the long grey limousines that were an ordinary sight in that modest driveway. And they floated the Swansons to nine months in Florida.

Going to Swanson's was one of the few errands outside the property that Mrs. Porter did alone, or could do alone, as every other destination needed a car to get to, and she didn't drive. She did indeed often pass the time with Mrs. Swanson, as Theo reflected, and, furthermore, she had once or twice mentioned having met somebody else there, a woman who spoke Czech with her. Mrs. Swanson told Theo, "Oh yes, yes. Sure, sure. Mrs. Brundage from Southampton. She is a widow, a Czech who was married to an Englishman in the oil business, I believe. She liked your mother very much. They had long talks in Czech." Theo drove out to Southampton to a huge, shingled house on the dunes and learned from the housekeeper that Mrs. Brundage had sailed on the Queen Mary from New York the day before with a companion. The second day passed this way.

On the third day Theo telephoned Bill at his office in the Medical Center. Why hadn't he called Charles, the son, instead of Bill, the son-in-law? Because Charles and Margaret had just left for a trip to Maine. He just waited for them to just leave, and then he called Bill.

"Bill, something a little out of the ordinary—I thought I'd better tell you. My mother seems to have effected an escape." Theo waited for Bill's response. If it had been Charles, he'd have shot back "When?" and then, "Tuesday! For crying out loud what the hell have you . . ." It was the logic of the legal mind. So, as he had known that Charles was setting off, he had waited a little longer to be sure he had set off, and called Bill. Bill said, "When?" too, then heard the story, and then came out to Moriches without telling Caroline, and they talked the thing over.

ffffffff CHAPTER THREE *ffffffff*

THIRTY years ago you took a wandering, tarred road, your car wheels sometimes popping the tar blisters on a sizzling day, to the flat meadow land on Great South Bay, and you were in duck country, by which was not meant the shooting of them but the raising of them. The economy was ducks, potatoes, and some summer people of middling prosperity who, through the Great Depression and through the thirties, supported middling-modest summer places in the town of Center Moriches, where the population might double in July and August, counting the help brought along from New York. In East Moriches there were never many more than a few hundred souls, the younger Porters being among the rare people on visiting terms with this village. Many inhabitants of East Moriches were living out a long life without ever once taking the trip to New York, two hours to the west by the Long Island Railroad.

34

They were accustomed to the seasonal migrations of chauffeurs who drove through their half-block of upstreet along
this unusually unremarkable last stretch of country before
the approach to the rich and handsome Hamptons. For East
Moriches, the Porter breed was the single live contact with
the sophisticated urban world and was evidently deemed
sufficient.

East Moriches was not beautiful unless you were a Porter
grandchild looking backward in time to your summer holidays, and your mind took that road, from the city to the
farmhouse, which was not all tar after all but, in places, con-
crete broken and only mended with linear designs of tar.
Angela would retraverse in the mind this homeward pathway
with the sign at the town line:

Welcome to East Moriches
The Friendly Village
With a Low Tax Rate

This announcement was at once courteous and disinterested,
in the spirit of a white calling card left by a visitor who
came round when he knew you would be out. Passing the
welcome sign, one was allowed to experience a physical sen-
sation consonant with the abrupt decline in taxes. Taking
the ungraded curve too fast, you might just miss landing in
a duck pond packed white with waddling, quacking ducks.
Some did not miss. Just there as you entered, the Friendly
Village could actually lay claim to a bit of special beauty
for a couple of hundred yards. The tallest black-green white
pine grew dense at the road on either side, and then suddenly at that curve there was the fine whiteness and fluttering of the ducks. Great verticals of pine-green and a ruffling

35

sea of feathery white. For the rest to be said for this village, there were large shade trees along the roads, and there were small frame houses mottled under their shadows, and here and there a stretch of meadow, golden from the summer sun; small, unaffected, common country beauties. Probably nothing could be said about the winterscape.

Just before the sea of white ducks came into sight, a dirt road led to the left into the pines, a short, solemn curve of a road that brought you to the cemetery. About a year before old Mr. Porter died a clever salesman had sold him a plot in this cemetery in a package that included the erection of a modest monument. ("It *is* a modest monument," Theo commented in his calm, wry voice at the funeral. "It's not in a class with the Taj Mahal.") Papa had not asked anybody whether it was a good idea, but each of the children volunteered the opinion it was a damned foolish way to get taken. (Charles, actually, was the one to be taken. Charles paid a bill of three hundred dollars for it.) Unfazed—never did the old man seem fazed by an outside view—he had had constructed on this plot a rather tall plinth, a replica along the lines of Cleopatra's Needle standing about five feet up from the base. The "needle" was supported on its low platform by wedges in the likeness of four stone crabs, their claws maintaining a defensive-aggressive posture. Moriches Bay was known for its crab beds. Therefore, what might on first sight seem an inappropriate selection of a tombstone for a small, submarginal farmer on Long Island, New York, could upon closer consideration be an apt memorial to an indiscriminately patriotic man of (two-acre) property with a throbbing booster spirit coursing through his veins, never tapped by Elks or Rotarians in a village of such little esprit it didn't even have Elks and Rotarians. On the front face of the plinth he had inscribed:

36

ADAM (PROHASKA) PORTER
born Podiebrad Bohemia
January 8, 1869
arrived Port of New York
October 11, 1891
American citizenship
October 23, 1897
died

On the left face of the plinth was the heading "relict" in small letters, beneath which:

ANGELINA
born March 5, 1880
died

The other two sides were left bare, but he would not be surprised if Theo found himself with no place to be put, and you could not tell who else.

This plinth business was the subject at the time of a lot of negative comment, and, in fact, all negative comment. Nobody had heard about the "relict" until it was cut. It seemed for many reasons a bizarre choice of word, not the least because Papa had little credence in his own mortality and was exceptionally hale and came from a long line of long-livers, while Mama was in frequent retreat with vapors, cold cloths on the forehead, palpitations, and the whole gamut of unmentioned women's disorders.

"You could say it was very gracious of him to let her have the expectation that she would be the survivor," said Theo. "You could say that, if you really believed he knew the word *relict* indicated he was prepared to go first."

Angela always thought the hubbub over the plinth was

37

very funny; but then, she had thought her grandfather *was* charming. He made a good story, but he did not, thinking upon it afterward, make a good husband. Of his seven grandchildren—Fanny's two in Rhodesia, Caroline's four, and Angela—he undisguisedly preferred Angela, and she responded with her whole heart to his bias and giggled at her own mother's assurance that she was her grandfather's favorite because her father was the son that had the money. When she heard, out of the clear sky, that he was dead, it was the first terrible pain of loss she had experienced. He had intended to take a turn onto the main road, and he wouldn't wait but bolted, as was his wont, right onto the sole route that carried through-traffic from New York City to Montauk Point, and the driver who hit his flank killed him instantly, killed them both.

What could her grandmother have thought about herself, about being "relict," both before she was and after? It was generally believed that she was as impervious to the consequences of her husband's more flamboyant decisions as she was unconsulted beforehand in the making of them. Did he ask her at the time of the Prohibition Amendment what she thought of his closing his two modest saloons on Second Avenue in New York City (his single source of income) and moving year round out to the farmhouse? He closed them and moved her. And the family simply assumed that she was well content to live forever in Moriches, remote from all those cousins and aunts and uncles who used to come in for coffee and cake on Sunday afternoons when her children were small in their family house, which was then in the rural Bronx. It is on record that, in the course of the years she lived in Moriches, two or three times some outsider, one of those cousins or aunts out for a rare visit, did ask her straight out, "Do you like Moriches?" And each time she said straight out, "No." Until after her flight, no account had

been taken of this bit of evidence that there was an undercurrent of resistance in her to being endowed by other people with a soul that did not protest and a character that
found it sufficiently fulfilling to submit wholeheartedly to
one bully and five children. For the observer, the fact that
she did not like Moriches might have been neutralized by
the fact that she was not cowed by her tyrannical husband.
She might have been contemptuous but was never heard to
put her contempt into words. Silence and pursed lips were
her way. When he got too demanding or when she got too
tired of it, she would say she was sick and go to bed, and so
somebody else was corralled to make his dinner, which he
did not like at all. It was the kind of leverage she had with
him.

There was a scene Angela remembered to be repeated
through the summer Sunday mornings of her early life that
testified well enough to an independent streak in her grandmother. She *would* go to church. Out of the kitchen door
she strode in her Liberty print—wearing white cotton gloves,
white oxford shoes newly polished, a natural straw hat with
pink buckram camellias and a bit of veiling at the front. She
carried a prayer book. There was always somebody to drive
her to this church—a small, brown-shingled Presbyterian
church with an untended lawn, overgrown by scrubby pine
brush, and a minister lent for the summer by the congrega-
tion in Center Moriches, who preached three sermons in
three different towns every Sunday morning. Somebody
would drive her to the service and pick her up afterward,
but rarely did anyone sit through.

This was because the religion of the family was a strict
atheism without modifications, superintended by this patriarch who regularly emerged those Sunday mornings onto
the kitchen stoop in his shirt-sleeves, his arms crossed, to
see off the relict-to-be with a loud, half-respectful, "Damn

fool!" It never rippled her. That is to say, she never appeared
to be rippled by this homely variant of *Godspeed*. The one
courtesy Theo regularly performed during her last summer
at the farmhouse was the driving to and from church every
week. Her continued attendance seemed proof that she did
not go to that church solely to flout her husband's assumption of supremacy by affirming the existence of a being yet
more supreme.

Still, she was not a believing Christian. After the war,
when Charles and Margaret spent a summer in Europe trying
unsuccessfully to trace her, they did learn that on the day
that Hitler invaded Poland she and Mrs. Brundage had already gotten to Strasbourg with, it seems, the intention to
cross Germany on their way to Prague. Because of the violent
confusion of the time, the two ladies might well have crossed
the border had they not been pressed by some Czech ex-
patriates who were befriending them to reconsider because
Mrs. Porter, by Nuremberg laws, was a Jewess.

None of the Porters thought of themselves as Jews, nor
did they think of themselves as Christians, the grandmother
needing, evidently, a connection with God, attending her
church through an absence of choice. That is, she was not
considering a conversion to Catholicism, and, were she to
have preferred a synagogue, there wasn't one. Neither she
nor her husband had been reared in the Jewish tradition,
and, after all, if Angela was burrowing into her ancestry in
search of some inherited tendency to live outside the law,
she might have found root causes in the family circumstances
in the early years of her grandparents, family circumstances
that were not so much unorthodox as extralegal. Good
atheist stock generally derives from one of two European
traditions: the aristocratic, springing roughly from the Age
of Reason; and the radical-humanitarian, rising from the
ghettos of Europe of the nineteenth century. Neither source

accounted for the old Porters. Rather they seem to have been spun off from a quasi-criminal, foreign-born proletariat which, whether on one side of the Atlantic or after passage to the other, reproduced and nurtured its young outside a traditional community. If one thinks of the people in the world of Brecht's *Three-penny Opera*, it might be possible to imagine that they bore children, a proportion of whom survived infancy, some small division of *those* arriving at adulthood, taking the leap, and slipping into a conforming existence. The Jews who landed from the old country in New York, as American history records again and again, could and did find refuge and protection in formidably structured, transplanted communities, and their very strength is one major source of our invigorated culture. But there must have been those motley others who lived on the fringes, and their progeny withered, or didn't flourish, or did flourish but didn't write autobiographies. Angela used to beg her grandfather, "Tell me about how you met Grandma," and he would say, "Well you see, I had this cousin who was really kind of a no-good bum, and he was sweet on your grandmother's sister Trudy. So one afternoon I kept him company while he waited outside the church. You see, there was a settlement house that was attached to the church, and they were helping all the young immigrant girls to learn English by bringing them into the choir. So that's where I met your grandmother. She came out with her sister, a beautiful young girl she was, and I said to myself, 'I'm going to marry that one.' "

"Did you tell her right away that was what you were going to do?"

"No. I gave her a little time, but she didn't need it."

"When did you first kiss her?"

"Why, that very first day! I walked her to her door, and I kissed her!"

"That very first day!"

"Certainly."

Yes, he was an autocratic man. If it were Angela's intention to read her grandmother's story for little prophetic signs of a soul with a life of its own evolving concurrently inside the woman who played mother, who played wife, ought she not to observe fairly that she, Angela, had also married an autocratic man? She believed that in this *recherche de temps perdu* for the woman from whom she sprang, with whom she was entitled surely to feel the closest blood ties, that she would discover herself to be retraversing the broad road her stalwart (if queer) grandmother followed. She wanted to meet evidence that she was retraversing her own forebear's road, if only symbolically, for the friendly comfort of it. She would excise time and hold close to her heart that earlier woman who went first. It was romantic to do this. It fit well to call her grandfather a bully, because her own husband fit the word and, in fact, fit it more accurately. Charlie, her husband. Charles, her father. She would be willing to make something of that coincidence of names, but it was just that: nothing could be made of it. On the other hand, by designing, for the benefit of her own personal story, a grandfather who was arbitrary, arrogant, and without the least tendency towards self-examination, by making him a husband who might very naturally drive underground a woman who had the will and the wit to find the way down into it, she was drawing Charlie—a most modern, a most contemporary, successful middle-aged academic still (now in 1970) destined to enjoy to the end of his life the emotional maturity of a late-adolescent male. When she married Charlie, they were both twenty-four, and he was a late-adolescent male.

But would it be useful to say that her grandfather with his panache was really a predecessor of Charlie, the Perpetual

Boy? It would, she thought, be thinking anachronistically
to ascribe to that Victorian character an immature personality, as though to suggest that he had this particular trait in
an exaggerated form not characteristic of other householders
of similar circumstance. Was her grandfather's sense of his
own masculinity absurdly exhibited to camouflage a fear of
impotence, or whatever? No. And there was no parallel to
Charlie. When Charlie was a fool, he was a fool surrounded
by all the knowy people who could read him psychoanalyt-
ically, watch the mechanisms of his adolescent personality
under stress, see him naked. When her grandfather was a
fool, he was surrounded by people who might mention he
was a fool, but they left his clothes on. Moreover, it was
unlikely that, when her grandfather was at his most impossible, her grandmother would sigh, "Oh! If he would only
grow up!"

*A*S a consequence of Theo's call about Mrs. Porter, Bill drove directly out to Moriches and did not return to his home until late. The next morning, without yet telling his wife of her own mother's disappearance—because of Caroline's characteristic of causing one to want to delay communicating with her—Bill called his sister-in-law Jo at the number where she could currently be reached. Bill always had Jo's number—and it changed not infrequently— but he had never before used it. He asked her whether she would be able to meet him for lunch at one—at the French Café in Rockefeller Center, because, being very rarely in New York (although he lived and worked in a suburb just outside it) he had not an idea what was elegant and chose what a man would who was annually assigned a visit with the children to the Easter Show at Radio City.

"There's a little family matter I'd like to talk over with you," he said, and she thought that he must be planning to tell her he was leaving Caroline.

"We were both on time that day," Jo said to Angela—Jo now, in these talks they had after Theo's death (1960), still

44

accustomed to fold herself into three parts for sitting, Jo moving towards the end of her forties, reaching her very handsomest peak so late. Her long, straight, black hair had sufficient white hair in it to be remarked, but the whole was now drawn back in a wide bun flattened into place by a large buckle of bamboo and bone. Her pale blue eyes were cupped beneath in darkish hollows that let her look as though she knew hard use and was all the better for it. Some people have irregularities in their appearance which become them, and time accentuates the irregularities, which become them the more. There is a point, of course, where the good fairies quit. Bill's appearance was like that too, although Bill was really homely, while Jo was really handsome. And if Jo was among the small number of aging women who remain sensual females well beyond the time allotted by their fellow women, Bill that summer of '39 when he was forty-five looked closer to sixty. He leveled off there. At seventy he looked closer to sixty. A big man with thick, greying hair, he had a head, a carriage, a walk that suggested he was the present representative of a line of stock which developed the animal parts by hard-working flection in co-ordination with a rapid refinement of the wits. He could, for instance, have come out of the pits of the coal-mining regions of early nineteenth-century England, but as the rebel, as the leader, as the radical. Examine his face for the marks of delicacy, for the touch of the exquisite that seems to record itself in the expressions of sensitive intellectual people sometimes, and there wasn't really a trace. As he was not intellectual, being in fact barely educated outside his medical training (a much-admired, much-cherished inadequacy striven for to this day by that profession), there was no reason to think nature remiss in leaving him with what, in the slang of those times, was descriptively called a mug. Albeit a lovely mug: and the whole of him, somewhat humped in the shoulders, distinctly potted in the belly, a slight roll to his gait, took the eye of the women, and even the eye of the men.

"I caught sight of him coming up Fifth before he saw me, and he was so elegant in his city suit. I don't know—to this day I think of that man as a sort of classless noble, and wherever he turns up, whatever door he comes through, why he, you know, vindicates the most sanguine Darwinian view. There he is, that great, strong mutation come to reinvigorate the race. Wonderful. He's just meant for procreation."

"He did that!" said Angela.

"Well, yeah, he—but I was having a wider view."

"Why, Caroline and Bill were the only ones I ever knew in that generation with four children. I remember when I was a child and felt called upon to brag about something notably bizarre in my family, I used to say, 'My Aunt Caroline has four children!' With us, my generation, it's a commonplace, but when I was growing up, our kind of women didn't have more than one or two. Curious, to this day, when I'm not with her, I'm still fond of Caroline—probably out of gratitude for her having four children. It was our family sideshow."

To Angela, Jo was the looking-glass opposite of her older sister (Fanny she did not remember), all the way to her being as dark as Caroline was fair, as gaunt as Caroline was round. She was opposite in the point of her emotions, was love-filled and, in fact, too love-filled. It was a flaw.

"He was walking with his eyes cast down." Jo resumed the narrative. "But then when he looked up and saw me, he grinned. He has such a good grin. We shook hands, and he said, 'You look beautiful.' He touched me so. He always touches me so. We had a table by the window and ordered our drinks, and I was so sure the thing had something to do with Caroline that I wasn't in any particular hurry for him

46

to tell it. And you know, he's practically inarticulate, so I thought, finally, 'He'll say two sentences like, "Caroline has moved out. I didn't make her happy." ' And he said, 'Your mother seems to have taken a job.' "

When Bill had gotten to the farmhouse, Theo had told him in his laconic way what seemed to have occurred. Two laconic men, they shared a communications system that had them transacting their business, as far as actual words went, in the briefest few minutes. But the talking was interspersed with long silences during which some kind of nonverbal processing might be going on, in order that the exchange of information be finally recorded with the fullness, the color, the touch of detail that the more verbal variety of person tries to say out. They drove on to Southampton to interview the housekeeper, first having called to ask for that favor and bringing with them a load of Swanson's pastry, and they were invited to sit down on the deck with whiskey and soda and no ice and Danish pastry, where the housekeeper, who was no mean example of the above-mentioned more verbal variety of person, told them about Mrs. Brundage, by whom she had been employed these seven years, and brought out photographs of Mrs. Brundage, and newsclippings too. The great surf of the Atlantic was in front of their eyes and the white sand all about, and behind them, the huge, handsome shingled house stanched of color by the salt air and water. The house seemed to have sustained little damage in the hurricane. Many of the houses on the Dune Road had been washed away to the foundations.

Who was Mrs. Brundage? To begin with who Mr. Brundage was, he was in oil, in investment. "But he was a lawyer," said Mrs. Crouse, the housekeeper, as if to assure the legitimacy of his occupation in that prewar world where the International Set put their hands to nothing whatsoever and were wrongly admired for their indolence. "But he was

English," she said in explanation. Mrs. Brundage was his second wife, much younger than her husband, and he had met her in London and married her there, and, in fact, they were both British citizens and carried British passports. She would not ordinarily know much in the line of passports, but they were always using their passports, and so she got to know more than you would think about things like visas. Mrs. Brundage said she was thirty-six, but she was forty-two.

Both men echoed, "Forty-two?" with surprise, thinking of her as an old woman, and out came the photographs of a large, firm, broad Slavic face, good-looking, a broad mouth smiling a twist ironically, a stagey smile, and piles of hair compressed into countless curls, elaborately arranged and of an orange color. "She's redheaded," Mrs. Crouse noted, "and she flares up quite a good bit, but underneath she really doesn't mean anything by it. Just, that's the way they are, the ladies of Europe. They wave their arms about a good deal, and a lot of nonsense is said, but they don't mean anything by it. It's the faulty language, I think." The men let that pass, meaning and all.

Mrs. Crouse knew about Mrs. Porter. At least she knew this much, that Mrs. Brundage was very keen to visit Czechoslovakia and had been advised this was impossible "because of your Mr. Hitler," but nothing would do until she got at least back on the far side of the Atlantic—and here the three heads turned to look across to the far side of the Atlantic. ("The sun just shone down so hard on that water and drained it almost of all its color. It was the palest blue," Bill told Jo. Because of the sea, and for some people, there bursts from them a need to mention intense feeling. The Porters, to their widest reaches were a sea-loving people from a shore-living position. "Beautiful. Nearly drained of the blue. Like your eyes," said Bill to Jo.)

"Poor soul," Mrs. Crouse had said, "She didn't have anybody she could talk to in her native tongue. It was two, three summers ago she came in from the city one day all excited because she'd met this lady, she said, at the pastry shop in East Moriches, who spoke the Czech language. She did delight in it."

Nonetheless, the relationship between Sophie Brundage and Mrs. Porter seemed to remain desultory and at the will of chance, so to speak, until this summer in question, when they must have begun to move, with their mutual language, toward a more intimate convergence of needs. They must have done so, since what followed did follow. They had sailed on the Queen Mary the very afternoon of Mrs. Porter's leaving her letter. Indeed, Mrs. Crouse knew Mrs. Brundage was to stop on her way to the pier in East Moriches for Mrs. Porter because she, Mrs. Crouse, had been sent to warn the chauffeur they would need the larger car on account of the extra luggage.

"Ever since Mr. Brundage passed on, two years ago this September twenty-first it will be, she's been very much alone, dear thing. I sometimes wondered what she would do with herself and whether she'd keep up the house. They didn't have any children of their own. There were three sons by the first marriage, but, of course, they're grown and married, and they've come out every summer just as regular with their own little ones, but she never really felt quite true to being the grandmother. Well, she was too young, for one thing"; and Mrs. Crouse, a grandmotherly woman herself, asked the world to be reasonable. "So she didn't have anyone, strictly speaking, of her own, and there was nothing to stop her from picking up and taking off. They had an apartment in London anyway. Only she wasn't going to London this time."

And where was she going? A point and crux of the interview.

"Well, now, I don't know how far she thought she could get towards where she wanted to go, which was Czechoslovakia, which is a country quite a way into Europe, besides which overrun by the Germans. The fact is she was quite determined to get to—Prague, is it?—no matter what was said against it. She wasn't what you'd call a reasonable woman, being foreign. 'Mrs. Crouse,' she said to me, and we kissed each other goodbye very warmly, 'I'll let you know where I am as soon as I know myself.' So that's how it stands, Mr. Porter," she finished, turning to Theo, "and I'll certainly be glad to get in touch with you when I learn more."

"But she never did learn more," said Angela, "because the war broke."

"Bill and I, we sat on and on that day at lunch. We drank whiskey, and then we had a bottle of wine. It must have been something like a 1934 Burgundy. Wouldn't it be nice to have a '34 Burgundy right now? And he was so gentle and nice and happy doing this naughty, sophisticated thing —drinking a long French meal in the middle of a working day. So then, I finally said, 'Bill, what did Caroline say?' "

" 'Nothing. She doesn't know.' "

" 'You don't think she's going to get curious after a year or two and wonder what the hell happened to Mama?' "

" 'I'll tell you the part of that letter she's going to have a fit about, and that's Theo's getting the property. I'd like some way for her to get to the end of her life and never know that. It's always been set in her mind that Moriches is her inheritance by virtue of being a superior breeder. She weighs us up, Drinkwaters against the Charles Porters, or Fanny. You and Theo don't amount to anything. To understand how Caroline's mind works, you got to have a feeling for an agronomic system of values. She should have raised livestock, and her pigs would be the cleanest and fattest, and she'd breed a prize bull. I am a very unsatisfying substitute for a prize bull.'

"And if I hadn't had so much wine," Jo said to Angela, "I wouldn't probably have told him how I had thought he was meeting me for lunch because he was going to leave Caroline. And he said, 'I couldn't ever do that.' "

CHAPTER FIVE

*W*HEN Bill did walk through his own front door late that Friday afternoon, he was a spirit larger and happier than life, his usual self buffered by an airy nimbus of French wine fumes, and beautiful Jo, and leaving a twenty-dollar bill on the plate, and forbidden Jo whom he had tasted. (They had eaten and they had drunk and it was oral and he seemed to have tasted her.)

His house was a house of waxed floors. The rules for living in it focused upon the feet. You wiped them. You took care that you did not slip on Friday, waxing day. (Bill skidded a little moving through the living room to the kitchen.) You did not scatter the braided scatter rugs. Credit accrued from polishing shoes, a terrible debit from being found with them up on the upholstery. It was a two-and-a-half-story, four-bedroom house, a bit cheek by jowl with its neighbors in a planned garden city in Garden City, Long Island. The attic with dormer windows was the "half" which you could finish yourself—Bill had long since finished it, and the two older boys lived up there—the whole providing hanging space for eighteen pairs of starched white-organdy ruffled curtains. A large reproduction of Breughel's *The Harvesters* hung above the couch in the living room. On the baby grand piano were group pictures from other years of the children, "taken professionally." There used to be a bridal photograph propped against the books on an upper bookshelf with a very pretty smiling young Caroline in a white dress cut in the unlovely flapper style, and a long stringbean of a boy in ill-fitting tuxedo, a very hayseed groom. One day one year Bill quietly threw it out.

Bill found Caroline in the kitchen cooking on four burners. There were always hearty, well-balanced dinners, one indistinguishable from the other, Bill would have said unfairly. There were as many as twenty combinations. Ham, spinach, mashed potatoes; or creamed chicken, rice, string beans; but never chicken and spinach. At 6:15 on Friday nights this atheist family sat down to fish, and, ordinarily, the predictability of the fish with a weekend at home to follow brought Bill way down. He was that night way up, and even charitable. He put his arm around his big, clean-aproned wife, patted her on her fresh-set, brittle curls, and told her to come on in and sit down, there was something he had to tell her. He expected a No she couldn't now, Bobby had orchestra rehearsal, Billy had scouts, Annie was going to the school dance; but they settled into the living room with sherry.

"Did your mother ever talk to you about a Mrs. Brundage from Southampton?" was the way he led her toward this untoward story, and he was gentle and she heard him out very reasonably. Yes, she'd even met Mrs. Brundage one day last year at Swanson's—a rather wild-looking dyed redhead, all ruffles and beads. They had only said "How do you do?" She, Caroline, circumambulated the strange implications dwelling in her mother's action, that central and uncanny fact; her moveless, willess mother had willed and moved. Instead she directed her attention to the outskirts of the story and could not believe even Theo was so casual as to let three days go by without telling anybody. He must have been drinking. What did Charles say? Had they cabled? She would call Jo right now. All of this Bill parried, hedged, deflected, with a success that charmed him. His spirit stayed winey. The children came down to dinner, and he kindly threw her a fishbone ("This is swordfish!" he said, pleased), and when the several parts of the household, animate and inanimate, were dispatched for the night, and the two were once more back to talking the thing out, they both felt an unaccustomed closeness, like people on the same side. He had not mentioned that Theo was to have the property.

The bad Caroline then had the need to say, "If you wear your best suit to work every day there'll be nothing left of it!" and his once-more-besieged soul broke through their mutuality like a jack-in-the-box through tissue paper and tore it up. It was in her nature to be ever vigilant in monitoring the small liberties taken by those who belonged to her, to peck at one or another of them as if they were wriggling little creatures who had again and again to be tucked back under her wing. There she was, looked upon with envy by many women because of her having something very like a prize bull, in a husband of such brawny dimension, but it is not every woman who recognizes a prize bull, or wants to, and from the evidence of her treatment of him she took the bull for one more chick, the naughty wayward one. Caroline, who had a powerful intelligence, ought not to have gone into animal husbandry as Bill suggested. She didn't understand the nature of beasts at all. She ought to have gone, where she wanted to go, into medicine and beyond, into medical research perhaps, or she might very well have made as good a clinician as Bill, or better.

54

That she was thwarted and reduced through the early years of her childhood is likely; it is on record that she was thwarted and reduced—by her father's bad luck, or the luck of a bad father—while in college, where she was first in her class. Suddenly, in her third year, he lost his money playing the grain exchange and could not pay her tuition, and she wheeled straight around, renounced her ambition to go into medicine, was implacable and would never reconsider.

Caroline now has two granddaughters who are fierce for the feminist movement (and both in medical school), but in the old days before liberation the most redoubtable of women exercised their native ferocity inside a castle with a name like 493 Elmwood Drive. And they kept the keep with a most untrusting eye against the encroaching world, against the enemy who were, roughly speaking, family, friends, and neighbors. Caroline made marriage her 'property,' her world. Taking a vengeful, reductive position, she mastered the practice of domestic science better than anybody and was once more the first in her class. That powerful intelligence along with a powerful rage were concentrated on reducing large worldly concerns to small dubious significance ("Nobody can convince *me* Charles is planting fifty-six saplings for the benefit of mankind! Margaret wants the property!") and to paint small concerns so large as to cover the whole canvas. It was her mission to make the inversion of values her life-work.

She read, however, and was not apolitical. On the contrary, she politicized everything indiscriminately. She took an unflinching *political* position in favor of at least one green vegetable, at least one musical instrument, the dropping of the quota for refugee girls at the University Nursing School, knowing where Bill was, the restoration of running-boards on automobiles as a safety measure, protective legislation for migratory workers. With equal fervor she was against the arms embargo, wearing sneakers every day, Margaret Porter, cigarettes, her boys getting drafted, not knowing where Bill was. Were there really sufficient waking hours for the infinite number of daily things to be weighed for their virtue or their sinfulness, to be sent aloft to build the Good, to be cast down, despised examples, never to be forgotten? Her world view was painted in moral colors and in two dimensions, a secular Last Judgment with Mrs. William Drinkwater, three-time president of the P.S. 39 PTA, in majesty holding the scales.

About Bill, Angela was later to understand that it wasn't the waxed floors and the balanced meals and Caroline's clucking and plucking at the children that were hard for him: it was her constant need to order, to arrange, to supervise, to correct him—to reduce him. An old male story there. Charlie had not so long ago said to Angela, with quiet bitterness, "You always put me down!" and she had been shocked, believing she had passed the years propping him up. Or was it the same thing? When somebody says "How are you?" you might answer, "Oh, I have a bad cold," or "Oh, I have a good cold." The same thing.

And the fact was Angela liked Caroline, or at least had admired her aunt, when she was growing up, for representing in the flesh and in her own family, the one-hundred-percent American mother. She was the model for her design in life with Charlie. *Now* she saw beneath the hearty, wholesome, joking aunt the Wagnerian fury. Now she saw the large-bosomed woman having to be large-bosomed to contain the oceanic emotions that swelled and receded from a spring tide to a neap in a rhythmical cycle as remote from outside control as the gravitational pull of the moon. And Caroline was married to a King Canute. He would feel the tensions rise, feel it with his fingers in the very air of the house, and scheme to distract, to disperse, to diffuse this furious energy before it burst. Impossible to do. Nearly always impossible. Fearful explosion followed by some weeks of calm.

But that American Mother whose Thanksgiving turkey *had* to be at least twenty-two pounds; whose oval maple dining-room table with the lazy Susan in the middle was *always* extended by two leaves; who had a house filled with her cousins who rode bicycles to school, had paper routes, played trombones in the school band, sneaked cigarettes, and passed on to her, Angela, fantastic information about sex, fantastic (but closer in the end to the spirit of sex than the "factual" information which controlled her own responses) —*that* American mother moving through a bustle of laughing, smart children and the dearest, funniest Uncle Bill, was Caroline too, Caroline the Best.

Caroline the Worst was unleashed by her hearing the postscript of her mother's letter. Theo! Theo was to have the property! Over her dead body was Theo to have the property, she said in a voice that turned sharp and shrill ("There's nothing to get so excited about. Not even your mother's body is dead."), and she flailed out against Bill the target, how unfeeling, how crude he was, how absolutely predictable it was that he would take anybody's part against her! She was a harried knuckle-cracker when her blood was up. She pulled and pulled at her fingers, and clawed at her wedding ring which was locked fast in a groove of flesh. She was a frenzied foot-tapper, beating to the same rhythm as their dog, who was a tail-rapper (which was the sort of detail Bill sorted and catalogued to keep himself detached while she worked her maelstrom). Oh, she would give anything to see Margaret's face when she heard Theo had beaten her at her own game—it would be almost worth the whole thing.

Then Bill lost his detachment (predictably, too) and told

her she was out of her mind to think Margaret with her
elegant taste could have the slightest interest in that shabby
two acres of rural slum. His defense of Margaret released
(predictably) that final long spasm of hate and bitterness and
sexual jealousy from her in which she said terrible things,
made obscene and lurid accusations against Margaret (to the
effect that she was in love with Bill, chased him shamelessly,
made him look such a fool, and, finally, that he, Bill, loved
Margaret), and after that hauled out and counted from her
miserly memory every hoarded hurt and affront she had
borne through Bill's being the fool about women since 1920.
She wept. She would pack her suitcase. At last she was
spent. The next morning she was quiet, smiling, reasonable,
calm, patient with a silent, stoical husband, and went about
her domestic chores as if in fact she could not help but be
admired for exhibiting a show of real sportsmanship, because
the appalling things she had said about other people the night
before, she was ready to forgive and forget. And she called
Charles in Kennebunkport, and Charles and Margaret took
the very long pre-thruway drive back to New York, not
stopping for the night.

At ten-thirty the next morning, which was Sunday morning, the beginning of World War II, Bill and Caroline parked
on East Sixty-third Street and walked through Charles's front
door, actually front doors. The downstairs door with a
Good Morning to the doorman, the elevator door with a
Good Morning to the elevator man, the apartment door with
an affectionate pat for Bunch, the short, round family housekeeper, a Negro woman of the palest hue who wore gold-
rimmed round spectacles and a uniform of blue-grey 'good'
cotton with white trim. "How're the teeth?" Bill asked her,
with what Caroline thought was his usual excessive familiar-
ity. Bunch said she was getting used to them and smiled

58

broadly, flashing for him this double row of large shining white tiles. Charles had bought them, and called them the China Clippers.

No waxed floors, but all dark-blue carpeting, and on top of that small oriental rugs. No skidding. Charles collected the oriental rugs, Margaret the pictures. There were woodcuts and etchings mostly, a few watercolors (one John Marin), and over Margaret's couch a large standing nude of a slovenly creature, in oils, by Robert Henri. Margaret in a modest way supported the American School.

Caroline with no difficulty scorned the idea of letting one of those pictures into her own house, but her outward self was nobly calm as she entered enemy territory through the foyer and crossed the long living room to the far end, where there was a wide bay window the width of the wall, with its long panes opened to the misty morning summer sunlight. Beneath the open windows there was a low table of a wood as dark as ebony, and on it a Sheffield silver coffee service identical to Caroline's and white china cups and saucers of the most modern Swedish simplicity—a far cry from Caroline's Royal Doulton—and Jensen spoons. Around the table chairs covered with blocked linen flowered prints were drawn and in one of the chairs was languid Jo smiling up with a bemused smile, first at Caroline, who did not look into those watered blue eyes and drown, and then at Bill, who did. The doorbell and Theo, whose voice had the middle-western twang of Elmer Davis, radio news commentator, and unaccountably always did have that twang, from his earliest years in the Bronx.

Margaret said that Charles was still on the phone—Margaret, who, if she were in love with Bill, disguised it this morning by looking sternly out of love with every one of them equally. Stiff with keeping her annoyance under control, she looked very grand and lovely for such a little angry woman. She wore an off-white linen dress with a design of small dark-blue flowers, as though she too, as well as her chairs, were slipcovered for the summer in the best possible taste. Mother and Mrs. Brundage, she told them, had gone through customs at Cherbourg that morning. The cable lines were being reserved for use by the government because of the international situation, and Charles was seeing whether he could do anything through somebody he knew in Washington with the FBI.

"Well, what the hell would he want to do, for Christ's sake?" asked Theo, looking at Margaret as if she were on the other side of a frontier where the folkways were different and largely unintelligible, although they no doubt contained their own rationality. In fact she was over there by herself, since Theo certainly spoke for Bill and Jo, and wherever Caroline was on this issue, it would not be where Margaret was.

Now Charles came into the room. He was a tall man of forty who walked with a slight irregularity, always keeping his left hand in his suit-coat pocket as if to support his left leg, which had been a little crippled by a childhood fall.

"Your father walked over to us that morning holding his head so erect the way he does," said Jo to Angela, "and well, I want to tell you he was our leader. There wasn't one of us except Margaret who thought he was right, but, anyway, we passed him the command. He was always a commanding man. He seemed to draw his command from a private source of dark quiet. Those beautiful brown thoughtful eyes, why, they'd look at you so warmly, while he told you so firmly that your judgment had been so irresponsible as to bring into question whether it was safe for you to be walking around."

"I used to bang and bang against his rationality," Angela

said, "like a child banging against a locked door. He was the exemplar of a godlike sanctified liberalism that I couldn't breach. Argue with him? It was impossible. I would come back from college and I would go to him and say, 'The American Press is a bought press: only PM is free. Everything else is the reflection of vested interests.' He'd turn his full face towards me as much as to say, 'All right now, I'm giving you my fullest attention, the very same fullest attention I'd give to the president of the Campbell's Soup Company were he to seek my professional advice.' I suppose that was too much attention. The force of so much attention pulled into line like that, backed by regiments of reason held in reserve—it scattered my wits. He would let me run on, and once or twice he looked as though he would try to break in, but gave it up, and I would be talking a lot of nonsense. I knew it. Finally he'd say, 'Angela, you're talking a lot of nonsense,' pick up his paper, and dismiss me. Now, thirty years later, the whole country's in the argument. The young have breached that sanctified liberalism, but he isn't its exemplar any more. He has gentled. But then, in those days, it was just the two of us."

"Yes, for him it was just the two of you. The first thing one saw in Charles was not that he was a walking compendium of American Constitutional Law and the Puritan Ethic, but how absolutely crazy he was about his daughter, about you. I always sensed in him an enormous capacity to love and be loved, and he was so shy of showing it, of letting anybody pass through. His kindness, his reason, his integrity were sentries, were posted like sentries, and they wouldn't let passion out and they wouldn't let passion in. And with you, this love-filled, compassionate, irrational female child, so safely his own daughter, well, I think all that aching for a *giving*, unrestrained love, for a need whose very existence

he would have refused to recognize on logical grounds—
well, all that flowed right to you. Your mother, well, you
know your mother married the sentries."

"All told, they have not been unsuited to each other, and
in fact, the one stretch apart, they've been happy."

"Your mother has been happy with the sentries."

"And my father?"

"I only remember when you married Charlie and he tried
so hard to like Charlie that I wondered, how ever would he
be able to bear it, losing you."

"I know how he bore it."

⁄⁄⁄⁄⁄⁄⁄⁄⁄⁄⁄⁄⁄ CHAPTER SIX ⁄⁄⁄⁄⁄⁄⁄⁄⁄⁄⁄⁄⁄

*M*ARGARET was never to review the first chapter of her mother-in-law's story without affirming that there was no question, had it been Charles who found his mother's letter, that he would have stopped her before the boat left the dock, or cabled the captain after, or done the executive thing to do. No question. Nobody questioned it. Bill or Theo or Jo only questioned why. Later, one by one, they departed from the logic of that necessity to stop her. What was the compelling need in Charles, that classically private man, that rational, non-intrusive, kind, supportive son, to reach out and stay his mother's choice if he could, merely because that choice was inexplicable to him? Why would he have stopped her? Because he certainly intended to proceed beyond assuring himself that his mother was safe, sane, and had enough money; and to proceed beyond assuring his mother that she could draw upon her son for any need, to go all the way to the end and stop her.

He could not bear anomalies, that's what it was. He could and indeed did adapt to Jo and what appeared to be her spinning out a life story of consecutive romances unsanc-

63

tioned by law or by anybody else, and Jo was a dear favorite of his. But Jo was never anomalous. Her position was consistently illegitimate. There was never anything irregular in her irregularity.

"My father," said Angela to Jo, "did not blanch at a matter of simple unorthodox behavior."

"No, but at a matter of complex unorthodox behavior."

Charles took a deterministic view of human nature, which view he understood to be corroborated by Freud. What marked him off from other men, what made him among the grand ones was a lovely largeness in the way he allowed each man the assumption that he acted from an interior logic of his own. Psychoanalytical theory concorded with his view here too. He saw that was what Jo did. She proceeded from an inner logic. That was what his mother ceased to do by her flight: she departed from the logic of her nature. She diverged. (That she departed from the country was of no moment.) Charles hooted Angela down once when she accused him of denying the existence of free will. But Angela was probably right. He believed in a strong will and a weak will but not a free will. When somebody was seen actually to change course, why, that was a warning sign of psychic disorder. That person would have to be relieved of the responsibility for his own direction: had to be rescued.

"Were a great calm to have befallen Caroline," said Angela, "all the people who had to do with her would loll happily in her springtime: only my father would have had his fine brow furrowed until he had seen her restored to hysteria."

"He'd have been right. Probably he'd have suspected a tumor. Some malignant reason would have to be the cause of an abrupt shift in behavior. However, my mother's shift was not abrupt, but probably a long time in coming."

The second chapter of Mrs. Porter's story was more surmise than substance. Upon her landing in Europe, it blew up. All the inquiries Charles had made informed him of where she was not. His colleagues in the law pursued for him the financial resources Mrs. Brundage would be expected to draw upon, and themselves drew upon a blank. She had had accounts in London and in Zurich, of which she had closed the former on the twenty-eighth of July previous to her departure, and had not touched the latter. As the weeks and then months passed, the family began to settle on an uneasy presumption that their mother had not left France. This became an uneasy presumption indeed, as France began to crumple; but as there had not been a trace, not a word, each of her children was left suspended, and allowed himself the hope, according to his nature, that she was tucked up in some safe little fold. There was of course very little evidence produced by the German onslaught to sustain this hope, and if what was known later had been understood then about the implacable progress toward the Final Solution, there would have been even less reason to hope. However, hope is not a term in the law.

Uncertainty itself sometimes puts an unbearable stress upon a person, but the Porter nature bore the stress through the long war years, or seemed to. Charles and Margaret sailed for Europe in July of 1946, directly after Angela's wedding, and they returned six weeks later having experienced two disconnected encounters, one by the oddest chance, reviving and bolstering the uncertainty concerning Mrs. Porter's well-being (or being), and adding to it an uncertainty concerning the well-being of Margaret.

Angela went by herself to meet the boat and remembered nothing whatsoever amiss about her mother. On the contrary, the sight of her two elegant handsome parents passing quietly through the pushing crowds, the steaming heat and piled luggage and crated merchandise—through all the muscular sweaty movement of disembarkation and customs inspection under the arching metal roof of the pier—the sight of their notwithstanding calm so pierced her with the knowledge of her betrayal of them, her loss of them, that the memory of that afternoon left her for good with a wrench of pain for herself: not at all for her calm mother. Her mother was not calm. Of the conversation Angela could only recall her father's telling her about the thick morning fog.

It was the *Queen Mary*, and she was anchored for hours just outside the Narrows, and they watched at the rail while the ship's garbage was dumped into the sea and became the center of an ugly effluvium, an ocean of bobbing oranges and waxed milk cartons and cabbage leaves rippling outward through the steaming morning sun. It was naturally a distressing last feeling about one's ship. It was distressing to have been delayed, and Charlie, who had come down at the appointed hour with Angela earlier in the morning, refused to spare the time from his work to return. This left her unreminded of that boyish, comic charm of his that had won her hand, and which she could not manage to conjure up in the quiet presence of her mother and father. She had caught sight of them at the top of the gangway, and tears, love, despair boomed through her. In the moment's fright at such emotional regurgitation, she remembered to have swallowed everything, tamped it all down, sealed it. That's what she remembered: that by a furious act of will she was not distraught. But Margaret, her mother, was distraught.

That is to say, Margaret was distraught for *Margaret*. When she was with other people she looked pretty much herself, but Bill, for instance, perhaps because for him words were an awkward means for the exchange of feeling, noticed telling signs of distress immediately upon their return from abroad. Her eyes were a little rounded by pain, by bewilderment—it is incredible how much the eyes record—and he thought, what an irony that the touch of doubt softened her

66

expression, made her lovelier now as she was approaching fifty, than when she was younger, surer, colder, and in firm charge of the direction of the world.

In September Margaret began to visit a psychiatrist. While a move of this sort is of little moment today, it was still, after World War II, a move that sent terrible spasms of anxiety through all one's relatives (Is she crazy? Is it catching?). To be reduced to this desperate expediency was humiliating, had a leprous tinge, and you kept the thing a dark secret. Not Margaret. She might have lost her mind, but she had not lost her sense of noblesse oblige, and she announced as a matter of public policy that she was undergoing psychiatric treatment. Her nature was to lead, to educate, to accustom the people to accept new truths; and she kept so open her daily life and thoughts that if she had a bulletin board nailed to her apartment door, it might read:

Tuesday, the 11th

9:00   ACLU [She had been a volunteer at the Civil Liberties Union for twenty years.] "The question is whether we should enter as amicus curiae to defend that Nazi? I think we should."

12:30   Lunch with Helen Winkler [the friend who had urged her to see Dr. Wise.]

2:50   Dr. Wise

5:30   'Friends of the Museum' cocktails/dinner with Charles.

General Concerns: Should Angela send back that Altman's coat?

Has Charles remembered to check Bunch's Social Security business?

It was unjust that the soul of this open responsible Citizen Margaret should not have been the beneficiary of a policy that was meant to bring every sort of hidden ugliness up out into the air and light to be healed. And Charles, of course, did remember to check the Social Security business, because if they were nothing else, Charles and Margaret, they were splendid joint administrators of a most successful and esthetic life with far-flung interests. Were they nothing else together —and, more pointedly, was she nothing else beneath the exemplary citizen, handsome wife and mother? It is to be noted that when Margaret, the last night on the boat, burst into a lacerating, wretched, accusatory hate-streaked weeping that went on nearly till dawn, Charles was sickened to despair, but he was not shocked as if it were a sudden aberration. It was not anomalous. It was the end of a sequence that went back several years.

As concerned the psychiatrist, Caroline said it was the menopause. Bill said for Christ's sake it had nothing to do with the menopause. (It probably had *something* to do with it.) People who liked Margaret—and she was liked, she had good friends—believed that Angela's marriage was a greater blow to her hopes and her pride than she had let herself know. But it wasn't Angela's marriage (which didn't help, however), and when they were all down at Moriches for the Labor Day weekend, to give a good airing to all aspects of those two encounters that reflected upon the fate of their mother, Margaret turned privately toward Bill and said, "Do you remember telling me that summer just before Mother went away that I shouldn't be working for nothing, that I should refuse to do a job that didn't pay?"

Once more it was that lull in the afternoon, and once more the lawn chairs had been drawn under the maples which, while they had a young, man-planted naïveté about them because they were too short to be awesome, and too much the same green, did nonetheless provide considerable shade, and retrieved respect for Papa's property and vindicated

Papa's judgment. And Margaret's judgment. To Caroline's benefit. For Caroline did not have to suffer the disappointment over her mother's treachery in the matter of Moriches—although she did suffer it—because Theo had not only packed up and left the farmhouse that very fall, but he had asked Caroline if she would be willing to take on the burden of keeping the place. Caroline was not easily deprived of a grievance and was able to be manageress of Moriches summer after summer while retaining a resentment against her mother, and a kind of defiance toward Margaret, to whom she continued to attribute terrible predatory intentions.

Margaret saw Bill walking across the lawn, the now green well-sprinkled lawn, and left the circle of chairs to join him as she had seven years before, and felt Caroline's jaw tighten, as she had felt it before, and when she reminded him of the words that he had said to her, as if they were a sort of landmark at the beginning of her self-appraisal, tears filled her eyes so fast and fully that she had not time to cover herself. "It's just self-pity, Bill, it's just self-pity. Don't give me your sympathy!" But she had his sympathy and his love, and his arm around her, a slim little woman a third his size.

He loved Charles as well, and it was to Bill that Charles turned with the story of his mother's trail and his wife's travail.

On the south side of the property was the brown shingled cottage which gave onto a little (green) lawn and a wide rolling yellow meadow, beyond which was another duck farm watering itself at the edge of Great South Bay. You could not see the duck farm over the rise of the meadow, but you could hear the quacking when something upset the ducks (it takes very little to rattle them), and smell them in the right wind. Angela liked the smell. Along the south side of the cottage ran a screened porch, the pleasantest of places on hot days, always catching some breeze from the sea and always dark from the branches of a huge elm. The trunk of this elm was what the Porter grandchildren leaned against through the years when they squabbled and plotted and played: it was always home base. Bill and Charles had sat upon the porch in green painted wicker armchairs for hours that morning. The old screens that had been patched and repaired like a crazy quilt and had their little holes stuffed with white cotton had been replaced with clean new ones by Bill. Angela thought it was a little like painting over a mural—a corny wallpaper mural, for instance, that covered one wall of the bedroom that was yours through your childhood—painted over.

"We both sailed on that depressing note about Mrs. Brundage," said Charles. "Her money in the Swiss accounts was just lying there, never touched. And nobody had heard anything more of her than of Mother, which was to say nothing, zero, which in the case of a person of considerable wealth is significant, where it might not be so with a woman who had, as far as one can make out, two hundred dollars, period."

"Was Margaret anxious to make the trip anyway?"

"Yes, she was. That is, she seemed to be. And things were all right on the crossing, civilized, you know. And then the day after we got to Paris we had the appointment at the Sûreté, where we learned nothing again, except it was their opinion, given the conditions of the times, the sealing of the borders, that nobody would have been easily able to cross into what had become enemy territory, and there was no record, uneven as the records were, of their ever having left France. They had entered at Cherbourg on September 3. That was the last fact."

"What about the American journalist?"

"That was strange. We were staying at an English hotel on the Rue de Rivoli, and we'd gone down to have a drink before dinner that evening in their American bar—scotch and no ice—and this Hammond, a young fellow with a beard, kind of crumpled, meaning to suggest Hemingway, no doubt, he'd been drifting around Europe since he'd been demobbed and . . . well, the funny thing is he wrote spy stories. So his mind, don't you know, rather leapt up when it beheld our Cold Trail. It was his idea to take the Orient Express from Paris toward Prague, as far as one would have been able to go, which was Strasbourg, the last express stop."

"And Margaret seemed willing to do it?"

"Well, Margaret really liked Hammond. He was interesting. He was knowledgeable, for one thing. These expatriate colonies—he was the one who described them. There must be hundreds of them—Polish, Czech, Romanian, Russian—people who fled the East for political reasons, people of all classes. They seek each other out in some cosmopolitan center like London or Paris, and they build a little replica of their old world, more conservative, more isolated from organic change, more socially stratified, because for one thing they're walled in by language—and it's an old population. The young don't stay. Hammond said that when Hitler moved into the Sudetenland, Czechs poured over the borders, and because of geography, there was a small Czech—or had been a small Czech—colony in Strasbourg."

The two men on the porch had a bottle of Champagne Cognac that Charles had brought home for Bill, and they were drinking it out of kitchen jelly-glasses.

"The next morning we were on that train, and Bill, I can't account for it—I can't account for it." And Charles was stopped by an emotion he was unaccustomed to express. He leaned forward and propped his tanned elbows on his grey flannel knees and clamped his forehead in his hands, his fingers making furrows through his fine dark hair, and read his lines from the floor. "I had such an unreasonable feeling of exhilaration. In spite of Angela's marriage, and in spite of this specter of concentration camps that we could hardly have shrugged off . . . well, it was partly the train. Handsome—the appointments . . . polished mahogany and etched crystal for the lamps, and brass fittings—and everything was upholstered in a dull brownish moss color, like lichen in winter but more velvety. Lunch was being served and the white tablecloths were blinding white from the sun coming through the windows and the shadows flickering, and Margaret was beautiful, exquisite, part of it all, and I took the whole scene, made it stand for the whole domain of my life really, all tapestried, and I felt like a Renaissance prince: that I could order this splendor for us by command." He lifted his head and turned his face to the yellow meadow and saw the sunshine on the white tablecloth and the water trembling in the crystal water-glasses. "And then I caught in the fraction of a second her expression, Margaret's expression as she looked at me with something like revulsion."

Charles got up and walked the length of the porch where he regained his composure. Bill felt immobilized by the intensity of his compassion for Charles, for Margaret, unable to utter another word, perhaps for life.

However, in a while he was able to ask, "Did she say anything?"

"No."

"But she was aware that this—uh—that this thing had happened?"

"Yes. Well in fact that was the lifting of the lid. We never have mentioned lifting the lid. We've only counted things that have flown out. But that was later."

CHAPTER SEVEN

*I*N Strasbourg they had gone to the *mairie*, where Margaret made their inquiries in her very good American French. First it had to be determined that there were several hundred Czech nationals living at the present moment in the city and environs. With patience and persistence on both sides, it was secondly discovered by the old clerk with whom she had to do, that the addresses of these nationals tended to fall into one or the other of two small neighborhoods. Once the clerk had tumbled to this pattern himself, he was delivered over to the chase and called in a colleague, greyhaired and large-mustached like himself, and they both put on their visored hats and walked to the window the better to talk and think, looking, Margaret said, like two roly Marshal Pétains, only nice. Out of that conference emerged the recollection of a young Czech gendarme, and he was summoned.

His name was Jean-Paul Svoboda, and he had been born in France twenty-two years previously of a French mother and a Czech emigré father, now deceased. He was a hardly credible defender of the public weal, such a whey-faced boy did he seem, and in his uniform with baton he looked to American eyes like the assistant leader of the Middletown High School Band. After he had been introduced to Charles and Margaret and what had grown to four or five sympathetic members of the staff—nods, stiff bows, firm handshakes—the old clerk (who was not a clerk actually, but of importance locally and had the rank of Assistant Inspector), slowly and with great care explained to him what the Americans were after, and finally he finished with "Vous comprenez, n'est-ce pas?"

"Si-si, si-si! Je les connaissais bien!" said the young man, and Charles, who always felt he was a hairbreadth of a syllable behind when he was listening to French, first doubted, then replayed through his mind, what he had heard. "I knew them well! In fact, I didn't know them well, because I was a boy then, but I saw them frequently, and my grandfather was great friends with them. That is, he wasn't friends with them, only Mrs. Porter." He pronounced the name *Mme Porté* rather than *Mme Portère*.

"That 'Je les connaissais bien!'" said Charles to Bill, the medical man. "I so little expected to come upon any trace of my mother. They pricked me those words, as if they'd burst an abscess, and I felt washed with relief, I felt drained in that second of a heavy pressure that I hadn't even been aware weighed on me. You know, I don't think about my childhood, I don't think about my boyhood, which was dreary and frustrating and unsuccessful, and I don't think about my mother in any usual sentimental way. I never thought 'Do I love her?' or 'Don't I love her?' I took it for granted I loved her. I felt responsible for her, but more as if she were my client. Well, that's why I'm such a successful lawyer." He smiled. "I care about my clients, and they feel it. I'd do the same for my own mother!'—that sort of thing." And he laughed at himself.

"I never wondered," he continued, "whether I was a successful *son*, and I never wondered what my mother felt about me. A feather to her cap, I suppose I thought. After all, I was

74

a small, over-serious, over-sensitive boy who spent three years in the eighth grade, and Mama used to be summoned to school by the teacher and cry, and my father would come after me with a stick and tell her I was destined to be a bum and come to nothing, and she would cry some more. Well, and then I turned out to be a pretty grand show. And they got my check every month. It was papa who was destined to be the bum."

"How did you ever get out of the eighth grade?" Bill asked him.

"There was a citywide examination and I got the highest mark you could get. Of course I knew the stuff pretty well by that time."

Jean-Paul Svoboda brought them in a taxi directly to the home of his grandfather, a small man in his late sixties who wore a trim goatee and a white cotton coat, double breasted like a man's overcoat, which was the kind of protective smock that a butcher or a baker wears to this day. Old Mr. Svoboda was the proprietor in fact of the *patisserie* over which he lived, but he had people working for him, and Charles and Margaret and young Jean-Paul moved upstairs and downstairs several times through the day, following the old master baker, who still had to make rounds, though he didn't have to make bread. Whenever they arrived downstairs, they all settled at one of the little marble-topped tables where they drank pots of strong coffee with rich cream and ate endless Bohemian pastries made with plums, cherries, poppyseed, hot out of the oven, and got heartburn. Charles said it took a week for them to recover.

Mr. Svoboda spoke a serviceable French, but as he became engrossed in the search through his memories he reverted to Czech, and his grandson revealed himself as 'a dear worthy boy,' in Margaret's words, a caring collator who picked his expressions carefully, turning again and again to his grand-father to confirm that something would be said in the right way.

At the start of the war Mrs. Brundage and Mrs. Porter had taken rooms in a pension since razed by bombing, a very nice pension with perhaps ten or twelve guests, probably all Czech-speaking. Mr. Svoboda would likely not have met them at all, since the pension was several blocks from his home, but for the fact that his old crony lived there too, a man who came from the same village in Bohemia. This man's name was Čapek and he worked as a printer for an emigré Czech-language newspaper which was at that time published in Strasbourg but had a considerable circulation throughout Western Europe—among Czechs, of course. Čapek mentioned the two women as soon as they'd turned up because it was clear that Mrs. Brundage was first of all, very well-to-do and, second of all, very high strung, and she was a long time in accepting the conviction that a war which was of no concern to her would offer her nonetheless, obstacles that could not be bought off. She was determined to get to Prague, but one could not get to Prague. She was a tall, good-looking, red-haired woman, often imperious, but with a warm smile, altogether unreasonable. She talked with great emotion and much gesticulation, and for many weeks, and perhaps months—it was a long time ago—seemed to live in a feverish way very near to hysteria, chasing after one or another contact or possibility, official or unofficial, which might lead her toward her goal. After some time, however, Čapek realized that she had become calm, quite calm. She stopped walking on her toes as if ever prepared for instant flight, and instead seemed to settle into her rooms, would buy inexpensive little household things the way people do who live in furnished places over a period of time to try to be fond of them, to stamp their own mark on them. All the while she was calming and settling in, the city and the country and indeed the world were breaking up in terrible disorder. Men were going into uniform, factories were shifting to war goods or closing, there was scarcity of some things,

76

food was beginning to be short, families were picking up and leaving for the south.

Mrs. Brundage both settled in and at the same time was often away, sometimes for days, and this left Mrs. Porter (again Mme Porté) rather alone. And well, as it happened, Čapek took an interest in Mrs. Porter, in an altogether honorable way, you understand. In the general confusion of the times, they had lost a number of workers at the printing plant, and Čapek took to bringing copy for her to proofread, and before you knew it, there she was, reading away all day long at this language she had scarcely seen since she was a schoolgirl. There was a great deal for her to learn in a technical way, but she picked it up so quickly that in a matter of weeks she passed for expert, and Čapek had her paid by the piece. "And it was during this time that she started coming with him over to my café for coffee in the evenings, and you would have been astounded to see her change before your eyes from a very quiet, reserved person to one of considerable energy and wit. She seemed to have got hold of her old language, and it unlocked more than her tongue. She told me once that was what happened. I'd see her a good bit. I had lost my wife. Of course she was a little older than I was, but she was quite fine-looking. She kept her hair very short, and it was still very dark, some grey, but dark and wavy. Very nice. Of course, it was just companionship, you understand. Nothing more." And his head flicked up quick as a bird, his face very solemn, and he winked.

It was preposterous for the Porters to conceive of their mother as the cause of a wink of this Gallic nature. The cut hair, the hair cut short and wavy so as actually to be thought becoming—why the very word *becoming*, gratuitously offered like that, uninsinuating, of course, might have suggested an attractive aging woman of the twentieth century, but not of the nineteenth. And, what was more, she had taken to

77

wearing a trenchcoat of some sort that she had bought in Strasbourg, having had with her, evidently, nothing warm enough for the changing seasons. It was simply impossible to visualize their mother in a trenchcoat. It suggested a waist, and a waist, a woman. Simply impossible.

"One evening," said Mr. Svoboda, "when I accompanied Madame back to her rooms, I chanced to ask her where she got such a name as Angelina Porter, which was in nowise Czech. You perhaps will not understand," he told Margaret and Charles, "that in those bad days there was a kind of unspoken agreement not to ask personal questions about the past, for political reasons. If you don't know something, well, then, you can't be made to tell what you don't know. So it was a cautionary thing.

"She told me that as to the Angelina, her father, when he was a young man in Bohemia, had been restless, a wanderer, sometimes taking off on his travels with the excuse of some wares to sell—ribbons and lace, doilies, embroidery—you would call him a pedlar?—sometimes more vague and with no excuse. He'd leave their little village—this was before they emigrated to America—and right away head south for Italy. He loved Italy, he loved the opera and had a fine voice for the open road himself, and he named his daughter Angelina. He would have moved them all to Italy if there'd been any way to make a living there."

Charles said that he was nearly numbed by the unfolding of this story, that he found himself rubbing his fingers against his thumbs beneath the table to test whether his extremities were affected. At that point Mr. Svodoba was beckoned by the lady at the cashbox, and as he strolled back toward them with his white coat open he was singing, quite audibly singing the Toreador song from *Carmen*, nodding towards his customers, his arms stretched out to the fingers to conduct the orchestra, his head tilted, rocking, his eyes laughing, a great roué.

"You know, we would sing arias sometimes together. She could still carry a tune, and it was amazing how much she remembered of the words. She didn't understand the Italian, of course. *Tosca. Tosca* was her favorite opera.

There had never been so much as a phonograph in the Porter house. It was absolutely certain that Papa had never taken Mama to the Metropolitan Opera House. Charles would have been prepared to swear that the whole lot of them was unmusical, tone-deaf, uninterested, but a chord was touched in his memory and he heard the echo of his mother humming. His mother, after all, had been a great hummer. And later Jo told them all quietly about when she was growing up by herself, the last of the children at home, and Mama would be behind the nearly-closed door of Theo's room, with the radio on. Winter Saturday afternoons, which were sometimes so long and lonely through her childhood, she would tiptoe through the hall and crouch down by Theo's door for hours while the opera was being broadcast from New York. The voice of Milton Cross would bring her to.

Angelina Porter was certainly not a Czech name, but Mr. Svoboda had inquired about only the Angelina, knowing that the surname would derive from her American husband. Only once did Mrs. Porter offer him a picture of her past life, and then the roughest sketch. Her husband had been a Czech too, with the name of Prohaska, but when he had arrived in America—a young man there to seek his fortune—and the immigration official asked him whether he wouldn't like a fine American name, this suited him admirably, for he was prepared to put the Old World behind him forever. That was a common enough story. She told Mr. Svoboda something about where she had lived, and about her grown children, that they were established successfully, but he noted her clear distress at these recollections and helped her soon to change their conversation.

"So you are the oldest son." Mr. Svoboda nodded knowingly towards Charles. "The lawyer. Her favorite child."

Charles felt himself resonate fathoms deep. He was unaware that he had such depths to himself. He neither enjoyed this discovery that he had subterranean passages nor did he approve. That is to say, he approved of self-knowledge and was loath to indulge other people who gulled themselves, but his own pride was based in part upon a personal hard self-reckoning. And he had thought, these last few years when he began to doubt after all that he knew Margaret, that of course he at all events knew himself, knew where he was.

Where he was at this moment was standing with his hands in his trouser pockets, his back to Bill, facing out toward the meadow, a tall man, built on a tilt.

"Margaret's going to see a psychiatrist," he said to Bill. "I don't know what these fellows can tell you, but if I went to see a psychiatrist I'd tell him I'm suddenly a very lonely man. A painfully lonely man."

Bill felt himself to be nearly disabled by love and sympathy. There was no man he cared more about, and if he had caught rumblings of some interior distress in Charles, or more properly, in Charles's marriage, he was not prepared for this awful acceptance of defeat. He filled the jelly-glasses to the top with cognac, and with a nod they drank it down.

"That's the end of the bottle," Bill said, in the interest of hearing the human voice.

"That's the end of the bathos. I want to tell you about Mrs. Brundage. She must have been some girl."

ttttttttt CHAPTER EIGHT *ttttttttt*

*I*T was natural to assume that Mrs. Brundage felt the need of a duenna, that the antimacassared figure of Mrs. Porter would provide suitable cover and buffer and protection. She could hardly have been thought useful administratively, as a person employed to look after tickets and reservations, to see to the laundry and the buying of aspirin. Mrs. Porter, a great consumer of it, had never even bought her own aspirin. Yet she must have dealt successfully with the United States government in the matter of her passport. No, Mrs. Brundage wanted a duenna, wanted the comfortable docility of this elderly woman, a woman of few words, but those words, happily, Czech, and no doubt believed it befitted her station to shepherd and be shepherded like ladies traveling in a James novel, Slavic ladies improbably traveling in a James novel. That is what the Porters thought.

It was natural to assume that an elderly companion suited Mrs. Brundage's perhaps dated sense of European propriety, but in fact, as the story developed, propriety worried Mrs. Brundage very little. She wasn't notably indecorous, but her single concern, which evidently she had quite frankly communicated to Mrs. Porter in Swanson's Bakery, was to rejoin a man in the diplomatic corps in Prague whom she had met early in that spring of '39 at a house party in Southampton, and with whom she had had an amorous relationship. So it would seem that neither had propriety been an overriding concern of Mrs. Porter.

Indeed, the fact appeared to be that in Strasbourg, when Mrs. Brundage in the course of her frenzied and abortive efforts to reach the diplomat found relief and appeasement in the arms of a French perfume manufacturer, Mrs. Porter was perfectly glad for her and, as Mr. Svoboda described it, was not the least judgmental. And when the perfumer prepared to flee the advancing German army with Mrs. Brundage, and Mrs. Porter refused their urgent plea to accompany them, it was in part because she, Mrs. Porter, had already thrown in her lot with Čapek and the dwindling number of people still working the press, and in part, as she told Mr. Svoboda, she wished Sophie her joy and her privacy, for she was a woman who suffered and was not whole without a man.

So they went their separate ways, those two women, because naturally, as Mr. Svoboda described it, the press would have to flee too, and go underground, and towards the Ides of March that is what happened. One day they were all gone, and Mrs. Porter with them. She never gave him a sign that she was leaving, Mr. Svoboda said. "We were warm friends, your mother and I, but I will tell you that everybody, everything came second to her great romantic reunion, if I can be permitted to use such words, with the language of her birth. I believe that she found in that language a key to the rediscovery of her own soul." Mr. Svoboda knew nothing about her fate, although he had inquired after her at every opportunity. As far as he could tell, the newspaper never put out another edition. Only of Čapek had he heard. Killed fighting in the Resistance in 1943.

Charles said that he and Margaret stayed on in Strasbourg for a few days in order to absorb and assimilate what they had learned. He became determined to see whether with official help some trace of that little group attached to Čapek might not be uncovered. Margaret became determined to return home. He supposed now, he told Bill, that he should have tried to make some provision for her to sail earlier and alone. But booking passage at the last minute was impossible.

"It would have been a simple matter to book passage sailing west at the end of July," Margaret told Bill later that afternoon. "I should have insisted."

"Well, but you wouldn't have had your hair done on the *Queen Mary.*"

"No. But, Bill, I had it done, and I was undone by it. I was sick from holding myself together those weeks in France but then when the hairdresser told me about cutting her hair on the passage—a rite of passage on her passage—why, I came upstairs to our stateroom, and Charles was just dressing for dinner . . . it had got so I couldn't stand to be with him, poor Charles, . . . but I respected his right to know what I'd discovered. I said, 'Charles, I have just encountered the most astonishing coincidence,' and then I started to sob and I lost all control of myself. I said things to him that he could hardly believe, never forgive."

Almost everybody agreed it had been an astonishing coincidence for the hairdresser on the *Queen* who had attended Margaret to have been the very man to have cut off Mrs. Porter's hair. He was an incessant chatterer, this hairdresser, as Margaret described him, a slim, middle-aged, hipswaying, knee-dipping parody of himself and Margaret was barely listening to his talk about wig-making, the climbing cost of human hair, how in Spain the priests were supposed to be making fantastic money selling the hair cut off novices at the nunneries. "It was terrible drivel, terribly silly, but then he said that every once in a while some passenger would come down and want to make a wholly new person of herself, and would have all her hair cut off."

And so Margaret came to life and asked, and learned that he would never forget her mother-in-law. First of all, she was an old woman, whereas his experience with drastic cutting had been confined to the young, usually mere girls, and that, second of all, "the red-headed friend" was pushing to have her dyed and permed, but that he insisted on just washing and combing it into place, taking money out of his own pocket, but it was in his nature to be selfless and also he was an artist first. And third of all, the difference the cut made to her appearance had to be seen to be believed. And usually after such a thing the customer is in a terrible flurry—Oh, they shouldn't have done it! Oh, if only they could glue it all back!—but Mrs. Porter was very quiet, the other lady doing all the talking, but when she got up to leave she turned to him, pressed a dollar into his palm and said, "Thank you. I am very pleased."

"I don't see that it's *such* a coincidence," said Caroline from her chair in the circle under the maples, "After all, they were both sailing on the same boat, and they both went to the beauty parlor." Neither Theo nor Jo, who were sitting with her, seemed prepared to defend the coincidental nature of the story. "It seems to me," Caroline continued, "that we don't know any more about Mama now than we did before. They might just as well not have raked up the past and saved themselves a trip."

"You really feel that, Caroline?" Theo asked lazily.

"I really do feel that."

"You *feel* once more inappropriately," Theo said. "You ought to see somebody."

"It's Margaret that's going to see a psychiatrist," Caroline replied primly. She could see Margaret and Bill strolling and

84

pausing off near the cottage. Charles was down at the bay swimming with Angela and Charlie and some of the young Drinkwaters. "Evidently the marriage was too much for her," she next opined. "Personally I think Angie was darned lucky to catch Charlie Lewes."

And Jo thought, "I hate Caroline and Caroline hates Margaret and Margaret hates herself."

"Also," Theo added, "you think inappropriately, Caroline."

While, in the meanwhile, Margaret was saying to Bill, "It has nothing to do with the marriage. I'm not *interested* in Angela. I love her, but I'm not interested in her now. She'll go her way. She has to go her way, and I wouldn't envy her no matter whom she'd chosen. I'm bored with the young. It is my life, and the vacuity of it that has finally unstrung me. I am an impoverished woman! If I had to start over I wouldn't know what to do; and I don't want to start from twenty, but I do want to start from now. I remember so well that day we were in Maine and you called to tell us she'd gone away, just seemed to have stepped out of her life like that. Well, it was the beginning for me. And she was nearly sixty! I am forty-seven."

"You're a beautiful woman, Margaret, inside and out," Bill said. "You'll be all right. I know you'll come through this." But she offered evidence as if to say he was too sanguine.

"I am my own do-gooding mother all over again, in spite of everything. Worse than my mother. I am a kind of courtesan. Worse than a courtesan, as I don't even provide carnal pleasure. I can't bear to be approached any more. I'm terrible to Charles. The American Civil Liberties Union is my *hobby*. How degrading that word is!"

"It's not reasonable to knock yourself like that. You know that place wouldn't have made it without you," said Bill in anguish once again that day, and he patted her shoulder and bent over to look her in the eyes, and pulled a long curl of hair from a crease in her neck and hooked it around her ear, and made a series of encouraging noises, the whole with love and the intent to jolly up her self-esteem.

"These young lawyers back from the war, they come down to the ACLU and they're not interested in our old philosophy. They're onto a new tack. And suddenly, I'm not interested in battling for our old philosophy either. I want to get out, to leave it all to them."

"Don't get out until you've started talking to that Dr. Whatsisname, will you?"

"And if I quit the ACLU I won't have a hobby. I'll have nothing. And if I leave Charles, I won't be a housewife, I'll be nothing."

"Margaret, for the love of God, don't do anything until you've had some time with this doctor."

"I don't have a god. I have nothing," she repeated, but she turned and smiled to reassure him, and said, "But for the love of you, Bill, I will wait."

The things that Bill knew and the things that Jo knew would eventually be what Angela would come to know, so that she could reflect that at the time of her mother's—what it was called then, albeit somewhat uneasily, was 'nervous break-down'—just when her mother was becoming ready to find herself no more than a courtesan, Angela was sitting in her economics class at Smith, hearing the following sort of advice from a most fake-aristocratic old Englishman, Mr. W. B. Hornesby: power and excitement for women lay not in the vote, not in the job, not in bed (very daring), but in the *salon*. All they had to be, these girls, were elegant, knowledge-able, beautiful, fascinating, and the great decisions in art and politics and finance would be brought to terms in their draw-ing rooms under, implicitly, their direction.

The girls called the course "Economics 316a: Saloon-keep-ing." They laughed at the Proustian Decadence. They were not unaffected by the implicit injunction with the highest intellectual overtones to Go thou into the world and Look Stunning, for they had grown up through the years of the Hollywood star system and could not help but want to be stars. Angela said that, as her grandfather had been a saloon-keeper, success would probably come naturally to her. But then, quite seriously one night, she told her dearest friend that it wasn't her grandfather but her mother who was a natural for saloon-keeping. She gave lovely parties and mixed the worlds of art and law, and men to this very day loved her and thought she was beautiful, and she *was* beautiful. "But she is really a courtesan," said Angela, all on her own: and it cost her some pain to say it.

"Hornesby is a ass," said her friend. "There's no life-role worth the respect of a woman's consideration that isn't worth the respect of a man's. Would your father want to ornament a salon? 'Not in bed' indeed! He's a faint-hearted fornicator, old Hornesby! Does your mother sleep with those men who presumably make their decisions at her feet?"

"No, no, no certainly not," said Angela sobered by the thought.

"Well, then she can't qualify for courtesan. It is the *sine qua non* for the title."

It was a coincidence that Margaret and her daughter should arrive at the word *courtesan* in such similar context. Submit the word coincidence to Caroline, and once again she would reject it probably in favor of Revealed Truth.

Angela admired extravagantly her petite and elegant mother who did everything so easily and so handsomely. Her admiration imperiled her, for she was hopelessly ill-equipped to be petite, to retraverse her mother's path. Angela was large and plain and, above everything else, unremarkable. People would ask (she thought), "Don't you know Angela Porter? She was with us at the café last night. She's a wonderful girl," and the fellow would say, "Which one was she?" On the basis of her general unremarkableness she rejected as impracticable the injunction to go out into the world and be stunning, but instead must have turned, she thought later, toward her Aunt Caroline for a model, an otherwise unremarkable woman who had made anyhow her mark as a multiple mother. That was open to Angela.

During those years of her young womanhood when she resolved to be insignificant with good grace and dignity, she drew some comfort from the belief that she came from remarkable people. Her father, her mother, her uncles, her aunts, and above all her grandfather, all remarkable. Her grandmother was not on this list. It was not that Angela regarded this grandmother who disappeared as so unremarkable that she did not put her on the list: she forgot even to omit her.

The overlooking of her grandmother was an example of the curious way one unconsciously selected the impressions one wanted from a reasonably noteworthy sequence of events. Initially, with her grandmother's entry into her odyssey, Angela was in college and out of the stir of family talk. Seven years later, when her parents came back from Strasbourg, Angela was entirely absorbed in the protection of her marriage, as though she were mother to a fragile infant, an infant with possibly fatal defects the symptoms of which she refused to acknowledge. All her mind was given over to explaining the symptoms as benign. And to whom? Who was attacking her marriage, who despising her for an unworthy choice? Well, without firm control, herself. With firm control against any tendency to delve, to burrow into herself, she listened to the story of other people, not delving or burrowing there either, only skimming. What she recalled best about the Strasbourg trip was her father's description of the beautiful train from Paris, and the reason why was that it recalled to her so vividly her grandfather's story about a trip on that train that he took before Angela was born.

"Tell me about the time you took the train from Prague so you could go back to the little village where you were born," she had asked her grandfather, again and again. He had gone to lunch in the dining car, and he described to her his sitting at a table by himself, how fine the food was in those days, how beautifully polished was the silver, the glassware, the woodwork, how delicate the china, how clean and white the napery, that you felt like a prince when you traveled in that way—and this was very much the echo of what her father would later say. "And all the time I was having my meal, there was this young man sitting some tables down and I would catch him staring at me before he looked away. Well, after a while, I can tell you, I became uneasy, and hurried with my coffee so that I could leave for my compartment. And as I was getting ready to pay my check, this fellow jumps from his seat, strikes his hand on the table, and cries out, 'Un Gottes willen! It's OOncle Adam from Amerika!'" and her grandfather would slap his knee and punch out the line. She would have wanted to take that train herself one day. On to Strasbourg to find the old baker and sit in his café and hear from him the strange tale of her grandmother? No, back to her childhood in Moriches before the foreclosure of her choices.

ffffffffff CHAPTER NINE *ffffffffff*

M ARGARET was not *interested* in
Angela. Young people bored her.

Caroline felt frequently compelled to announce, "I have to
sacrifice my own need for my children's. They come first."
The need in question was always worthy, reasonable, inexpensive, modest, and renounced unblushingly. Nobody could
understand how she could say such a thing and not blush.
"Caroline is not stupid," somebody or other would insist as
if to clear up right away the likeliest misconception. About
the time that Angela was coming into maturity, certain psychological phrases were sifting down into the folk wisdom,
and one of the most handy was to explain anybody's aggressive behavior by saying he was 'insecure.' More or less everybody betrayed himself as insecure, and it was the word used
regularly to explain Caroline. It was probably fair in her case.

Insecure or not, how she could seriously say something so
tacky as "I have to sacrifice my own need for my children's;
they-come-first"—bright woman as she was? Well, banality is
a terribly likely consequence of the under-use of a good mind.
That is why in particular it is a female affliction. One does

suspect that a woman like Caroline who has deliberately wrapped her outward-reaching impulses in Home and Family bunting does take some sly pleasure in scattering platitudes into the ranks of the unbelievers. In her delivery one detects a touch of cynicism. And Caroline was married to a man who was the greatest unbeliever of them all, who would not go to PTA meetings, who would not be a den leader, who was unmusical, unpunctual, and probably unfaithful because women approached him as though he belonged in the public domain. He certainly was forever out there, old Hail-Fellow Bill, cruising around in the public domain, soft lights, young nurses, and God knows who else, being generous and attentive and useful to everybody but His Own.

Her mother's departure was hardly likely to make Caroline less secure, and in fact reinforced, fairly enough, her sense of the unreliability, the untrustworthiness (Papa's property to Theo!) of people. *Beware of Greeks bearing gifts* was her attitude to people. She looked out beyond her children, beyond her stoop, and she saw Greeks, and she saw Bill trading freely with them.

With children Caroline was divine. She was the arch brownie-baker, and the house was filled with Boy Scouts and band members and ballerinas from the farthest reaches of Garden City. Her boys would prove a great credit to her, would be prize-winning scholars (they all went to Princeton), would be medal-winning soldiers (two were in the War), and would go on to graduate school, from which one doctor and one lawyer (and one biologist). They bore every outward sign of success that all those undeserving mothers who were not avowed sacrificers wished anyhow for their own young. The one girl, Annie, four years younger than Angela, was a cheery homebody and her mother's comfort, and washed the dishes (Angela never washed the dishes), and in time would not want to go away to school. All heart and a straight B average, Annie would leave Queens College in the middle of her sophomore year to marry a student of the documentary film (who later drank) and to become in the New York Telephone Company the highest-ranking, highest-paid woman they ever had.

Caroline liked the young, and when Angela was young, Caroline liked her. She expressed this liking in abrupt half-sentences such as, "I surely thought you were going to be the world's gawkiest-looking bride but . . . ," and her fondness for the daughter was no doubt warmed by dislike of the mother. However, she did offer Moriches for the wedding. And so Angela had been married on the lawn between the farmhouse and the cottage in a ceremony officiated by a Justice of the Peace who read from a beautiful script that her father had written. It was a lovely simple wedding, enormously expensive to mount, all the simplicity having to be ordered by Margaret and delivered from New York. It was a small family wedding extended to a few young people, Charlie's father and mother being a tacitly understood embarrassment to the Porter *amour-propre*. Red roses were everywhere. Bill had begun training roses over a split rail fence he'd put up, and they were thickened out wonderfully by a greenhouse in Westhampton. Jo was her maid—or matron—of honor.

It was easy to count out Charlie's family, but not Charlie, a slim, limber, collar-ad handsome, as it was then called, graduate student just Angela's age and just Angela's height. He was the only issue of M. M. Lewes, financial wizard, consulted by President Roosevelt, a familiar at the White House, it was let out by the Leweses, if one could become familiar very fast in two visits five years apart, added the Porters. His marceled mother, who pampered the wizard, wizard, jr., and herself by turns, was a vain woman of that breed who overate and whose face and stomach fattened but whose legs mysteriously didn't.

She wore the sheerest silk stockings, her skirts too short, the highest spike-heeled shoes of suede or satin.

She was a woman about whom it would be difficult to say whether an extraordinary native intelligence had been narrowly channeled into the smallest concerns, *tant pis;* or whether a very modest endowment appeared capacious in an arena that encompassed only herself and son and husband, *tant mieux.* "Where do they come from, these Leweses?" someone was heard to ask Theo. And Theo shrugged his shoulders as if to say he knew very little about them but gathered that Mrs. Lewes upon her marriage converted from Catholicism to Narcissism and, it seemed, never looked back. "A Saul of Tarsus sort of thing, you know," said Theo. The wizard himself had nothing to say socially, was charmless and harmless. They were among four people who drowned when a pleasure cruiser capsized in a storm off Florida about two years later and the *Times,* in a good-sized obituary, noted that he would be missed for financial reasons; but beyond feeling the jolt of a violent death, people did not appear to miss him otherwise, neither Mr. Lewes nor his lady. Angela didn't miss them. Charlie didn't seem to miss them either.

How ever could Angela have picked Charlie? She picked him because he was handsome, popular, careless, bright, and picked large, plain her. However could Charlie, who was charming and spoiled, who was called "very egotistical" by the girls he didn't court, and "a guy who could date any girl he wanted," by the girls he did, pick Angela? Well, of course because there was a lot of substance in Charlie and also because at a critical point he had suffered a severe check in his free-wheeling assumption that he could have anything he wanted. He had been turned down at Harvard, Yale, Princeton—*all* Caroline's boys went to Princeton, one reason for her generous attitude to the certifiably lesser Charlie—and had gone to (equally estimable) Amherst in two sessions separated by the War, in which he was in the Battle of the Bulge and from which he felt truly fortunate to have come out at all, and had in the end graduated *magna cum laude*. The rejections, the War, the times in general, perhaps, had a permanently chastening effect, and this man, who seemed destined to be forever impossibly boyish, was to keep that rendezvous (to use Churchill's words in Churchill's time), but not wholly, because he became, already while he was at Amherst, a serious scholar, and he remained a serious scholar whose contribution to American studies matured remarkably through time even if he did not.

Later, looking back upon the years of her successful 'handling' (an exposing word) of this man, Angela thought: I belong to the best in the genre of managerial woman. We stage such very good marriages. We cook with wine and Provençal herbs and serve a buffet against a backdrop that is book-littered and with wall-hangings and Baskins and Shahns and Eskimo sculpture ("And what's that?" "Why it's said to be a carving from a gatepost, India—only early nineteenth") and African masks (Well, I have an aunt who lives in Rhodesia and she has been . . .")—the sort of woman whose children get into Harvard and then drop out of it (and this was prophetic): her sort.

Behind-the-scenes women (what heartily and proudly was to be looked for and found in back of every successful man!) hadn't they arrived in middle age having mounted marriage and family life wonderfully well? Hadn't they created a most benign environment for the best possible growth of the husband, a domestic setting from which the most gifted children would be proud to flee? And then what happens in that child-centered life when the center goes? Why, everybody has a climacteric, by which she did not mean a biological one like the menopause.

If one looks up 'climacteric' in Webster's *Second Interna-*

tional—that dear concerned dictionary—the definition will prove to be immensely gratifying to Angela's sort of woman. A climacteric, among other things is a point in human life in which some great change in constitution, health or *fortune* is especially likely to occur—"The critical years are thought by some to be the years produced by multiplying 7 by the odd numbers 3, 5, 7 and 9." Oh, delightful, dearest dictionary and spiritual guide, it is thirty-five and forty-nine you get by this, unbiological ages, where things fall apart for *metaphysical* reasons. Well, and her sort of woman manages beautifully to hold her sort of man together so that he works proficiently in spite of dips, of climacteric troughs of doubt: at thirty-five he takes a year or so to lower his sights—he is not producing on a Nobel level—and at forty-nine he has an ugly struggle over the inconsequentiality of his entire life-interest. (*He* does.) She supports him. She stands by—until their eighty-first year which, says Webster's "others add" to the critical years of multiples of 7. These are the good marriages that won't fall apart unless at forty-nine she has a climacteric which has her examining the consequentiality of her entire life interest.

They would never fall apart, ordinarily, but the world was falling apart, its final decision to do so seeming now to have been made in about 1960, while in 1970 the dissolution having proceeded amazingly, it called out to women, rather generously and grandly called out, "You may as well come from behind!" as if the prison were stormed to free the political prisoners and in the end they were letting out lifers too: a scene from *The Heart of Midlothian*. Angela could not now be the woman behind the successful man. The '60s were a climacteric period for Angela and for the world both.

Charlie had not said "Get thee behind me!" Not at all. From the beginning when he looked for her he looked behind, but he hadn't sent her there. If it were a psychological truth that marriages were made, if not precisely in heaven, in the sub-conscious (the very next manufactory of inscrutable reasons), then she would be able to say about her choosing Charlie that he answered her advertisement for someone who absolutely could not acknowledge wife as peer, but who, at the same time, would buckle and sulk without the maintainance and sponsorship of a strong woman. Her marriage and the ducking behind him to hold him up was, in effect, a 'holding operation' from which they both gained tremendously. She knew she grew beneath his shelter, that she owed to him the time and cover provided, the sense of emergence from a formlessness to a somebody, of triumph over her own young self, that she was grateful and for a long time never meant to leave him, meant to stand *beside* him until they were eighty-one if necessary.

At her wedding her mother was in beige and in a nervous state, and for many years thereafter rather abdicated her directorship as far as concerned her relationship to Angela. Angela, filled with love and admiration and inadequacy at the thought of her mother, was anyhow forced by the 'breakdown' to experience a respite from the superintending Margaret, and to lay the beginnings of her own marriage and motherhood by herself. This perhaps explained her temerity in having one baby after another in the fashion of her Aunt Caroline, which she subsequently wondered if she could have done had her mother been well and at the controls. The years of Margaret's suspension of interest left Angela in an esthetic vacuum as far as the design of her marriage went, without a statement of policy, as it were, and she had to fill it catch as catch can with what she saw later as an amalgam of Margaret and her grandmother and Caroline.

The first home that was Angela P. Lewes's was the small upstairs of a wooden row house, this row one block from the Sound and the salt spray and the hovering gulls, and very far and inconvenient to the university in New Haven. The neighborhood was an Italian enclave next door to a honky-tonk boardwalk, and for most of the year the houses and their families together effaced themselves, drew in, muffled in sea mist, but in the spring when the new sun burnt the mist dry there was a great burgeoning of human life and plant life and car, bicycle, and motorcycle life. Angela and Charlie would have moved but for the sand and the Sound, the sewery Sound that stood in for the clean sea. The salt smell held them there for the five years they were in New Haven. It was the only five years of her life that Angela was with a single exception friendless, living outside society. She painted, printed, sewed, read, cooked, cleaned and had babies with great intensity, cultivating the smallest inches of her time fastidiously as the old Italian men in her neighborhood tended their small patches of yard, extending the possibilities of its yield marvelously, even roofing them with trellises for the wine grapes, growing wine grapes in the very air.

That a bright, educated young woman would cultivate domesticity with such remarkable intensity is now rightly seen as an appalling misuse of woman. Right or wrong, it was seedtime for Angela. "I learned two things in those five years," she said later to Jo. "That I had the greatest potential to be an excellent domestic and to be a third-rate artist."

"And you read."

"Yes, and of course I read . . . from which everything follows."

And there was nothing unique about the misuse of the young Angela. To be a married student then was a new phenomenon. There was, furthermore, a certain chosen quality about being the wife of a married student. Marriage and parenthood were undergoing then, as it now seems, a fake revival, and the young educated woman, for the most intellectually advanced reasons, willingly, joyfully contracted herself to the smallest concerns to make an art of her life, her roles, her children.

"There was one morning when the thing was settled," Angela said to Jo. "Christina was two, and we were fog-bound by the window. I was pregnant with Adam, and I was doing a woodcut and watching the fog press against the pane. It was a large gull I was cutting—very large, from the under-side, and I was gouging his gull throat, and I knew all at once that I would never gouge out of art anything that would al-low me to say 'I am an artist.' 'I, artist,' was a charade. But 'I, mother' wasn't, and I turned to the having one child, nearly two children to . . . retrieve my dignity." This was one of those conversations Angela and Jo had in the library of the Northampton house in that early winter of 1960 when they were waiting for Theo to die upstairs. It was a watershed of a time for Angela, or what the *Britannica* says it would be better to call a 'Water Parting'—"the boundary line be-tween one drainage area and another." When one is living such a metaphor one does not, of course, know it. Now, ten years later, when nothing stays her, when she is fully on her course, Angela is witness to the fact of her own Christina's living in a loft in the Village, calling herself an artist, not having yet said 'I am a charade,' not having children to re-trieve her in case it comes to that. "Oh Tina," does Angela say, "if you had a husband and children . . . ?" or "Well, Tina, my dearest child. At least you do not have the problem disguised from you." Which does she say? She says the second. To herself.

*J*O, that last born of the old Porters, grew through a silent childhood to become as tall and as dark as her oldest brother Charles, and oddly beautiful with hair as black, skin as white as a princess's in a fairy tale. There was from her earliest years something that caused her to be thought of as a sort of lovely changeling, a genuine and natural spirit set down by the elves for reasons unfathomable (if not cynical) in the Porter cradle. She was loved and left free by her hard-nosed, rational, achieving brothers and sisters, and by her hard-nosed, irrational father, and by her withdrawn mother, as though they bowed before her, having been lightly brushed and left a bit sanctified, and with the hint of doom. This long-limbed free spirit had been a loving little girl and then a loving big girl, and by the time she was a loving woman, it was too late to consider how to impose the conventional and legal restraints upon the expression of her nature. When she was seventeen, in the gentlest most unprovocative way she told her mother and father that she would be off to New York on the morning train to study at the Art Students'

League, having just signed herself out of the high school that afternoon, and that she would stay with Charles and Margaret for the present.

"Didn't they make a fuss?" Angela asked.

"Not too bad. Papa said, 'That's a damn fool thing to do! You going to spend your life painting pictures? You'll live in a garret!' and Mama sighed and drew her lips together and nodded and said finally that I was to go upstairs and get my slips for her to mend, that she didn't want me to go to Margaret's with torn underclothes."

Jo departed from the Charles Porters soon after to live in something very like a garret with her drawing instructor, but in a matter of weeks she had eased away from this man toward the novelist, Frank Mulholland, then in his prime (forty. Forty? Forty.) whom she met around a crowded table in the Russian Tea Room and with whom she lived, on and off, for several years in a farmhouse he had in Wilton, Connecticut. In fact she never quite finished living with him. He is one of her ports of call, still, now in his 70s. In the early days before the war Mulholland would drive Jo down to Moriches in his Cord, a rich man with no running boards, toward whom the Porters never became chummy, nor were they hostile, and really the only mark he left after seven years of fairly regular association was on Caroline, who fixed her irritation on the abandonment of running boards by the automobile industry, the fault of the soon-defunct Cord and, by extension, Mulholland. As Mulholland was divorced, Caroline did ask Jo why she didn't marry him.

"No need."

In a sense Jo was born needless: she sought neither the law's guarantee nor society's blessing for any love she had. The two sisters, Caroline and Jo, born twelve years apart, were polar images in this. "No need," said Jo, for marrying, and Caroline was scornful. Caroline had no god. She believed instead in the iron law of marriage.

"I may be old-fashioned," she would announce, "but I do not believe in adultery!" Marriage was a legal contract to which the woman, as cosignatory, agreed to much the nastiest lot in life, in exchange for which the man owed her sexual fidelity. Why sexual fidelity? Why not love? She called the whole complex business love and believed she took title to it when she signed the contract. To be sexually monogamous seemed to be for her a severe and punitive price a married man must pay because those were the terms of the contract. Fidelity, legality, money, adultery, geometry—all these were the hard, clear terms with which she hypothesized marriage. Jo, on the other hand, didn't hypothesize marriage at all, because of her seeming unconflicted capacity to love more than one person, many more than one person; and adultery, fidelity, geometry, legality, money, were all alike subjects that rarely urged themselves upon her serious consideration. Her dislike of this sister, which took root very early in her childhood in reaction against her ruthlessness about obedience, waxed with her love for this sister's husband, and rested not upon Caroline's being the shrewish wife, but upon Caroline's tenacious conviction that she was legally entitled to her shrewishness. Caroline needed the law. Jo had no need.

Jo was not *exclusionary* by nature, the way almost everybody else seemed to be. She must simply have been born latitudinarian. And she was nonhierarchical. It wasn't that she refused to be impressed by rank, but that she didn't notice in this laddered world what rung one was clinging to or reaching for. And finally, she lived in a timeless present. Jo was inexplicable to her world, but not to ours. It was as though she were pulled out of that future for which she made no plans, brought backwards in time by some agency, by the elves, arriving to play her part thirty years too soon for it, before it had been written. Her world was charmed and disconcerted by Jo, and it let her make her private path through, stepping backward from her the way it does for lepers and for saints. But she was not a leper and certainly not a saint. She is explicable to this world of the '70s, as consonant as Angela's children with disestablished love and caring, with their egalitarian disrespectfulness, with the nowness.

On the underlying always-interesting question of sensuality, who of them all was brushed with it in any especial degree? Angela thought about herself that she was not a sexual creature, and Jo thought *she* was not, and they agreed Charlie wasn't, for instances. But on what evidence? Not on outward signs. Angela, at least, had never slept with anybody before she was married, but Charlie? Hundreds. And Jo liked to touch whom her heart warmed to; and toward warm women and children and men she would reach out with her fingers to their cheek, or sometimes lips, as though she were blind and her sensuality (indeterminate as was the question of it) moved the more urgently through her remaining senses. And, not surprisingly, the finger-touching and the great, palest-blue, listening, caring eyes, the large jaw so fine a setting to a fine mouth, and of course the sinuosity of her long body—all that caused the men to want to touch back. From time to time there would come a man who wanted her very much, and his wanting evoked her wanting to give him what he wanted, and she did. She turned toward men with interest and affection and love, and came to them sexually, the sexual possibility a bonus dimension (as against a woman) in pursuit of deep love, caring, friendship.

Jo's first move away from the art instructor and toward the novelist was a figurative veering off from the plastic arts toward the novel, via acting and then writing for the theater, and thence to other forms of fiction. At the time of her mother's disappearance she had sublet a small apartment on West Fifty-seventh Street from an actor she knew who was having a spell in Hollywood, and she had cut down from the full-time to the partial mistress of Mulholland of Wilton, a mutually agreeable diminution of their time spent together.

It is a fact that if you are an anomaly to other people, *they* think a lot about how odd your choices are. You, the anomaly, give much less time to that. After her talk about her mother with Bill at the French Café that late-summer day in 1939, Jo walked up the Avenue and into the zoo and sat by the seals for a long time, musing about, and anguishing over, and longing for not her mother. Bill.

Bill had been a romantic figure for her, how far back into her childhood she could not remember. She was the kind of little girl who saw a sitting father as something exactly up-holstered for her comfort, and in the evenings when she came upon her father reading the newspaper, she would duck under it and rest against his chest for renewal, and her old father, adjusting his daughter's head from his line of vision, held her and read on. But Bill, when he was a young tall bony man with yellow hair, her grown-up sister's husband, wasn't cushioned in a way inviting to a child, wasn't an auxiliary papa; but she, anyway, headed for him whenever he was around, climbed up against him and, as she recollected with a tremor on this seal-watching day, liked to run her hand slowly along his wide chest to fit her fist into his armpit. She could scarcely recall, now, his being yellow-haired and slim. She looked at a seal half flopped onto its back with its great round belly up to the sun and thought Bill's belly must be very like, that she would like to bury her nose in it. Not sisterly thoughts, those.

The impropriety of lusting after one's sister's husband was not altogether inoperative in Jo, for whom propriety was usually a threshold too low to trip over. However, she kept

Bill a wraith in her fantasies, an increasingly blubbery wraith who awakened her and led her into intimacies, never when she actually saw him in reality, but always just after having been with him in the flesh; then back across the barrier to her fantasy world she would rush him, safely disembodied, to act his part in a daydream.

The barrier between fantasy and reality was what she walked through the day of her father's funeral in Moriches in the spring. The barrier in actuality—and, as the subject is the division between the disembodied and the bodied, an esthetically appropriate barrier—was the high wrought-iron fence that surrounded the cemetery through whose gate she passed that day, behind Bill and Caroline and their children toward the open grave up ahead, where she could see the hearse and the men hastily setting the coffin down beside it and driving off.

She had felt the loss of her dear father very deeply, especially in this cemetery where they had walked together hand in hand many times behind the Memorial Day parade, the pines rising very tall and very black, the sunlight filling the well of the clearing where the little gravestones were sinking, through the years, through the centuries, into the graves they marked. Distinctly she remembered the sound of the rifle shots saluting the dead, a frightening noise. Her father would warn her and she would cover her ears and press her head into his body (into his belly?).

Bill's thick skull, thickened by his thick grey hair, was in front of her, and he hadn't had a haircut lately, and the white hair over the roll of his red neck made a fringe on his coat collar. His big, rounded, stooped back strained at the seams of his suit, but then he tapered marvelously downwards. His hips were slim and his legs were the legs of an athlete.

They straggled, the family, untidily along the bottom end of the grave, and waited while townspeople and friends of her

father joined them, and then Charles, who was standing between Margaret and her mother, crossed to the other side to
read the burial service he had put together, and she, in the
shifting—yielding to an overwhelming need to touch—moved
toward a little space open between Bill and their little Annie,
and put her hand around his thick tough upper arm—solid as
a hod-carrier's—and felt him press it against the side of his
chest. His back to her, he didn't, anyway, wonder whose
hand had sought him.

She needed to touch the people she cared for. And Bill, in
his way, was a toucher of people. His arm readily reached
around shoulders. When little children were about, his or
anybody's, he stooped to pick them up. He always bussed the
older women. He patted younger behinds. On his rounds at
the hospital he sat at the edge of beds and held people's hands.
He wiped their foreheads. So they were two touching people,
she thought as she sat with the seals and played with the word;
and their romance, heretofore the figment of two separate and
self-contained imaginations, each as integral as two raindrops
on a leaf, could or might at the most delicate touch come to
make one romance, as would happen to the raindrops.

Ought she not to have remarked how inappropriate was this
reactivation of her longing for Bill on the very afternoon she
had discovered that her own mother had so incomprehensibly,
so flatly, left her without a goodbye? Why, she was suddenly
virtually orphaned, with her father's death not five months
before—a change in status that deserved a tear of its own.
And ought she not to have tweaked her conscience at elimi-
nating Caroline from any consideration of at least loyalty?
Not Jo's oughts.

As to her own mother's incomprehensible departure, Jo
comprehended it. She was the only one of Mrs. Porter's children who knew intimately, or rather intuitively, the later
woman, the one in abeyance, and were she asked to explain,

for the edification of her bewildered family, why *her* Mama was not quite *their* Mama, she could do it. She had talked to Bill at lunch very easily about what it had been like for her, what it probably often was for that last and unforeseen child, born to a woman who had years before completed her cycle of childbearing and infant-rearing. In the dozen years between Caroline's birth and hers, her mother, buffeted, matured, had become a much more private person. To tend this unexpected infant Jo visualized her crossing backward and forward over a great distance, a field of time. But very far from leaving with this last child the sense that it was an unbearable intrusion reluctantly care for, she laid down in her from the very beginning a nearly beatific regard for silence and privacy, a capacity to love without clutching, to love without needing to redesign, to reorder, to alter and improve the one who is loved.

"Does that explain me, Bill?" she had asked him over their wine. He had watched and listened to her so fixedly that she wanted, finally, to hear what he was making of it all. His eyes were green, she noted suddenly. Behind his glasses and his narrowed lids and the creases and lines of humor (and age) and the great fair eyebrows, she had never noticed the color of his nearly-hidden eyes. "I mean," she went on, "when I love someone I feel less inclined to tamper with him, not more."

"And less inclined to marry him, not more?"

"But I have loved not a few men. If I married, why, I would seem to agree to eliminate or foreclose or confine myself . . . Of course I can say this because I don't think I will have children."

In addition to the explanation that Mrs Porter, by the time she had borne Jo, was a mother once-removed, so to speak, from the centrality of maternal absorption, there were less supposititious facts to account for this increasing distance she seemed to allow between herself and everybody else, with the partial exception of Jo. Jo was eight when her father arbitrarily and unilaterally made the decision to remove them all to Moriches year round, and this in effect plucked his wife from the busy populated old immigrant neighborhood of her young womanhood, and rather slapped her down into the long empty falls and winters and springs of that remote Moriches. Her gradual withdrawal into herself, which went so largely unnoticed as only now to be a reconstruction of her last twenty years, her retreating to Theo's old room, her taking to bed with the vapors (a clever escape from the old man into hypochondria that her sympathetic children admired) all these symptoms might now be called Depression.

"I think you all saw her as a resigned woman," Jo had told Bill. "But the resignation . . . well, she rather dramatized the resignation. She invited you to think of a figure in a mourning picture, with herself now mourned, now mourning, wilting by a stylized willow and a stylized urn. She seemed to mark out for herself the longest possible old age through which she would solemnly, sweetly enjoy the long slow decline into death. Her *role* was the Resigned Woman, but beneath she was neither so resigned nor so old."

On the Fourth of July when they had all gone down to Moriches, Jo had found herself alone for a while with her mother in the kitchen, and she had put her arm around her and said, "Mama, you know, I have this really very nice apartment in the city now, and I want you to come and stay with me for a while."

Her mother had pulled gently away and said, "I can't live your life, my dear, and you can't live mine."

"I don't like to think of you by yourself out here all winter. Theo can't stay on."

"I won't be by myself out here. You can rest assured about that."

"Well, what will you do?"

"I am still making up my mind what I will do."

And Jo said to Bill that it occurred to her at the time that Mama was seeming pretty nippy. Not in mourning. That the long mourning might prove to have *preceded* her loss.

"But the evidence," Jo said, "was confusing. On the one hand she was quite obviously letting the house run down, and on the other she'd got a new kitchen clock. She'd thrown out Papa's crazy clock. I thought that was a sign of sanity."

Angela was to latch on to this replacement of her grandfather's clock as a significantly precise, decisive step that her grandmother had taken out of the background of her own life and into the center of her own life. The second-hand of this clock swept slowly from 12, around the bottom and up to 8, stopped, short, and flung itself in reverse back to noon. Stopped—short—and she threw it out—when the old man died.

1111111 CHAPTER ELEVEN *1111111*

*I*N the mid-'50s the center of Porter family gravity shifted from Moriches to western Massachusetts, and the cause of this certainly was not Charlie Lewes's joining the faculty at Smith. Angela had put the Porters aside after her marriage, whether they noticed or not. But her Uncle Bill, who had become Chief of Medical Service at the University Hospital in Queens, accepted the position of Dean of the new University Medical School being (they wish) built in Springfield, Massachusetts; and his second son, Will, who was a biologist, meanwhile became a member of the department at the burgeoning UMass in Amherst. Still, after all the moves had been made, Angela saw these relatives rarely, and then more likely in Moriches, a whole day's trip away; Moriches, into which Caroline long since had sunk her stake, regarding 'the property' as *private* property, entirely her own. Once in a great while, on a Fourth of July or a Labor Day, there would be a remnant gathering out there because Theo was east, or because somebody yielded to a nostalgic whim; and some Porters would gather to form the skeletal clan, but whichever Porters they were, they never thought of themselves as coming down to Caroline's, but coming back to something not overtly cared about that belonged to them all. It was Theo's returning home to Angela in Northampton to die in the fall of 1960 that was to prove magnetic in causing the scattered household clusters spun out through the years, and largely self-contained, to draw in and regroup themselves, to reconstitute along bloodlines, and with a little the sense of unseverable ties, not at all reminiscent of static agrarian societies, the blood being much too thin, but nonetheless a notable social phenomenon in an era when the nuclear family itself was breaking down swiftly, attachment to the extended family being roughly abandoned with no time to grieve about it. Porter blood was running uphill.

It was Jo, with nomadic ways not unlike Theo's, who rescued her ill brother from a hospital in Los Angeles—because she was writing the script of a film at the time—and brought him east with her—because she had finished the script. Her own apartment being unsuitable for patients for every reason, and the farmhouse being closed up cold and empty for the winter, she ticked off the alternatives—Caroline up in Springfield, to whom it would be unfeeling to assign anybody; Margaret, but Margaret was working, so absorbed in the law and still fragile that one wanted not to jostle her; but, on the other hand, Angela!—the notoriously blooming housewife and mother, in a great handsome house with disciplined children who could be kept quiet.

The friendship was born between Jo and Angela out of Theo's dying. Jo, who had been so much older and so exotic and unattainable, was now a contemporary. Angela had caught up. She had lived very fast and caught up. Jo was forty-seven and Angela was thirty-eight, the same age.

Angela had been profoundly shocked by the experience of having Theo decline upstairs for those many weeks, because she had anticipated, unconsciously, that he would die if not beautifully, *philosophically*, looking on his own death with some detachment and humor. He was instead petulant, querulous, ungrateful, sometimes seeming to cling to living, sometimes impatient to die. He had been such a fine, independent, unwhimpering man, *big*, and he was dying small. She had read the diary of a woman guillotined during the French Revolution, who was the daughter of a great general. They are in prison together when she is nursing her father through the long days of his last illness, and she records this fact: how nobly he lived and how pettily he died.

Well, was it petty? Theo lay there in Adam's bed shrinking toward his own bones, jaundiced, drugged, the cancer finishing him up, and almost every evening his brother-in-law Bill would drive up, often without Caroline, and take his seat in a rocking chair next to the bed and not say anything at all sometimes. Bill could do this: be silent. It was regarded in the family a phenomenon in a class with having two heads. Theo, looking like Gandhi under the sheets, would pluck the air with his fingers, and roll his head slowly from side to side in little jerks, in search of things flying through the air. Sometimes he complained that bugs crawled up his walls and Angela would sweep her arms across the wallpaper for him and ask was it better? No, and he was annoyed with her that she didn't see the bugs. Finally she unhooked a black-and-white lithograph from the wall and hung up a large brightly-colored poster of Paris—Notre Dame, and the Seine—but the bugs crawled right over it.

By its own curious economy Theo's mind was still working very sharply, and very critically. Eventually he ceased to eat anything, but while he was still being persuaded to sip some soup, he told Angela, who was holding the spoon, that tomato-based soups were always improved by oregano, sweet basil, a touch of sugar, and when she read the political news in the *Times* to him out loud under his direction—John Kennedy had just won the election and was selecting people for his administration—Theo would comment short and sour, "He'll never get off the ground with those men." It was prophetic. One day Angela passed the door while Tina sat for a few minutes in the rocking chair, and she overheard her ardent daughter, who was then about fourteen and who'd just swept her own young arms across the wall, tell her uncle of her plans to be a writer too, that the only way she could have a "meaningful life" was by becoming a writer.

"If you continue to use the word *meaningful*," Theo said in the small raspy voice left to him, "you might as well give up all thought of becoming a writer. You will have lacked the ear." And he searched the walls with his eyes and his fingers plucked the air. It was the first time Angela heard the meaning of *meaningful*, through this dying brain, and had she ever used it before, she never used it again.

It was not pettiness, but the economy of his dying mind that rid itself of all extraneous energies and emotions, that made him seem petty. His humor went right out the door. He suddenly was never funny again, and one couldn't successfully be light with him. Before he lost his wits he lost his wit, and then it can be seen very starkly what human burdens wit carries in the service of love.

"I'll tell you, Bill, it seems odd to me," Angela said one night when he was upstairs dying and they were downstairs waiting, "that he, in the end, let this death take its own slow pace. Instead of intervening."

"For some people it looks as though there's a time where they're still in command. Then they reach a point when they deliver themselves over to being cared for. They have to intervene before that point or they won't do it. With Theo you would think he wouldn't tolerate the indignity of this seemingly inevitable characterological decay that he was promised."

"There's always a lot of talk about not letting nature take its course. But I'm not impressed by how brave people are." That's what Caroline said. Caroline was there that night. Jo said she thought when she'd taken him out of the hospital in Los Angeles that she might have intervened against his intervention, did they think? They thought possibly. Bill went up once more to say goodbye in case he was awake and when he came down he said, "Now do you want to hear something strange? I looked through the door and he was sleeping, and I was just about to turn away when his eyes opened wide and he said right into the air, he said, 'Mother swallowed the pills.' "

"What does he mean by that?" Caroline snapped out in her angry voice that was usually angry even when she wasn't.

"It doesn't mean anything at all," Bill said. "People revert in their thoughts to themselves as children, to their parents, when they're going like this. I see it every day at the hospital."

Theo died. Jo knew Theo as brother much better than Angela knew him as uncle, and said she was to cheer up, he wasn't really ever noble. "When it comes down to it, he was a little mean-spirited, you know." But he wasn't mean-spirited to Angela, and it was entirely unexpected and a little wicked that he had rewritten his will to let Angela inherit Moriches. His electing to die among his own inspired a mild but durable taste for *belonging* throughout the extended family; another sort of bequest.

Meanwhile there was the technical difficulty of burial. Theo was after all to find his place marked by his father's plinth, beneath the right face of the plinth—and the grave had to be prepared in the frozen ground of January, and Angela, leaving the children to Charlie and Mrs. Hamsun, drove all the way out to Moriches with her father and mother, and Jo and walked through the wrought-iron gates over the frozen rutted mud into the cemetery she knew very well, which was bare and wintry and, of course, seemed very much reduced in size. The pines were shorter. Bill and Caroline had come down, with their daughter Annie and their son Will.

There was a heavy grey sky that morning, and a fine snow began to fall very fast while Charles—without whom none of them could ever have been dispatched, neither married nor buried—read "The Lone Striker" (Frost), during which they all grew so cold and so moved, and the claws of the crabs wedged beneath the tombstone collected white mufflers of snow.

There hadn't, after all, been a grave dug, and the coffin rested where it was to be later sunk blanketed with a terrible-looking pall of fake grass, Easter Basket grass, that was rapidly being hidden by the tasteful snow. Her father recited quietly in his fine voice, referring to his volume of Frost now and again, but drawing mostly from memory. Was that the first time, at Theo's graveside, that she watched her still-handsome tall father, standing mildy askew with his weight off his damaged leg, hunched against the cold, reading through dark-rimmed glasses with such characteristic composure, was it the first time she realized clearly that she no longer needed to flee from him, to rescue herself and fly from the intense love she had for him? At thirty-seven had she finally grown up? She had been watching through this fall and winter not only a dying, but a coming to life. Their own Tina, square and squat and homely little Tina, whose whole body and mind had been waiting and waiting for the time to sprint free of childhood, did, before their eyes and in a matter of weeks, shoot beautifully toward the shape of the woman she would become. Angela felt in herself a stirring like that, an adolescent awakening, imbecilic for her age, the first clear sign of the sea change that was to come. She looked at her father nearly as a peer, and wasn't frightened of her love, and what is more, she looked at her mother, in brown fur, elegant even in galoshes, her hatless mother becoming snowcapped, her lawyer mother becoming successful, and noticed that she, the daughter, was free, that she, Angela, was free of the guilt of failing her. Nearly.

Feeling improperly giddy for the occasion, and light (but not elegant) in her heavy boots, she edged slowly around the far side of the gravestone for a fresh glance at her father, at everybody, and read her grandmother's face of the stone:

relict
ANGELINA
born   March 5, 1880
died   January 3, 1957
in
Aix-en-Provence, France

Her father wanted a bit of Frost on Theo's side:

> "The nearest friends can go
> With anyone to death, comes so far short
> They might as well not try to go at all."

They had been leafing through the volume of poetry coming out from New York in the car that morning, and Margaret wondered whether Frost's choice for his own epitaph, "I had a lover's quarrel with the world," might not be more tidily incised on such a tall narrow face as the pyramid presented. But Theo didn't love the world. The sentiment would fit the stone but not Theo. (Not Frost either, as it has later developed). "Well, I don't know how you're going to jam all those words in, that's all," Margaret said to her husband with a mild edge to her voice, and Charles said, "We'll find something shorter," and let it go, and they were all right. They were all right for a long while now, as a consequence of a great caution each observed.

How did they relinquish their hold upon her, that father

and mother over Angela? Well, she knew, she knew, and her eyes gazed over her grandmother's grave and back to her father. They had driven down together, just her father and herself, with her grandmother's ashes in a small shipping crate, on another winter day, only on that day they were alone, everybody else hearing too late to be able at the last moment to pick up and attend the final act, or rather afterword, of the story of this wandering woman, their progenitrix. Only Angela knew the ashes were in the wind. Charles told only his daughter. This fell about oddly.

On a bitterly cold morning in early February 1957, Angela had driven Charlie over from Northampton to Harvard, where he was to lecture at ten because Charlie had broken his leg skiing and couldn't drive himself. She had been amusing herself window shopping along Brattle Street and was heading for The Commander to warm up with coffee, when out of The Commander came her father carrying suitcases and shepherding a woman toward his car, and they seemed, father and daughter, to see each other simultaneously. She could only think later that what must have occurred was that *ping* of release that Jo would describe. What she found herself *doing*, nearly without affectation, was laughing at the delight of meeting him so unexpectedly and hugging him, and *not* saying, "What in the world are you doing in Cambridge?" While her father, with aplomb, said, "What the hell are you doing in Cambridge, Ange?" and smiled affectionately and introduced her to Mrs. O'Brien. "I'm on my way to pick up Charlie," she told him, and "I'll call you tomorrow morning," he told her. And Mrs. O'Brien and she warmly shook hands goodbye, as they had just warmly shaken hands hello, and Angela tracked back up Brattle Street, not cold any more, but definitely warmed by all that dopey warmth, and by her unbelievable sense of exhilaration, of feeling she'd been sprung. Still with half an hour to spare, she did a thing nearly as unprecedented for her as bumping into her father with, evidently, a mistress: which was to see in a shop window a handsome coat in charcoal grey and buy it on the spot for eighty dollars, and wear it to pick up Charlie.

The next day she wore it to New York and on for many winters. She wore it with pleasure for marking the following: her departure from the no woman's land of not having any tastes (good or bad), her first large purchase without Charlie there to say whether she liked it, her release from the dull steady ache of having betrayed her father's love, from which he would never recover. He was recovered.

The next morning he called to say, "Look here, Ange, those ashes turned up at the dock yesterday and I was just going to take them out to Moriches and dig a hole and stick them in and no fuss. Do you want to come with me?" And she'd taken the train to New York that evening, and had a late supper with her mother and father, everybody grinning in a very happy way, even Bunch. "You look wonderful!" each one said to the other in the course of dinner, and everybody did. Next morning her mother went to work—she was back at the ACLU in a most executive capacity—and she and her father waved her off down the street as they waited for the car to be brought round.

"Where is she?" asked Angela, meaning her grandmother's ashes.

"Where's who?" asked her father, thinking that Cybele O'Brien was who.

"The ashes," said the daughter, hearing in her father's voice that she had been misunderstood.

"In the trunk," said the father, and they got into the car and drove off.

They went on in silence for some time. At last Charles asked, "Has this upset you very much?"

"What? Grandma?" She deliberately misunderstood, and they laughed.

"You don't have to tell me *why*, Daddy. I know why. You don't have to tell me anything."

But Charles wanted to assure his daughter how worthy was Cybele to be her father's mistress—a fatuous desire. He confined himself to the barest data, or rather, he covered his passion in the most unimpassioned way, giving Angela the sort of information about Cybele that you need on a passport application. Her name was Cybele Wheeler O'Brien and she was a fabric and furniture designer for a large Cambridge firm, and her husband was an electronic executive in Worcester where they lived, and she had two teenage children. They talked impersonally about Cybele as if they were talking about a new will or insurance policies that would not *disturb* Angela's security but would *affect* it. But then finally Angela asked "Why does she stay with her husband?"

"She loves him."

"But why does she need you then?"

"The heart has it reasons."

"How do you feel about Mother?"

"I love her."

"Well, what about Mrs. O'Brien?"

And he hesitated before he said, "I adore her." Then she hesitated before she asked, "You can go two ways?"

"Mmmm."

"What about . . . loyalty?"

"Well, you don't go two ways *easily*."

Again there was a longish pause before Angela asked, "When did you . . . How long have you . . ."

"Seven years."

"Seven years! And you're still agog after seven years! Oh, my father, it's impossible to believe!" and she laughed with delight for him.

118

"Well, my dear, it is a liaison that is clandestine, immoral, and illegal, all attributes that serve to prolong that kind of thing wonderfully."

Angela never told Charlie about her father. She never told a soul about this until she told Jo and Jo said, "Yes, I know."

"How do you know?" asked Angela, astonished.

"Well, Bill knew."

As to old Mrs. Porter's ashes, a hole was waiting for them in the frozen earth, and they buried them quickly, crate and all. Charles had the plot, that square of Porter earth, that other bit of Papa's "property," sown with violets instead of grass. That was the ground cover. It must have been lovely in May, but nobody was down in May any more, and nobody had seen the violets.

They were eight mourners for Theo now, mourners made black by the blizzard that was whitening everything but the underside of the pines and the people. Charles finished, and they set off quickly toward the cars, moving dark and silent through the white, a sight the very farthest from a day in May. Angela and her father stayed behind by the new grave for a moment and Angela said, "You've never even seen the violets."

"Oh yes, I've seen them."

And she thought, well of course he would have come down to satisfy himself that it was all right. She heard the satisfaction in his voice.

"With Cybele? Have you come down with Cybele?"

"Yes, we come down in the spring."

She looked full into her father's face, and he looked full back at her, his smiling eyes nearly closed for love, or possibly for his several loves coalesced.

Charles the father had not found it nearly so difficult to achieve a detachment in his love for Angela as would warrant her guilt at abandoning him. In fact his need to feel so deeply fond of her was happily deflected on arrival of her babies—an assuagement of such a need not unique in the history of grandfathers. Charles the son, the best-loved son of a mother whose flight he would never really grasp, was a cordial trustee to her memory: he planted the violets. But this man, in whom one might descry a particular gift for loving, and whose capacity in this was tapped so late, was delivered over to a steady bewildering joy in his having Cybele. For a second his daughter surmised something of that joy he had, that complete love he might know with Mrs. O'Brien, complete without her, Angela. There are many people, evidently, who are keenly aware of being two selves, of being simultaneously the self who interacts with life outside, and the other self who watches. In Angela, who felt herself acutely to be two, the watching self noted that the other self was pained at being displaced from the center of her father's absorption. Furthermore, the pain of displacement was mingled with the pain from omission, the pain from never having had such a love herself.

*T*HE eight mourners were marooned in the farmhouse, confined against their will by the blizzard that established itself rapidly and frenziedly at the moment of Theo's burial. The greatest urgency to return home that Bill and Caroline Drinkwater felt, that Angela felt she ought to feel —the enormous preference to avoid the dankness certain to be lurking in all the bedrooms of the farmhouse that Charles and Margaret had—this mute but sincere shared desire to escape, for crying out loud, that barren God-forsaken uninhabited winter end of the island cut no ice with the blind white sky. Jo, alone, who was disconnected from time, from the rhythm and order of ordinary households, was amused to be captured. Will Drinkwater—you couldn't tell what he thought. He was as quiet as his father, as disconsolate as his mother, Angela believed, but she was wrong. His sister Annie made do. That would be for her epitaph. No flipping through Frost to find something for Annie. Annie Made Do.

To cover the annoyance of being crossed in their plans, they each conjectured aloud What *could* they have done had it not been for Bill's wonderful forethought about having Mrs.

Howell from the village not only put up the furnace and turn on the water, but prepare dinner for them. Caroline, whose need to be gracious was very attenuated and spent itself on census-takers, Fuller Brush men, grade-school teachers, wives of new interns, Bill's arch enemy the superintendent of nurses at University Hospital, and other such intimates—Caroline, who had been entirely against the idea of opening the farmhouse for the funeral party, had the pleasure of assuring everybody that she had been entirely against it, and that if Bill hadn't overridden her they would not now be there, whereever else they would be, would they? The dinner of pot roast and potato pancakes and applesauce was in the event so exceptionally satisfying as to pitch them out from their gloom and into a regular carnival of affectionate bonhommie—the dinner or Bill's Burgundy.

This day of the funeral had tumbled on through its hours, heaving up unpredicted events and moods, beginning with the sobriety becoming for burials; pausing at the wine-induced hilarity which spent itself too, followed, it seemed, by a headache everybody avowed he had, while a tension grew inside the house as the early winter night closed them in from outside.

"Possibly we are in a whodunit," said Angela to Jo. "In that event Caroline cannot be the corpse. We need somebody subtler."

"Yes, but we'd all turn out to have a motive," said Jo.

"Even Will? (who was the second Drinkwater son). Do you know, I really don't even know him. What is he like?"

"I'll tell you about Will," Jo answered dreamily. "He's a close one." But Will had turned up just then to ask Angela if she knew there were several cartons of what were presumed to be Theo's personal papers and probably manuscripts which Caroline had stored in the course of the years in the attic and which seemed, he thought, to fall within Theo's bequest to her. Will was the longest, lankiest of the three Drinkwater sons, a listener like his father, who bent a little toward an up-turned face, sheltering it in a protective parenthesis. He was red-headed. Angela at the time of Theo's death had only lately seen much of this first cousin. Will wore steel-rimmed glasses, bow ties, one color-free corduroy jacket; was absorbed in his subject, biology, and secondarily in, of all things, tapestry, designing and stitching it. (Charlie had been awfully playful about this until Angela snapped, "What do you think embroidery is? A secondary sex characteristic?") He was married to a woman from whom he seemed to spend nearly all his waking hours away. They had two daughters, little Suzie with palsey.

Will came upon Angela and Jo in one of the larger low-ceilinged bedrooms to which they had been assigned, each woman not only fully dressed but huddled in her coat, and propped side by side against the head of the one double bed, against, in fact, the most unyielding bedstead of metal pipes, painted chipping cream. The pillows had an unusual smell, mildew when frozen, they guessed. One lighted bulb of, at the most, forty watts hung on its wire down from the middle of the ceiling. There was a bureau—cream—no curtains, and a cushioned wicker chair with its cushion removed, and the heat had not made, as Margaret Porter was certain it would not make, significant progress toward the upper rooms, notwithstanding the physical law that it must rise. It would rise eventually but had so far lost against the struggle with a truly palpable cold damp front. The room with the blue forget-me-nots on its walls was not bare and unlovely in the summer, but when Caroline stripped and cleaned the house at the end of the season she really left nothing, not even the Woolworth lamp-shade.

"My father wants you," Will told Jo. "He's in Theo's room." Then Angela and Will were left alone and Will pulled a flask of brandy from his pocket and passed it over, and it was Angela's first experience with guzzling from the bottle. Immediately the brandy went to her brain and softened it. She would not probably otherwise have told him how distressed she had been that Theo had left her the farmhouse. Her impulse had been immediately to turn it over to Caroline, Will's mother, but Charlie (and here was the brandy working) said she might not. And she told this cousin whom she scarcely knew that the felicity for which her marriage to Charlie was renowned, drew a major share of its happiness from her nearly undeviating policy of obedience to him. This legacy of Moriches, for instance, was hers, and she wanted to give it up to Caroline. Charlie had said she was not to do it, and for the first time in her life she wondered whether she had locked herself permanently inside the confines of his personality so that her own could only flex and move in the room he allowed. And why had he wanted her to keep this place anyway? It wasn't money. They had money. She guessed it was that, in spite of this being the son of a financial wizard who had twice been to the White House, he came from nobody and no place, that his father and mother had risen, had advanced to their importance, isolated, insensitive, vain, shedding whatever past attachments they had had, and that therefore their lives were marked in almost no memories, as their deaths were marked by no stones. Charlie didn't need Moriches for his children, a human heritage from their mother's side. He took it for himself. Angela felt that he took *her* inheritance, *her* forebears, without a nod of thanks and made them his: a transfer of emotional property that was not legal and against which she had no recourse.

What she remembered most about this spilling over to Will was what a reassuring thing Will said, that the very fear that she had about being boxed and locked by Charlie would save her. It was like the Peasant's Uprising, he said—that when a man's life improved, however little, from the level of the barest subsistence, *then* he woke up and was angry and hoped. Before that, when things were the worst they could be, he was dead to hope. Will said, "You're stirred, Angela. What you have to do now is not settle again."

"I really love Charlie, Will. I shouldn't leave you with the impression that I don't love him."

"It's self-love that is the issue. You see yourself living for a long time under the dominance of a person, or maybe it is just an idea, and you are unaware that you've given up a part of yourself—as if you didn't love that part, couldn't trust yourself with it. But then once you see that you have given it up, why then, you know, you can't take your eyes off it: it will needle you until you've freed that part."

"And what happens to the hereditary lord of that part, I wonder?"

"But don't you see, *his* eyes aren't on that part. Once you begin to re-examine the hypothesis of a relationship, you don't stop, and you are guiltily absorbed in yourself and you worry, 'What about *him?* What is he thinking about all this?' And the truth is he isn't thinking one thing about it. It's not his obsession at all. It's only yours. Using some care and some tact, you are quite free to free yourself."

"It sometimes looks to me," said Angela, "that a middle-class marriage is a careful mismatching of two innocents—and the game is called Making the Best of It, while in actual fact each one does a terrible thing to the spirit of the other. And they are cheered on to do this for the whole of the one single life-span allotted to them, and you wonder why they endure each other, why they stand for it? And the explanation is that they really answer each other's needs, unconscious needs, and are in fact often admirably suited to each other, and that, unbelievable as it might seem from the outside, they do really *love* each other."

"It's not a theory I cling to."

"Will, do you love Louise?" That was the brandy in Angela.

"No."

Jo came back, and Will went off to bed, and Angela asked Jo, "Does Bill love Caroline?"

"No."

It was that night, with the storm howling circles outside the house while inside upstairs the morbid cold remained unstirred by draughts that Jo told Angela who it was that Bill loved. And the story disabused Angela of one romantic notion she had about Jo, to replace it with another. It was Angela's conviction that this miraculous beautiful woman, Johanna Porter, for whom she had the most absorbing affection, was uncannily beautiful outside because she was uncannily beautiful in, and the moral of her was that her feelings of love and loyalty were not exclusive, that she didn't have to do what every other woman thought she ought to do, that is to say, love one man once and for all. There was an easy happy egalitarianism at the heart of Jo that allowed her to look frankly at many different men in the course of her life and touch them and be touched by them and lie with them. It was a wonder more people couldn't manage it, Angela thought. She herself couldn't, Angela thought. And she believed that Jo never had one overriding love, one overwhelming love, but this wasn't true.

Jo's story was more than twenty years old. She could look far back through the cemetery railings and remember that neck with the overlong fringe of white hair: at her father's death. Then the long lunch in New York with the response, the caring in those eyes: at her mother's flight. Then there was the following Sunday morning they had all gathered at Margaret's apartment to discuss What to Do about Mama, and in a short moment after having not decided, Jo contrived to be alone with Bill in the front hall, and in spite of a hundred different cool things she had calculated she might say, she heard her voice rush from her low and dry, "I want to talk to you again." The others were already bearing down on them. "It's foolish," came Caroline, high, loud and clear, "to stay in the city on a hot day. I for one," she announced, "prefer to sit on our own porch where there's always a breeze. Everybody's welcome." Everybody doubted it.

"Will you be in this afternoon? At four?" He was a calm conspirator.

Jo told Angela that she had watched the clock hands go round and round until time for his call, nearly out of her mind with excitement, and nonplussed by her own reaction. But he didn't call at four. Immediately she was sick with the tension tightening in her throat. She was suddenly feeling nausea and perspiring unusually and even thought it wasn't Bill, it was the grippe. And next, that it wasn't Bill or the grippe but her own fantasy, that Bill was an innocent—had merely a brotherly concern for her in her understandable distress in regard to her mother, and would do what he could but there was no urgency. She felt bled, gutted—no, *leeched*. The doorbell rang and, a bit out of breath, Bill told her the traffic was terrible that had held him up.

They were awkward and formal with each other and sat across a little table drinking whiskey and talking, their heads sometimes almost touching, a gardenia plant pushing up between them with three blooms thickening the air with their sweet odd smell. Bill dipped his nose in one from time to time. Unplanned, unpredicted, they found themselves talking very seriously about dilemmas, moral and immoral, but not about their particular joint dilemma, whether it existed, whether it was moral or immoral. Jo did not so much as mention her mother. It was Bill, who never talked, who talked. His agitation, his emotions that day had two sources, no doubt unlike and unequal, but where the one seemed dammed, the other burst and gave way. That afternoon Jo listened to Bill spell out his misery in his halting way over the dreary business of his oldest son's getting with child a policeman's daughter. Bobby had graduated from high school that June, was valedictorian, was to enter Princeton in a few weeks. The policeman's daughter, who frankly was not in fact actually sure that Bobby was the father, married the other possibility, who was persuaded by Caroline to do this Right Thing. Bill had known none of this. The collusion between Bob and his mother was insufferable. Caroline had brought him in when it was all over, "because you can never tell what you are likely to do! You are so short-tempered!" and Bob, while he expressed remorse and shame to his mother's satisfaction, did not to his father's. Bill thought his son seemed basically conscienceless, just glad it was over, that's all, not giving it another serious thought, but ready to look heartfelt and say with his nimble tongue any number of beautifully touching things that didn't touch him. Bill in a rage had taken the boy by the shoulders and shaken him violently and flung him against the wall. This resulted in a good crack on the head which gratified the father but not the mother, who in an "inevitable explosion" said that he had always picked on Bobby, that his children could never turn to him when they were in trouble, that "this sort of thing with that girl," happened all the time, was perfectly natural in fact; that he, Bill, was a great hypocrite when he knew very well why she'd married him ("I didn't for Christ's sake do it because you were pregnant!" "You knew what you wanted!") and that Mary Lacy "did it" for she didn't know *how* many boys and it was a wonder she wasn't caught before she'd finished the eighth grade!

A few days later Bill had gone to pay a call on Mary Lacy (that was), and found her a poor pinched thing, chiefly remarkable for having inexplicably excited lust in anybody.

What she seemed to be was dull, but kind and polite and un-complaining, still living in her family home, in her own bed, now with a husband in it, and not seeming to experience no-table anguish. Bill experienced the anguish for her and said that if there were anything he could do for her medically or whatever, he would consider it a kindness if she would let him. So that was the end of it, and two weeks had since gone by, and only the stony revulsion he felt against Bobby remained.

Jo melted with compassion for him, loved him for his misery, yearned to comfort him, but there was no passageway, they had not made a passage for these feelings, so the pro-priety of their association remained intact, and suddenly it was late and he had to go.

✐✐✐✐✐✐ CHAPTER THIRTEEN *✐✐✐✐✐✐*

*T*HE door that closed leaving Jo alone in her apartment left Bill alone in his obsession, where he feared he might stay forever, frantic to pull her against him but entirely unable to reach out his actual arms to the actual woman. And he was awash with doubt. Was he in fact reading her eyes right, those round open eyes of an unbelievably delicate color? He lived and breathed her. He knew her smell. He hated the gardenias for routing it so thoroughly, and it was with vengeance that he sniffed them. He was back in Garden City without registering the drive, had a supper of cold ham and potato salad without tasting it, drove a load of children to the community pool for Sunday Nite Swim, stood crossarmed by the pool edge talking politics with his right-wing dentist, somehow performed the rituals that preceded sleep, all of these exchanges with the outside world never once piercing through the obsession which swelled through the center of him from the top of his head to unmistakably his groin. Finally in the hot dark night he lay spreadeagle on his side of the bed, numb to Caroline on hers, when unaccountably, disconcertingly, she was moved to touch him on the shoulder

130

in a clearly placatory gesture and say, "I was wrong about Bobby. I'm sorry." It was impossibly, horribly hard for Caroline to do this, to give the smallest hint of a capacity to err. She seemed to believe that by some special dispensation she was excused from ever having to do what was routinely expected from the rest of mankind: to apologize. Certainly she did not excuse Bill or the children from begging *her* pardon. Through the tumult of his passion and passionate confusion Bill recognized, as though it were a great distance off, the still, small voice saying "I'm sorry" extracted by his wife from her conscience at a terrible cost in pain, and he wasn't touched.

The next morning, which was Monday, his sense of disconnection with real life was compounded by a break in his weekday routine. He was to take the nine o'clock plane to Washington, where he had been invited to sit on the ad hoc Hospital Administration Planning Commission and would return Tuesday evening. As Caroline with Teddy was driving him to La Guardia to wave him off on this his first flight, he was effectively deterred from cutting out to phone Jo from the airport. It was a hazy sunny morning, and the big propeller planes waited to be boarded right outside the central rotunda. You bought your ticket or checked your reservation and then walked through the doorway in 1939, when air travel was charming, unharried, unpolluted, and you, an adventurer, climbed the steps to the cabin door and turned around at the top so that your family could take pictures of you brave. So Caroline, bent over Teddy who was bent over the box Brownie, would paste into the family album this blurred and cockeyed photograph of "Bill—His First Flight." "It's too *bad* he couldn't hold it still," Caroline would say. "It's the spirit of the thing. He captured it perfectly," Bill would reply.

In the sky. He was on a trip, experiencing a disembodied

joy that they want today when they say they are going on a trip. The pilot, under the probably correct assumption that in back of him was a great body of human anxiety, would break in through the loudspeaker from time to time in a reassuring way to remark on points of interest. "Now if you look down to the left, on the highest peak of the Poconos is the last known eagle's nest in northern Pennsylvania. She has three eggs in her nest." Bill looked and scanned the beautifully undifferentiated mountainscape below him and said, "Missed it." His seat companion grinned. They had been sitting there with breakfast trays before them, and this fellow, who wasn't thirty and who'd left his food untasted, was drinking scotch. He had a wooden leg, he said, and the whites of his eyes were yellowed, Bill noted, and he was a veteran of the Abraham Lincoln Brigade, a cocky, brash, pointless, sad young wreck, Bill thought, who did beguile him through the flying time, did penetrate the mists of Jo, and he was grateful. He, Bill, had thought often in those years that, were he freed, he'd join the Brigade. The Porters, nearly every member of the whole extended clan for these three generations up until to-day, were absorbedly left-wing-edly political.

The veteran of the Abraham Lincoln Brigade told Bill wild bloody stories, all of them substantially true, and re-ferred several times to the night he shared a ditch with George Orwell. Finally, "You know who Orwell is?"

"No, I guess I don't," Bill admitted, at the very end of the era in his life when he didn't know anything, at the very brink of his coming to learn everything.

In Washington he checked into the Wardman Park and went off for the day to his commission. There he said so little and appeared so wise to his fellow appointees that they made him temporary acting chairman of Ad Hoc (AH) establishing an appropriately gingerly tentative approach to hospital problems whose solutions, when they were finally presented to the Administration, could be gingerly tentatively laid aside. He returned at the end of the day to his hotel room that had a wide window overlooking Rock Creek Park and on the sill of which was sitting a bathroom glass with water in it, and a gardenia. In nothing flat, he would have said, he was on the phone. "Was there a message for him?" No. "Do you have a Miss Johanna Porter registered?" "I'll ring you through, sir."

Then Jo said "Hello," and Bill said "I want you to come to me, do you hear?" He raced to the bathroom to wash off the day, opened the door in his shirtsleeves, still holding a towel, let her pass into the room, and the two of them stood apart stock still, looking at each other unsmiling, their arms hanging loose. Then Bill dropped the towel on the bed and moved towards her without hesitation and finally did pull the actual woman against him.

It was the end of irresolution for them and the beginning of a lifelong love that never abated, that was the keel to both their lives, that was constant and amazing to them and remained almost totally unknown and unsuspected.

"I never *never* heard a word about it," said Angela to Jo in the cold bedroom of the farmhouse on the night after they'd buried Theo. "Nobody knows? Nobody but me?"

"And Charles. He has known about it nearly from the beginning."

"My father! Was he shocked?"

"He was very funny. He said that in criminal law adultery inside the family was the most natural thing in the world! That's why incest taboos were so strong."

"Did he mean to be funny?"

"Sure. About a year after our . . . liaison . . . Bill felt that there ought to be some responsible third person knowledgeable about what was then quite obviously becoming the kind of double existence he leads—to allow some small protection for Caroline and the children—there were so many of them. . . . I mean, if the thing were ever to have come out, why, instead of everybody spending a lot of time expressing astonishment, why, Charles could take on Caroline right away."

"Well, now, that's very thoughtful, isn't it?" said Angela, turning it over lightly.

"An illicit attachment is infinitely interesting, ethically speaking."

"I begin to see that." Angela paused, then asked the unusually intrusive question, "Have you slept with anyone else since?"

"Well . . . a little."

"A *little!*" And Angela laughed and said it was delicious insanity that other people had tasted and were lucky. After a moment she asked seriously, "Didn't you ever want to . . . *regularize* the situation?"

"No, I guess I never really did," she answered. "In the first place, it was impossible, and in the second, I didn't want to anyway. I love the secret privateness of it."

"And not having children . . . ?"

"There again, it will sound odd when I say it, but I have loved not having children. I was pregnant once. In fact, Angela, I was pregnant at your wedding. And for a dreamy few weeks I simply gloried in the feeling that inside my body was growing a part of this lovely man. It was that lovely, foolish sense of being the, you know, holy vessel. But then I thought, well, that's all very fine, but when it's finished growing *there*, do you want the child that comes out? And I absolutely didn't want it. So I went to a coroner in Flatbush and he took it out."

A little later Angela mused aloud, "I suppose it all has something to do with your being a writer."

"You're a writer!"

"*YOU'RE* a writer," said Jo, and the words pinched Angela's soul with an exhilarating fear. Indeed, hearing this said from an outside voice, she felt herself plucked out of anonymity most abruptly and held up to the world, feeling some sympathy with the White King in the Tenniel drawing whom Alice holds pinched between her thumb and forefinger, and the king waves his scepter and kicks his legs furiously for balance, and his ugly mouth is in a great O of astonishment. It was not extremely astonishing, however, that Jo should say, "You're a writer," since Angela had told her during their watch over Theo one afternoon in the little room on the third floor, the room she had done over for a retreat for Charlie to which he had never retreated. She told nobody else.

"I'm a secret writer," she found herself whispering in a half-laugh unexpectedly. "Instead of drinking. I write instead of drink . . . although now I see one can do both."

Jo looked at her with such interest as Angela felt herself unaccustomed to evince.

"Why secretly?"

"Well that is curious . . . that it springs from the very openness of my nature. In fact the secrecy was by mistake. Circumstances contrived to keep me quiet (they would have to be powerful circumstances, wouldn't they?) when I was very eager to explain and show what I'd done. . . . Do you know, it is like my grandmother, that is, your mother—she was a silent singer. . . . More difficult, that, of course."

"How long has this been going on?"

"Well, I'm not really sure. One of the things that's happened to me is that my sense of time passing has gone awry. The present has become so heightened for me. I feel something like a tubercular patient in *The Magic Mountain* where they've all let go of time—because I suppose for them it is simply death to anticipate the future. But what's happened to me is different. It's not that death is in the future. It's that the present has become so vital for me. I feel more alive inside the characters I spin out of my fantasy at the typewriter than I do downstairs in the kitchen of my own life. . . . It's a secret vice to permit yourself to live in a fantasy, isn't it?"

"What do you write about?"

"About women. I only have heroines. Heroines and heroines."

"And you mean Charlie doesn't know anything about it?"

"And I'm also a secret reader," Angela, pursuing her own train of thought, had to limn in more detail the first outline of her truth. "Voluminously, and even voluptuously, I've been rereading everybody—*Middlemarch*, *The Idiot*, E. M. Forster—I pack it in, pack it in—I am so immersed in the reading as well as the writing that I sometimes don't know what I have written and what George Eliot has . . . very funny. . . . Not only mad but somewhat immodest, wouldn't you say?"

"But what about Charlie?"

"He was very angry with me when I let myself get pregnant with Angelica. It goes back to that."

"Doesn't he take any responsibility for making babies?" Jo asked impatiently.

"No," Angela answered firmly. "It is altogether mine," which she said and meant.

"Well, I don't buy that!"

"But if she'd been a boy. . . . He's been a very good sport about my giving him girls, considering . . ."

"Considering! Your giving him! Angela, I just don't know how you can think so primitively."

"So then afterwards the house was really, he said, a regular crèche and there wasn't one square inch that didn't smell of urine. . . . But that was a damned lie, you know, because our babies smelled beautiful. But anyway it was hardly, this house, a place for scholarly work, and so he spent more and more time at his office at the college, and so I made a surprise for him. I fixed this room for him up here. Nobody ever comes up to the third floor and it's quiet, and I had it painted and papered and had this carpet laid and surprised him with it for Christmas. And he was surprised. He loved it. He was so touched and happy about it, I thought, and he'd visit it to please me, but he couldn't use it until he'd got a typewriter in it, he explained. So for his birthday I bought the electric typewriter. . . . But as he still didn't use it I began to see that I was particularly insensitive about this."

"Weren't you angry?"

"I was embarrassed."

Angela was embarrassed to have seemed to want to rivet her husband to his house, and the room on the third floor was a gaucherie she was glad to see sink out of reference. Perhaps a year went by before she went up there to try out the typewriter, to use and not waste the idea of the room, as she told

137

herself—she who was frugal, who was not wasteful, a good housewife. Testing that typewriter on sentences and bits of plots and heroines, she ascertained that it worked very well, the typewriter.

Perhaps another year went by that way, typewriter-testing. She couldn't recall. Charlie had been caught up meanwhile with a new idea. He wanted to talk about it. She wanted to keep him caught up in it, to have him write it out, and it was as though there was between them only so much mental energy they could give over to talking about writing . . . so that it was enormously important that not any of it be deflected toward herself. It would be misconstruing Angela to put this to selflessness. Not telling what she did through the baby's naptimes, the "not telling" itself, the omissions, were like deposits that imperceptibly built her little reef of secrecy. When did she begin to cherish the very secrecy itself? She didn't know. When did she allow herself to recognize her own seriousness? This year of 1960 that she told Jo, when her last child was off to nursery school and the mornings were hers alone. Off to the beginnings of an independent life went Angelica, dear delicious child, true frosting.

And up until that year, up until the very threshold of that decade, Angela expected to progress in a seemly way through a dignified middle age to a wise old one, becoming elegant in lieu of ever having been stunning in her youth when she ached to be stunning, when she would gladly have obeyed the old faker Hornesby's injunction to go out and have a Charismatic Presence, with under- (but not too under-) tones of sexuality, beneath whose aegis the decision-makers made their decisions (and here she saw herself at the top of a grand stairway looking like the Victory of Samothrace, who was a stocky girl built not unlike herself). Orderly, obedient, rational, humane, responsible, gifted, law-abiding, the most above-board of human creatures—and pre-destined to remain all these things—she didn't.

She was certainly very slow to come to anything. She would write for hours and hours and in the end might have just a single paragraph. Very slow. She wrote on, and she thought in metaphors. For instance, at the beginning of the decade there had been too little rain in the Northeast for many springs and many summers. Charlie insisted upon setting up sprinklers on their wide lawns while Angela was in anguish to let the grass burn out to save the community water supply (bearing burnt-out lawns more philosophically than most because of conditioning, probably). The lawns did burn out, an irrelevant point, because hauling sprinklers around, evenings on end, required the kind of perseverance Charlie didn't have, or as Charlie recorded it, "She got so *aggrieved* I had to give it up!" Then, after the dry years, there were many seasons of heavy rain that beat down on the top of the earth and turned the Connecticut Valley lush and made the farmers rich and relieved Angela from tilting at sprinklers, but that rain didn't sink down in great quantities to replenish the subterranean supply, but mostly poured off the surface of the earth, into the sewers and rivers and out to the sea: there was no agricultural drought on the surface, but underneath, surprisingly, there persisted a geological drought.

Angela caused to beat down her own heavy rain on the surface of her life: and her son and freshly laundered daughters bloomed, her family increased and they multiplied, and the handsome house standing back from the giant elms became a center for the coming and going and feeding and consoling of students, and in the political season Democratic Headquarters for first Stevenson, then Jack Kennedy, for congressmen and mayors, and Charlie was popular with the young and an associate professor and in two years would be a full, besides being captain forever of the faculty softball team. But all of this was a little like the story of Job in reverse, because as she saw it quite clearly, and even cheerfully, she racked up these things, or to return to the metaphor of the rain, she poured things on hard, but very little seeped down to the core of herself, to what William James called "the hot place." Until she crossed into the '60s, that portentous neatly-bracketed decade, portending the apocalypse and doom and a lot of frank if impermanent joy, she had not discovered her *egotism*, a gift of such rich proportions as to indicate a latent genius for self-absorption. Was that all that was in the core of her, the hot place, an ignoble newly come-upon self-love? Meanwhile, whatever it was, it had certainly been latent, repressed and overlaid by those exigencies of life which consumed her time and mind, and left her busy and happy in her accomplishments and relieved to have not more than a minute now and then to look in and fear that there was nothing underneath, that she had no core, that there was no hot place.

Upstairs behind the secret reef she was undergoing a sea change of the soul, and there were unexpected outward signs.

"You know, I mean," she said to Jo in a later conversation, "I felt like St. Elizabeth."

"St. Elizabeth . . . the mother of St. John?"

"They had always wanted to have a baby and they prayed and prayed to have a baby and the time passed and they gave it up, and then when she was something like eighty-seven years old she discovered she was pregnant! Well, it must have been one enormous surprise."

"One would have to assume that."

"I've always gotten up in the morning and gathered the whole world together and put it in order, always with a sense of time and place for everything. You are what you are by forty. The alternates to yourself, what you might have been, the experiences, passions, that might have given you a different sense of being will have had to have taken place earlier, in your teens, twenties, early thirties."

"It's a deterministic view. Not unreasonable."

"I passed all those years a great gawk of a girl, so tall and square and plain, so fundamentally overlookable. Every once in a while when we'd be going out to dinner some place I'd ask Charlie what I should wear. He'd say, 'Wear anything. It doesn't matter what you wear. Nobody notices.' "

"Nobody ever looks at you?"

"Well, more accurately and more generously, he would mean that people look to me for deeper things than mere beauty, or of course sexual attraction, which it was implicit we both recognized I didn't have."

"And now it's quite the other way, you'll have to go to bed by day?" They laughed, but Angela even blushed.

"A middle-aged starlet. I'm just baffled by the timing. It was as if into the program of my life there had been written some unaccountable delay, and I got changed to a swan when I was thirty-eight. . . . Do you know I even cut a tooth then? For about a year I suffered intermittently with an awful pain while a wisdom tooth cut down through my upper jaw, and when it finally arrived, the dentist pulled it."

It would not be inimical to the spirit of Angela to use the analogy of the House that Jack Built to say This is the World that Angela Built, because, a minor point, her life featured houses: the Northampton house which was the great central documented success of the Lewes marriage, and the cottage in Moriches which they took over and redid as a consequence of Theo's bequest, a patched-up accommodation to the emotional requirements of Caroline, who was asked please to keep on at the farmhouse (and Angela gave over several months to the pleading) while the Leweses would reserve the cottage for August.

The world that the grown-up Angela built rested on a foundation of sand which, as she allowed herself to enter a loveless marriage, she saw at the time but did not let anybody else see. How had she got on to the sands, that fragile-nerved great barge of a poor girl? Finally Jo asked her how she ever came to marry Charlie.

"Well, it just rolled out that way. I didn't stop myself. I didn't intervene, don't you know . . . didn't intervene in my own fate. After I had graduated from college I was dismally low. There was really, literally, no direction I thought I would like to take. To cover this vacuum, the entire pointlessness of myself, I said I was interested in art. I somehow got the lowest-paying sort of errand-running job at the Museum of Modern Art and I very soon saw tiggers didn't like art. Well, I mean I suspected I didn't have anything more than a genteel flair for drawing and I began to feel I had no personal sense of taste whatsoever . . . it hung on to me for years, that feeling. I would have to look elsewhere, sooner or later. I knew that. And then, I also thought I'd better get my own apartment, but my mother . . . it was when she was beginning to break down. I was frightened by her sudden emotionality. . . . Then one Christmas there was an Opening where I met Charlie. He'd come with another girl. A very pretty dopey little chick. The three of us spent the evening together, going on down to the Village afterwards, and in the end he dropped the other girl off first, and took me to my door and did not touch me.

"So that was the beginning of the sort of *friend*ship, he told me frankly, he was looking for, as he had had quite enough of the *other* for a while. During this winter of friendship we exchanged thought-filled letters (He was back from the Pacific and at Amherst) and visits (and I liked to return to that college world), and he treated me with a dignity and equality that did not subsequently distinguish our relationship"—she said this wryly—"and spent all his New York time with me going to the galleries and often to the theater, returning me courteously to my door, meticulously not touching me. But"—and Angela smiled at Jo—"I was a very touching person."

"So then," she continued, "what must have happened psychologically was that my femaleness and my sexuality, combining in fierce indignation at being rated so low, marshaled their resources and quite obsessed me. That I could not arouse his passion was the thing that gnawed at me and the gnawing or lust passed for passionate love. And as to Charlie, when the friendship was indeed promoted to courtship, the change might very probably have reflected on his side a game that had grown to real love to his own surprise (with a shade of concern at the brow that's never left him). He asked me to marry him in May and between then and our wedding in Moriches I was liable to painful attacks of sobbing and retching late at night in bed. It was the single time in my life that I've exhibited overt symptoms of an undercurrent distress. I tried a little to be rescued by the stratagem of leaving my bedroom door open so that my father might be awakened by the racket I was making, but he never was. *His* door was closed. It was a night phenomenon. In the mornings I was quite all right."

She took a daytime dive at the wedding itself. This beautiful wedding thick with red roses she remembered only for its being the setting for the struggle in her own surging heart, a seeming mortal struggle that made her punchdrunk, numb, and allowed her to appear before her family and guests serene, or so she believed. She was dissolved by the profoundest most painful love for her father, and when he spoke the lovely words that gave her away to Charlie, and he looked up at her with tears in his eyes, it was an adamantine pride that kept her on her course. What could it have been but pride? It would not be true to say that the sight of the groom repelled her. She had a friend who told her that when she and her new groom were on their honeymoon cruise she stood by the rail with him one night and thought, "My God, I am married to a total stranger." It is the kind of remark that characterized one's first encounter with a mature insight. One returns to that insight again and again and it is always keener. One thinks at one's wedding that one ought surely to know the groom: one doesn't. And the groom? Looking through eyes that have learned to see women cut to the pattern of his mother, a young man in 1946 could scarcely be expected to *know* his bride, who, in the case of Angela, was like the earth on the first day, without form and void. Really, how else could she have emerged but disordered and chaotic, when her childhood and girlhood were riddled with improper suggestions about what a woman was, or could be, or should be. It wasn't her mother who taught her to tuck tail, to feel less, to be second. It was in the air she breathed. And are her own daughters now, a generation later, arriving in better shape? Is Christina, today twenty-three, in better shape? Much better shape about being a woman, with a much worse future to be one in. Perhaps.

The house that Angela built was built on sand into which she drove deep piles. There were the many children, and her so frequently pregnant belly might seem to have suggested that the real clue to the success of her marriage to Charlie was sexual. Angela had come to Charlie on her wedding night in a ramified over-all way ashamed, with the sort of shame about nakedness, about performance, that is a cultural shame or a class shame. This shame was reinforced by her need to discount evidence of her own sensuality, and to collect evidence that she was undesirable, and she must in some pitiable way have arrived at a sense of gratitude to Charlie for making the compromise of finding satisfaction in *her*, after he had known unimaginable (she couldn't imagine anyway) delights with so many voluptuous *others* before her. And erecting a philosophic point out of her conviction that Charlie had made some sort of sacrifice in the matter of sex, when against all natural desire he fell in love with her, Angela used the point to support the thesis that, anyhow, sex was of small moment to the educated mind. She entered marriage apologetic and co-operative and in a bind about the necessity for the whole business. She was her mother's daughter.

One pile she drove into the sand supported the partial myth that Charlie was a born dedicated scholar. The stake that it represented to both of them, the weight of success it bore and was still bearing, ought to be of some comfort to those who are not hopelessly pessimistic about the improvability of man. Those who took the dour view, as Freud took the dour view (but as Erikson doesn't) about the viscosity of a man's temperament, that it runs very heavy and not very fluid, were having to say dourly during the decade of the '50s, when the blacks were getting ready to spring free, that you can't legislate morality. As it turned out it is really very subtle, what you can legislate: you could legislate a climate of opinion more hospitable to the civilized generous urge in a people, and similarly with this marriage in question, Angela rather established by fiat that the purpose and importance of their lives would inevitably be her husband's intellectual achievements. And this domestic ambience, however fraudulent in the beginning, did indeed have the effect of turning Charlie from a boy-man who passed an awful lot of his first years in graduate school cradling a quart carton of chocolate-chip ice cream in his arm with a western propped in front of him, in a room borrowed from an anthropology major who was digging in Turkey. But the good Charlie, by Angela's insistent encouragement, nosed ahead and was eventually to establish his mastery of the history of the American Party System and be considered for the Bancroft Prize in 1968 for *The Bosses*, and Angela was long since relieved and grateful to him for giving her pride in him, and love for him. He was a distinguished scholar. He really was. The house that Angela built—a large well-constructed, rationally designed, sophisticated handsome house—provided the room for Charlie to achieve distinction. The house that Angela constructed had its entrances and its exits, and one day, to her own astonishment, she walked quietly out for a while. But what was the house that Charlie built?

ᚴᚴᚴᚴᚴᚴᚴ CHAPTER FIFTEEN ᚴᚴᚴᚴᚴᚴᚴ

*I*T WASN'T until the summer of 1962 when the Leweses took the cottage for August that Angela went up to the attic of the farmhouse to find the papers that Theo left behind. This tarrying is the natural but in the long run ineffectual defense of those who write and who have friends who write and colleagues who write and you ask and are asked to read manuscript and to say honestly what you think: it cultivates a delaying instinct. Angela had no trouble tarrying over the obligation she had assumed to read Theo's lifework, but one quiet summery morning in a pause between rounds of guests, the idea of the cartons in the other house arrived not unpleasantly in her mind. She corralled the two little ones, Josie (their own Johanna) and little Ange (both loving that attic, delighted by fright of that attic), and they climbed the ladder and opened the door into the hot small dark triangle made by the eaves, and with a flashlight found three boxes just where Caroline said they would, among the orderly and nearly dustless bedsprings and suitcases and waiting household things. Not a very interesting attic. No surprises. But she was wrong there. She was afraid of bats and so got the cartons and the children down quickly, and they were walking back to the cottage across the dewy grass, the little ones squooshing in their wet sneakers, when Angelica stumbled and her small box flew into the air and landed broken with its contents scattered. "There, there, that's all right," her mother said, "and we'll pick you up and we'll pick up the . . . letters," which in two moments, with a flip of the envelopes, she could see were written by her grandmother from Strasbourg in 1939–40 to Theo in Moriches (and forwarded to him in Denver), and all that time nobody had known a thing about their existence, as all that time nobody had known a thing about her grandmother's existence. It threw a damn queer light on Theo! She brought them to the hammock on the cottage porch and arranged the envelopes by their dates and read them in sequence. There were sixteen. What did they say and who *was* that woman, who was she! Nothing. They said *nothing* more than "My dearest son Theodore. This is just a word to let you know that I am well," that she is living in "a very nice clean Bording House," there are eleven guests in all and all Czech, and (soon) that the weather has turned cold and she has had to buy a warm coat, and (later) that there is talk of shortages of eggs and butter but that their cook does not seem to have encountered difficulties, but that there is a gentleman of her acquaintance who is a baker and he expresses concern and (in the last two letters) that they are thinking of leaving for the South. There is a refrain at the end of each letter: "Be assured that my health is good and that I have no need of anything. I think of all of my dear children and their families. With my love, Mother." No window into that distant self.

Angela found Bill and asked angrily, "But what in God's name did Theo mean by not telling anybody? My father was so concerned!"

"Theo meant to save her from the consequences of your father's concern. That's all he meant," said Bill.

"I guess I would have gone over to get her and bring her home," said Charles calmly, when he heard. Her father wasn't the least distressed *now* about not knowing then, and not distressed about Theo's ghoulish secrecy. She suddenly saw herself the only one overwrought about these unreported letters, letters that didn't after all tell them anything that hadn't already been long since unearthed and surmised. She was sitting on the porch that evening with her father and mother just arrived, and the Drinkwaters over for a cocktail, waiting for the little ones and Charlie to come back from the station in Center Moriches with Edmund Hardie, and she felt her stomach heave, felt the heat beading her, making her wet, felt her skin tight on her forehead and the weight of her heavy hair piled, knotted, pulling to the roots of her scalp.

She turned to her mother, her trim, tiny, lovely, still somewhat estranged mother (Margaret was now past sixty), who was biting her cigarette holder in a refined manner few could affect and who was watching Angela with an old, old expression of bemusement and tenderness her daughter had not caught on her face for years.

"Mother, wasn't Theo insane to keep it from you? That Grandma was all right? Wasn't that an irresponsible suppression of evidence?" Angela burst with a final appeal to the lawyer in her.

"Well, my dear," Margaret said to Angela in the gentlest rediscovered mother-voice, "he was protecting her from us."

They were all looking at Angela with a single expression of calm compassion, her father saying nothing, her mother, Bill silent, Caroline for once including herself with a human concensus, all assenting to the proposal that had they known where their old mother had gone to, they would all have combined to move heaven and earth to do the wrong thing on that mother's behalf. And how were they so wise now? How were they there conspiring to be so wise now, leaving Angela out of the conspiracy of wisdom, and bringing her to tears? Why was she crying?

Angela escaped to the kitchen (the grand new kitchen with its screened dining room that had been bayed out from the garage), and her mother followed her.

"I can't imagine why those letters should upset me so," she said to her mother.

"They're probably standing in for something else," said Margaret, and added, "Do you ever try to track down an emotion like that, to see what kinds of association it has? Where it's sprung from?"

"Is that what you learned from Dr. Wise?" Angela asked and smiled affectionately at this fine example of how orderly and serviceable became all her mother's knowledge. You put it into her mother and out it came, processed for use by mankind.

"Well you ought to do that," persisted the mother.

"I do do that," acknowledged the daughter.

Angela had really already tracked down the source of her tension to a psychiatrist of her own: E. C. Hardie. A friend he was, just a dear friend. She hadn't known he was coming down until that morning when they had been wakened early, she and Charlie, by two unappeasable, undeflectable flies that buzzed down in tandem at their heads, and got knocked at wildly, and left them tormented with seconds of silence, and woke them thoroughly.

"You have to get up anyway," Angela said to Charlie, "if you're going to Montauk with Adam to make arrangements about the boat." Adam was twelve, their second child, and ought to have been in camp as Christina was, but he wouldn't go off and be tough, and *wrest* things from life. He backed away, retreated from effort. This was the unsatisfiable child that she worried over angrily. He was lazy and spoiled —or was he frightened? Or was he numb? He was not a good sport, that child was not a good sport—and Charlie pawed over him, picked over him like a mother cat, and tested him (and Adam failed and failed). Charlie was too steeped in the soul of this one son, their one *small* child, nearly frail child, this *boy*, while the girls were giants, but this boy never had an unmonitored moment to be alone and grow. You grew privately, Angela believed. Adam isn't *tough*. It was her lament. But Charlie was tough, and Charlie spent the next five minutes leaping around the room in his undershorts flinging a wet washcloth at the flies. He was a good clown, agile, lithe, and determined at forty not to look fifty in ten years. To this end he was destined to take on two fads that would set her teeth on edge, to jog with the discovery of jogging, and to dye the grey out of his hair.

"You know, what I forgot to tell you, Ange, was that call last night was Edmund Hardie asking could he come down, was it all right?"

She had tracked down her emotion to Edmund Hardie, the source, or rather to Charlie and his need to diminish this old friend, a need in Charlie that she could nearly trace with her finger through the pattern of her marriage, back to the beginning when they were graduate students, the two men, this need that made Charlie look so small, made Angela wince and look away.

Charlie could love fiercely and not only himself, and during their first year in New Haven he made a friend of John Stein, who was a truly scholarly man, a friendship that went very deep for the both of them while it lasted, in which the one, the genuine sober-grounded John, felt lifted by the free-wheeling hoax of a student Charlie, while the other, Charlie, prized deeply John's witness to his inner worth.

John that second year began bringing Edmund Hardie around to supper on weekends, and Charlie seemed positively driven to banter over Ed's religion, wouldn't leave it alone, and the bantering would inevitably turn to raillery, come too close to a sneer. And what provoked Charlie? In the beginning it was a jealous clutching at John, Angela thought. He had to make an outsider of this divinity student.

"Where the hell did you pick up that *Christian?*" he'd asked John.

"Most appropriately, in the Divinity School," John said.

"How did you stray into the Divinity School?" Angela asked.

"That's where they give 'The Philosophy of Evolution.' "

"In the Divinity School?" Angela asked amused.

"Oh, they're mad about evolution. They never leave it alone, they tussle with it divinely. In fact, Ed is a testimony to their incredible success at conversion. He is their greatest triumph." They had no sooner met Ed, the Divinity student, than they'd heard he was already a renegade, and so from the very beginning it was unworthy of Charlie, unwarranted of him to insist that this caricature he'd drawn of an evangelical, still wet and blinking-eyed *rube* was Ed, was ever Ed, anything like him. Ed was always somebody else entirely.

Long ago Angela had said to Charlie, "I don't think it's right that you should kid around with him like that."

"He *likes* it," Charlie said. "He's a bit of a swish. They like that sort of thing."

"A swish!" Angela was shocked. "You mean a homosexual?"

She came back to the subject the next evening. "John said that what you said about Ed is preposterous."

"What?" asked Charlie, pretending.

"That he's a homosexual," answered Angela, controlled.

"He's a *repressed* homosexual." And Charlie laughed.

"Oh for crying out loud, Charlie. It's awful for you to say that!"

"Well save him, Angela! Go on and save him! There may still be time. You're always ready to save people!" He was angry and walked out.

To Angela Ed seemed not smaller but larger than her husband, first because of sheer size. He was three inches over six feet, a broad muscular man with a craggy face in which the lines were already deep carved, a face in high relief. He came from western Pennsylvania, from a small town settled by the Scots and the Germans to which his own mother and father had emigrated from Scotland upon the event of their marriage. Indeed it was the condition of their marriage, the terms on which a determined, not to say driving, sort of bride accepted the hand of the fairly reticent and somewhat withdrawn, and not ambitious elder Hardie, and they came to America, where Mrs. Hardie read the Bible and named her first two sons John Knox Hardie and Edmund Calvin Hardie and intended that her boys would succeed where their father had not. The withdrawn father made a career of withdrawal, rolling off for thirty years as trainman on the long-distance lines of the Pennsylvania Railroad.

Ed told Angela that in Scotland the one route out of the working class for a poor bright boy was the Church, that that was where the scholarship money was. His mother's translation to Pennsylvania was a mere bodily migration, he said. Mind and spirit she was bound to the mother country, classbound in it, never more than forty-seven miles from Edinburgh, and never less. She intended John, the firstborn, for the ministry, *willed* him on, whipped him with words, was spare with praise, always with the commission that when he once got up there he would pull them all through. He was killed at Guadalcanal. Edmund had followed silently in the wake of John, had earned a scholarship, like John, to a small

Presbyterian college in the south where, sheltered by his brother from his mother's attention, he took courses mostly in laboratory sciences. Then they went to war.

"But as I came back and John didn't, I naturally took his place." Through the years they were in New Haven together, Edmund would bicycle out picturesque in a black suit, the one suit he seemed to have, looking properly like a curate, Angela thought, peddling through a British film. He was her only company. They'd walk together wheeling Christina in her carriage along the empty winter boardwalk, swooped about by gulls, and she asked him questions about his life that nobody else asked, asked him questions that he had never asked himself, it seems.

"Well, were you *interested* in theology?"

"No," he answered, mild, pensive, "No," as if he were thinking the thing over for the first time, as if, when he was unexpectedly assigned his brother's shoes, directed to take his brother's road, he hadn't a prior intention to go somewhere else.

"I should think"—and Angela remembered with what ardor she rebelled for him—"that if your interest, your commitment, was scientific, that you would have found it terribly wrenching to pull yourself out of physics and put yourself into metaphysics! Didn't you balk? Weren't you wretched?"

"I can't say that I was wretched, no. I saw there was a lot of reordering to do, and I thought if I was going to get religion I'd better get out of the South."

"But you would have had to pretend to believe what you didn't believe," pursued Angela, still ardent.

"No, I didn't do that, you see."

"But just this fall when you came up here, did you believe, or did you disbelieve? That's what I can't see about you!"

"I didn't think about it either way, Angela. Not until after the first day of the first class when I began reading Darwin, his *Autobiography*, *The Origin of Species*, some criticism by Muller and other people. Then I believed them."

"But what about all that science in college, what about evolution when you were actually working with the evidence of it in the laboratory?"

"People can work profitably in a laboratory without once thinking about evolution. I never thought about it."

"I can't *believe* it!" Angela cried out, flinging her arms into the air. Believing and disbelieving were the major occupation of her own mind.

Edmund was the single significant friend Angela made those first years of her marriage. For whatever reasons, this man whom they continued to see in an almost fateful way long after they left New Haven continued to evoke in Charlie the need to degrade him a little, to unman him, but no longer from jealousy of John Stein. Charlie forgot about John Stein and the jealousy; it counted for nothing later. What she thought might have been at the root of the thing was that Edmund was a listener. He talked very little and he listened attentively. At the end of that first year when Ed had changed schools, shifted effortlessly, funds and all, atraumatically, from theology to medicine, in order, he said if asked, to go into psychiatry, why, the interest in that silent listening man was compounded for Angela. But perhaps Charlie was further unnerved by the listener: what the hell was he listening *for*, what the hell was he *hearing*?

It was fateful, Angela thought, how Edmund checked in with them, touched their base, through the intervening years. It was as if he was the instrument of a smirking justice that took Charlie's measure from time to time to see if he'd grown bigger, and proved that he hadn't. Proved to whom? Proved to Angela that her grand marriage, her grand life, would ironically represent her masterwork, her finest piece of fiction? It was Charlie who found Ed again after many years, Charlie who sought out this friend, met this fate more than halfway, established a ritual of visits, a litany of ribbing and ragging. It was Charlie who was fascinated to have this huge, rough-cut, courteous man near him, next to him, so that he could cut him down.

And Angela was fascinated by Edmund, at once dreading his pending visit and longing for it. Edmund was a lovely man, altogether another man than the one Charlie needed to deride. He had the beautifully quiet courtliness, the grace, the seeming *classlessness* of a man who learned his good manners very early, at the knee of a Victorian working-class mother, a mother who was satisfied that God had seen fit to put her in her humble station, or who was unsatisfied, either way. Edmund treated Angela with an Old-World courtesy and reminded her of her Uncle Bill; and more than that, he approached her as an equal, as if a woman were as equal as a man to him. He never married.

When Charlie had come back from New York those years ago and said guess whom he'd met? Ed Hardie! After a while she asked if he was married.

"No he's not married," said Charlie allowing a touch of smugness to sound. "Of course he's not married."

As to Edmund's connection with her grandmother's letters, they were in fact two pokes at the newly roused giant in her, her free and equal spirit. In the one instance the old woman was pursued by her caring children with a net of concern they intended to fling over her, pull taut, to make her un-free. In the other was the firm hand of friendship, Charlie's hand, clapped upon Ed's shoulder to pull him low and make him unequal.

Could one love and care, be loved and cared for, without the need to control, manipulate, *subordinate*? As wife to

Charlie, was the real question not that she had tried to improve him and hadn't, but that she had tried to improve him and shouldn't have? She did not come to her marriage free and equal: she had come willing, and craven. And now?

"You are the nicest man I know, Ed," said Angela, at once parrying the truth and fondling it. "It's curious that you aren't married."

"People talk irrationally about bachelors, Angela. You are saying, in effect, that the nicer a man is, the more drawn to marriage?"

"Well, the more suited for it, anyway."

"It would seem to me more logical to conclude that because I am so singularly nice the reason must lie in this singular quality about me, that I am not married."

"All right, I'll turn the thing around and put it this way: You seem to me so generous a person as to be able to forgive somebody and marry her."

They were sitting in four wicker chairs that evening in a corner of the south porch of the cottage: Angela and Ed, Jo and Bill. A lot of other people were eating and drinking inside and wandering about the Property looking for August shooting stars. This end of the cottage porch narrowed the distance between somebody sitting in one wicker chair

THE SEA CHANGE OF ANGELA LEWES

and somebody sitting in another. On this end of the porch the head didn't swivel, the eyes flick, the attention drift so widely and so often. It induced intimacy. It was where years ago Bill heard Charles's anguished story of his mother and his wife. They were drinking brandy then too.

Heavier, craggier, greyer than the curate on the bicycle, no longer restricted to one black suit, no longer out of pocket (although he supported his mother and a maiden sister), Edmund Hardie would have looked more like an aging prize fighter, not in the best condition, than a psychiatrist, but that his dented, weathered face was intellectualized by horn-rimmed glasses. The glasses, the seersucker jacket and the suntan trousers, all *de rigueur* with their sort of man circa 1962, were, Angela thought, an ineffectual disguise for Ed, who was not a sort of man at all, but *sui generis*, unclassifiable.

"I believe a bachelor is more disturbing to society than a single woman," Jo said. "They worry about his free time. And on the other hand, people cannot believe that a woman, given her choice, would not marry. People doubt that what I am is probable."

"A man who doesn't marry seems to administer a rebuke to society," said Ed. "I, as an example, elect *not* to bind one woman to myself. Monogamy, the Western world says, is normal and natural to the human species, and I seem to say, 'The hell it is. Not to me.' And as most men harbor a doubt about how normal and natural the thing is, why, they tend to get defensive about some guy who's resisted what I've heard Jo call 'the tyranny of culture.' In my practice you have a patient who is a bachelor, and you take his very bachelor-hood as a symptom—in the category of an abnormality. It is as if resistance to such an overwhelming consensus can never be a mark of health, can only be a mark of illness."

"Suppose a *woman* were to question whether marriage was

normal and natural?" Angela asked with agitation in her voice.

"Doesn't she?"

"Why, Jo! What about children?"

"Well, logistically, of course, monogamy and the double standard combined have been a very sophisticated as well as coercive mechanism for providing that children survive to the age of reproduction. But it's a mechanism that's not geared to the modern predicament. Look at all the women we know who are packing up their overnight bags and tootling off."

"Well, you're just writing The End to the whole human experiment, Jo. Abandon the sanctity of family and you may manage to keep children alive physically so they can reproduce, but when they're all grown up they'll be too distraught, too unbalanced to cope with the world."

"And so we are."

"Anyway Ed, are you sorry you have this bad symptom— wifelessness?" Angela asked, shifting away from the apocalypse that doomed her children.

"Better the symptom than the disease. Oh Angela, I could say to you either that I am too selfish and I won't give up my freedom, am not *prepared* to accommodate to anybody else's needs, or, I can say I'm too rigid and I *can't* do it. These diagnoses may satisfy others. Regardless, they are not the gist of me—if one can see where one's own gist is. Somehow, *somehow* I am able to love a woman without having to stake her out as my property. And the women I've cared deeply about—why, they all have a certain balkiness about them. They won't or they cannot make an exclusive commitment to one man. I am that way too. So like finds like, I suppose. When I am with 'A' whom I love I feel a great longing to express my love physically. And so do I when I am with

'B,' an entirely different human being, an altogether autonomous other self whom I love for that self."

"Jo is like that. Aren't you, Jo? The question is whether you are two anomalies or without the law—somehow unintimidated, not tyrannized."

"I am not like that," Bill said. "I'm left over from the olden times when you were only allowed to love one woman. So I love one woman while being married to another. I find it fills the time."

"See how you love your children, Angela," said Jo. "You don't feel when you have a surge of love for Tina that you've had to rob Angelica for it. You know, you are a woman of great heart. That is your trump suit. I suspect you can love more than one man."

"The question isn't whether I can love more than one man. The question is whether I can admit that I do. What would become of me? And so many people depend upon my orthodoxy, don't you know? I am the anchor for their sanity, I sometimes think. But they have play . . . they are attached loosely and they have play. But a good anchor doesn't have play. I have become increasingly impatient with the complacency with which other people are assured I am content to be an anchor."

"Angela, you're the finest kind of woman," Edmund said, leaning towards her to run his finger along her cheek. "The balky kind."

The next day there were only women and children, the men—Charlie, her father, Bill, Ed, Annie's two gawky gung-ho boys and pokey Adam—having left before dawn to go deep-sea fishing on a chartered boat. All day they would be on the ocean, and all day Angela wandered over the grass and took soundings. That is to say, retrospectively she remembered sending down sounding lines rapidly, half consciously throughout the extent and to the edges of the domain of her life, and she saw how matters stood. Circumstances were conjoining. Her heretofore latent self was aroused, at once broadly aroused, mind and soul; and pinpointedly aroused, sexually. Like Alice, she wondered who she was going to become, as she drifted among the very women there that she was made of, that were her female options, her alternates.

To begin with there was her mother, Margaret, down to Moriches with a full briefcase on a week's vacation. Margaret could never have served as the model for her daughter's cleaving to the hearth. She had become, in fact, a model for the fleeing from it. When she broke down, and with the guidance of Dr. Wise in time reconstituted her life, she did this by advancing even farther into the world. At fifty she went to law school. Subsequently she returned to the ACLU all peer and equal. As to her marriage, her anguish quieted in time, and she and Charles resumed their joint trusteeship of it. They cared for each other in their fashion, were loyal in their fashion. So what Margaret actually did by way of resolution was to provide for Angela a solid example of non-capitulation to the advice to lie in the bed you've made, to lie in it *indefinitely*. This example of her mother's self-rescue had remained in abeyance along with the example of her grandmother's while she had her babies and was nuzzled and encouraged by her Aunt Caroline. Now it cut into the forefront of her musings.

Of those women on the grass, Margaret had set up a bridge table under the oak tree outside the cottage and was working at a brief on her typewriter, looking, with her reading glasses, like a lawyer to be reckoned with or, with her teeth bared on the cigarette holder, like a lawyer to be bitten by, her two youngest granddaughters kept beautifully absorbed by crayons and their grandmother's sheets of white paper.

"I need the lellow, Josie. Please pass me the lellow," Margaret heard Angelica say.

"You got to say *yell*ow," said the golden gentle Josie, who didn't lisp, but on the other hand couldn't pronounce her 'r's.' "You just follow how I do it. *Yell*ow. It's not vewy hahd."

And Angelica agreeable and competently repeated, "Please, Josie, pass me the *yell*ow."

"Wight you ah!" boomed old Josie, which became among her grandmother's favorite stories. She saved it all day to tell Charles first. This sort of mutuality marked their lives.

So there was on the one hand the mother of Angela finished with battles and at peace. And there was on the other her Aunt Caroline seeming to settle into an extended truce. Caroline, presiding over the property from the farmhouse, the top house, had mellowed in her way through the years, had settled into a formula roughly expressed as three parts intolerable to two that touched you. She was not now bovine, whatever she had been in the fullness of her motherhood. She had become very lean, an *Indian* cow, if cow. In common with her sister-in-law Margaret, she maintained a monogamous ménage to the end, with a husband who didn't, but Caroline never knew this. It was different with Charles and his liaison. He, by indirection, by some sort of innuendo, was compelled by his underlying strong bond with his own wife, to have her understand how he had made his accommodation to their continued life together. Caroline lived another scenario entirely.

One by one her children strained at her tether, broke free, and landed beyond the range of her authority, but no sooner had the last done that, than the first was sending a grandchild back, and there were several years of heavy Drinkwater breeding when Caroline had her suitcase at the ready waiting to hear was it a boy, was it a girl? As time went on there were little ones on long visits, *sets* of them dropped off by their parents with a grandmother who kept them in line like a master sergeant, saw that their shoes were shined, that their hair was braided, that they ate their vegetables; and with a grandfather who would come home late for his supper, swoop up the lot of them, and cart them off to an unsuitable drive-in movie and they wouldn't get home until midnight! In summer the farmhouse was always dense with children. The Springfield apartment had bunkbeds in the two guest bedrooms. Caroline pursued the vindictive business of living unto the third generation, and the third generation loved her well enough. Children did. She had three daughters-in-law who did not, but only one who came to blows with her. And she had Annie, her own daughter, a steady good-natured corporal.

Angela was fond of poor Annie who made a whopping salary at the Telephone Company in 1962 while caring for two sons who were a credit to her, and also for one alcoholic husband. She was a bit younger than Angela, and pretty stylish ("You really have to be, in my job"), and her hair was rinsed and teased and later bouffant, and her skirts went up and up and then zoom, down, and she managed wonderfully, she made do with a Very Fine Attitude. Poor Annie had the most lovely relentlessly cheerful disposition, never seeing in her lot, in her headaches, anything that other people would not gladly trade theirs for, wish they had instead of their lot, their headaches: a beautifully wrong-headed assessment of other people's tastes and preferences. Her husband alternately worked and drank, and she lived with the fear— and here is where she earned her sad adjective—that one day he would carry out his threat and leave her.

Increasingly of late, Angela fixed a most respectful eye on Annie because of her whopping salary. The five women in from the grass were now eating sandwiches on the cottage porch: Angela and her mother, Caroline and her Annie, and Jo. Annie had been telling them about the great breakthrough in telephones now coming in decorator colors. She was half joking, or perhaps a quarter joking.

"That's all right Annie," said Angela. "Laugh all the way to the bank if you want to. I admire you *vastly*. For a woman to be paid for what she does is the supreme tribute. I get very down when I think I may be destined to spend my whole life dedicated to Good Works."

"I may be dim," Caroline interposed, "But I can't for the life of me see why you would want to blush for a life dedicated to good works! Although it's a little premature, I think, to count on being valued so highly!" and here Caroline gave Margaret, the mother, a hard look.

Margaret, who through the years tended to forget that a state of war existed between herself and Caroline, said mildly, "One might be concerned to find that one's life was adding up to being not much more than a kind of clubwoman, even if you are the only woman in the club. I mean, one might be justified, don't you think, in looking with some dismay at a lifetime of unpaid jobs?"

"My God, Mother, I work twenty-four hours a day keeping this show on the road!" Angela turned about-face as one will with one's mother. Also, she was still the secret writer, but then, it was an unpaid job.

"Well, my dear, it would be perhaps wise to wonder at this point whether it isn't the elegant hobby that keeps an intellectual woman with a lot of children playing house indefinitely, a very sophisticated sort of house, of course."

"That's a reductive thing to say to somebody, Mother!" Angela shot back in anger.

"Don't hear it that way, dear. I think you are very gifted. I think you are too intelligent to spend your life baking casseroles for Charlie's seminar students."

"I would have gone out of my mind without the Telephone Company," Annie let out—let out a bit of reality.

"I don't care what anyone says," Caroline bawled. "Running a house and bringing up four children are a full-time job!"

"They are two red herrings," Jo contradicted.

"It's not the *time* they absorb"—Angela struggled always to be on Jo's side and was surprised to be arguing—"They blot up your emotional energy."

"A house and four children add up to hard work, long hours, and little thanks, I can tell you that." Caroline told them that. Jo said, "The household is what you *do*, not what you *are*. It's a woman's problem. It's written that she shall be a catalyst, *strive* to be the best possible, most grateful catalyst for the release of male energies."

"Oh, Jo, for goodness' sake. How can you talk that feminist jargon?" Angela was hurt that they weren't agreeing. Jo went on, "You're a performer, you're an actress. Take away your roles, and is there anybody there?"

"But if I'm an actress and I play Nora—why, It's a very expanding lesson to play Nora. After I've been Nora I'm not the same again. I'm leavened, an expanded self. You sound as if a woman just stage-manages her life, unaffected, just directs and stages it. Like Mrs. Alving in *Ghosts*."

"That's right! That's what we do, stage-manage, direct, design the sets, pick the costumes, write the dialogue. And if you're very good you make everything much better. Just as Mrs. Alving does. She sacrifices herself, sacrifices Truth which is sordid, and designs in its place a beautifully ethical lie, for her son."

"You're saying I *play* Mrs. Alving, that I am the star at best of a . . . situation comedy?"

"I sacrificed my life for my children, but I don't apologize!" said Caroline.

"I admit to a lot of fake touches, Jo," said Angela, once more ignoring her aunt, "I mean I think I'm living today's *metaphor*—the metaphor of my time and my culture—that stands for the elemental rules for human survival, for reproduction and survival . . . I know I sound like Darwin for the Home . . . I mean, I just don't think I'm underwriting a lie, a life that's fake to the core. Do you think I am?" Angela asked Jo, half laughing. Angela felt that she was always half-laughing while she talked of late. Like a tic.

"No, I don't think *you* are," Jo answered, unconvincingly. "But I have thought one does—one must. And then again, must one?"

"Well, if we get too tired of this business we can play Hedda Gabler and put a pistol to our heads."

And at the end of the day when the others had left and only Jo stayed on, Angela said, "You know what Charlie told me before we went to sleep last night? He told me he thought you were beautiful and he'd never seen any woman keep her looks past thirty-five the way you have."

"And what about you?"

"Oh well, I'm his wife. And you know Charlie, he likes them fresh and wide-eyed: And she says to him, 'Oh Mr. Lewes, I'm absolutely fascinated by your article on the reform of the Electoral College. I think it's fantastic!' and he thinks, 'That's a beautiful girl!' Every year he's renewed by a fresh flock of students who adore him and move in on us, and there are girls who come back year after year to see him—us. I think they keep him faithful."

"He never takes one off?"

"No." Angela laughed at the idea. "Well, I don't know, after all. It never crossed my mind." And she thought about it for a moment, but Charlie seemed so entirely accounted for, the flattery and the stimulation of those bright pretty girls just the right amount of diversion, she thought. "I've never been jealous." Angela put that fact on the table, wondering about it all at once, as if not being jealous were an inadequacy, and then, by association with another inadequacy, she said calmly, "I'm not a very sexual creature. I've never been jealous and I've never had an orgasm."

"That's a funny coupling of charges against yourself," Jo said, laughing, intending to lighten this indictment.

"And the reason I believe I am telling you that," said Angela full steam and now flustered, "is because I am suddenly knocked flat by a tremendous wave of lust. I'm dizzy with it. I'm obsessed by it."

"It makes you look marvelous. Charlie is the only one who doesn't see it."

"It seems so silly, so inappropriate—at my age! And what will I do? I'm not even sure that Edmund . . . that I'm 'B.' Or what if I'm 'C'? I don't know whether, for crying out loud, I could stand being 'C'!"

"What is perhaps more relevant is whether you could be unfaithful to Charlie?"

"I don't know that either." Angela was stopped by the thought. "I'll have to see, won't I? And who is 'A'? That's what I'd really like to know."

"Don't you know who 'A' is? I thought you knew who that was. Rosa Benson Forrest."

"The piano-player?" Angela asked, startled, tasting jealousy for the first time in her life, a metallic taste, in the throat she noted, where there are no taste buds.

"Oh it's a very old story. They took up in New Haven, years ago. They keep separate apartments and it's always been an on and off affair. She's away on concert tours in Europe a lot of the time."

"I can't believe it! How come nobody knows?"

"Oh, you know Ed. He doesn't need to tell things. And she—well, we don't travel in her circles. They knew each other in New Haven first, and then she married somebody else—a Mr. Forrest, one assumes. Then she divorced him, but they had two children who live with their father, who remarried. Nearly her whole self is music, and she lives by a very demanding regimen. She won't marry, she won't tolerate entanglements."

"Where'd you get all this?"

"I used to see her sister from time to time. She's in the theater. I thought we'd talked about it. Funny."

"And she's forty and she's beautiful?"

"Well, I've run into her now and again—not to talk to— at these big things. She's beautiful in an ugly sort of way. She's elongated, she tapers, she has a cold oval face and a long throat which she cuts with a small chiffon handkerchief in coral or violet. It reflects well on her that she seeks out a man like Edmund. You wouldn't think, offhand, she'd be giving enough."

"You know, Charlie has let on through the years that Ed likes boys. He's curiously insistent about that."

"Very curiously."

////// CHAPTER SEVENTEEN ///////

*A*NGELA marveled at the facility, the guiltlessness, with which she stole hours from her Ibsenian roles—her silent secret slipping upstairs, the secrecy at first assumed by inadvertence, but then becoming integral to the writing, its cachet. She had thought of her divergence as unique, her abrupt departure after nearly forty years of constant presence surely unprecedented. But she was not after all unique even for a Porter, and her departure was very far from being unprecedented, and in fact, as fiction goes, a pale copy of her grandmother's: and from the time of that Moriches weekend of the letters and of Edmund there began to take root in her third-floor soul an obsession with her ancestress and predecessor. She effected an alliance with this cunning deep ghost.

Whatever upheaved through that mild weekend in the summer of '62 seemed to subside. What had happened between her and Edmund Hardie? In actuality nothing whatsoever had happened. In fantasy he joined a spectral grandmother to become another inhabitant of her secret life, the third-floor lodger. She read and wrote with a lust she had never known before.

"It's displaced sexual energy," she told Jo. "I'm rueful about it. However, I believe it keeps me faithful to husband as well as typewriter. I'm afraid that if I had a love affair I would rechannel my sexual energies into sex."

"I've found it quite the other way."

"What do you mean?"

"Well, if I've noticed anything, it's a rise in creativity rather than a lowering . . . as though I'd been, don't you know . . . inseminated."

"Is that so?"

Angela had four finished short stories and an essay called "Jane Eyre and Dorothea Brooke" by the fall of '63.

"And I do not want, if I can help it, to be a flower born to blush unseen."

"The thing would be to get an agent. I know a lovely man whom you might——"

"Oh, Jo, I am too fearful to take that step."

"Well, find yourself a nom de plume."

"I have found myself one."

Charlie and the children became accustomed to the idea that Angela had made a private corner for herself in the upstairs room, and knew she read in it and brought her sewing up, and wrote letters there. It was not remarkable, no more so than that her grandmother had taken Theo's room in the farmhouse. Nobody suspected her grandmother had the presumption to write, had the daring, dared.

"But then she didn't write," said Jo to Angela.

"But she dared. Finally, she dared."

The problem of the presumption of writing anything one would ask anybody else to read was nearly insuperable for Angela, and while it was as much in her temperament as it was in her mother's to expose herself painfully, to lay herself bare, in the public-spirited, liberal open way on every sort of issue nobody else gave a damn about, by the accident of the initial secrecy of these particular proceedings, she may very well have served herself a bit of forbidden mental privacy, a provision always heretofore tasted sparingly, labeled *Caution* on account of its addictive quality. Without question she felt herself to be extremely modest and shy about the pieces she had written, and never even would show them to Jo. But on "just this or that poor impulse, that for once had play unstifled" (Browning)—and it was exactly that, a poor impulse that darted past her red-faced shame,—she sent off "Jane Eyre and Dorothea Brooke" to *The New Yorker*, with the return address "Marian Evans, % General Delivery, Northampton"; and subdued resurgent waves of panic that billowed up into her brain by reminding herself that her anonymity remained complete.

It might take six months, she thought, to get an answer, but at the end of three weeks there was her rejection with the covering letter:

Dear "Miss Evans":
This work may be earnest, but it is also smug, and one must read through many pages before finding a single original idea or graceful sentence.
Yours sincerely, . . .

Certainly humility is an admixture with a strong infusion of arrogance, as is laid bare in the struggle characters like Raskolnikov and Prufrock had, and surely it was ill-advised of Angela just tactically speaking, to have chosen to be "Miss Evans," but the choice, it is nonetheless true, derived from the humblest part of her humility. It was even true that her admiration for George Eliot was not strictly confined to the books she wrote, but that she identified herself a little with that earlier woman, although only, she would have asseverated warmly to whomever she would have confessed this, *only* with her frailty: with those weaknesses and misgivings that come through her diaries and letters, as for instance her exorbitant need for protection and reassurance which she finally seemed to receive in all its rich exorbitance from Mr. George Henry Lewes. Well, and here it will be perfectly plain to see that while Angela could not be gratified by the protection and reassurance of her Mr. Lewes, Charles Francis, who was in this instance blameless, of course, she would take pleasure in calling herself Mrs. Lewes, with more legal, perhaps, but less emotional entitlement than George Eliot's.

So there was the Lewesness between them, uncontrived. As to Marian Evans, it was a plain and unobtrusive, unremarkable name, all except that it was George Eliot's, and it was to the plainness Angela went back, even with a little the intention of restoring worthiness to a plain name, restoring the right of such a name to be an author's name, averring the right of an author with a plain name to be a *woman*, or the right of a woman with a plain name to be an author. So she sent that plain name out on its own for a first sally only to have it greeted with contempt. She presumed so timorously to associate herself with George Eliot and she was smacked down for it in a second, and called smug. She did not, naturally, like one word of the letter beginning with "Dear" and ending with "sincerely," but "smug" was what stung.

A terrible coincidence, she would like to have thought, to have been mistakenly called smug again.

Angela was raking the first leaves on an Indian Summer day when she had to race in to the phone. It was Annie calling from her office in the New York Telephone Company.

"Angela, a sticky little family problem has come up and I'm turning to you" because—her husband was not too well and she didn't like to leave him—"besides the usual rat race at the office."

"Sure, Annie what can I do for you?"

"It's my mother and Louise. They seem to have had, you know, a little set-to."

Caroline and her daughter-in-law, Will's wife, were so hostile to each other that they always seemed on the verge of recalling their ambassadors, and it was a fact over which the rest of the family guffawed that when Caroline accompanied her husband to Amherst to see the grandchildren she "would not take anything by mouth," while on those rare occasions when a return visit was made to Springfield, Will and the children went in while Louise resolutely sat in the car.

"What happened?"

"Louise slapped Mother."

"Slapped your mother!"

"Well, probably she didn't slap her very hard."

"Well, what does your father say?"

"He says she didn't hit her hard enough. You know my father."

"Well, it seems to me a perfectly irreconcilable situation. Why do you want to do anything about it?"

"Oh, you know, there're the children—Sally and little Suzie—and my mother's getting older . . . Of course the whole blow-up was about Suzie. My mother told Louise she should be in an institution."

"*Again?*"

"She *should* be in an institution, but of course my mother shouldn't keep bringing that up after all these years. I mean, she's entitled to express her opinion as the grandmother, of course, but you know Louise is a very overwrought woman . . ." Every one of them should be in an institution, Angela thought.

"What do you want me to do?"

"I thought you could go over and see Louise."

"Annie, she doesn't like me much better than she likes your mother."

"Well, Angela, she doesn't like *anybody*," Annie said in a rational, persuasive way. "I wouldn't trouble you about this, but I'm afraid if I leave here——"

"Listen, all right, I'll go over there, Annie, but she'll probably slap me, and then Charlie'll go over and belt her . . . and . . . I think we should stop while we're ahead . . ."

"I knew I could turn to you, and I want to tell you how much I appreciate . . ."

Will and Louise lived on the second floor of a large Victorian house in Amherst. One always walked through their door pretending; pretending that the shabbiness and disorder didn't exist, that you didn't notice that the plaid canvas suitcase propped against the living room couch was still there from last time, that you weren't concerned to tear your hose on what you sat on from whatever was sticking out of it, splinters, or broken metallic fibers from the ruptured upholstery. Cats, dogs, hamsters, gerbils, white mice might shoot across the room. Thin little Suzie, with her poor limbs crooked and her whole self shaking, forever seemed to tremble in the eye of these whirling creatures. She was eight then, with a lean face and uncombed straggle of pale hair, and she would look at you with an expression at once dull and peculiarly cynical, the cynicism there, of course, from a muscular disorder. She wore limp dresses like the little girls in the photographs of Appalachian poverty in the '30s.

Their older daughter, Sally, was fifteen, a carrothead, a brisk, trim, pretty, frecklenosed girl who must have gotten a good seven years of her mother before Suzie was born and Louise began to decompensate. Sally was a kind, helpful, patient daughter to her, was always good with little Suzie, and was inevitably her father's anchor. She lived among the disparate beings and cared for them, but could not reconcile them.

Angela had first met Louise at her own wedding in Moriches. She and Will had been married unceremoniously the week before in the Town Hall in Madison, Wisconsin, where they had been sharing a sink for a year in the University biology lab, and they had driven East to present themselves to the tribe handily gathered for appropriately nuptial reasons. Neither Angela nor Louise remembered much about the other beyond Angela's thinking Louise was a bit bulbous in feature and had no rear end, and Louise's thinking Angela was rich and spoiled. Louise was neither rich nor spoiled and had grown up in a small town in Southern Illinois, the daughter of a Methodist minister with seven children who shot himself in the head in the rectory office when she was twelve. The family then moved in with the maternal grandparents. Louise seemed to have worked grimly to get out of there, earned money and scholarships for the University of Illinois and later for graduate study, fought her way out of religion and into the Communist Party, out of the Communist Party and into the biology laboratory: a serial believer. A serial believer must by nature experience a series of betrayals. She had lately been believing so fervently in the Spastic Foundation and Retarded Children's Classes that she had on several occasions called Angela for reasons of county financial and organizational support. Angela had written the checks, which was easy, and had attended with Louise half a dozen meetings of one sort or another, which was terrible; but in regard to her present mission of reconciliation, none of this was capital in the bank with Louise because Louise—and in this she was singularly like her mother-inlaw—did not let you store up good points with her, to be drawn against in case of need.

Louise answered the door. She was wearing dark slacks

and a maroon pullover and looked really pretty good, Angela thought, surprised. She had a bit of ginger in her.

"Well, I don't ask myself," she said by way of hello, " 'to what do I owe the pleasure of this visit?' "

Angela was always unstrung by incivility, by this breaking of the rules. She had no language to respond to it. Two lazy cats came slowly to the door to see who it was, and she reflected that Louise was very good to children and animals. She did love little Suzie. Probably she went out of her mind with loving her.

"Ah, come on, Louise. Look here, everybody's wanted to sock Caroline and nobody ever did, and now you have. OK? It's not such a big thing, that urge. No reason to blow it up that way."

"Ooooooooo," Louise literally groaned in rage, "you are so smug, Angela, so smug."

11111 CHAPTER EIGHTEEN *11111*

IT is hard to locate Charlie in this story. As it is written, Angela is the maypole and all these people dance around her, but she would have said otherwise, that he was the maypole, a suitably phallic image, the very *sine qua non* of a maypole which she kept bedecked with colored ribbons and spring flowers, around which she danced holding hands with the children. Her other self watched through these years as she began unloosening the hands, untying the ribbons, spinning off. Charlie spent these years letting her.

How much of the very successful congeniality of those two depended upon the coincidence of their later need to diverge as they had had, evidently, the earlier need to carve themselves into an interlocking whole? A lot. Blessed Random Chance was the patron saint, of Angela's Darwinism and to refer back to the hazards of the climacteric and multiples of seven (and to combine in the same sentence what was indeed contained in the same woman, an intellectual with a sprinkling of salt over the left shoulder), as Charlie moved into his middle thirties (5×7) there seemed to be a fork in his future. It did look as though he might choose just to ride out the remainder of his time on earth because, being a boy-man, it was apposite to think that everything there was to do had to be done when one was young, and he'd done it, and the rest was to coast. It was very common in the academic trade, when rank and tenure were assured, to coast, and Charlie, differing in one nice respect from many of his coasting colleagues, was rich (on account of the wizard) and might become the playboy of the Connecticut Valley. He liked to play. But he also liked to work, and by chance (he said chance too) he tumbled to a rich vein in the political science mine by stumbling over Boss Ed Flynn of the Bronx, that nugget. The hypothetical fork a man comes to in academic life is usually discernible years later, if at all, as the wrong choice he made; and his wife saw it all along. As to women, either their lives are thought to be forkfree, or their choices too trivial to be remarked upon, and years later the husband still never saw it.

Well, Charlie took the better fork, and eventually began to dig into his vein in depth, which accounted in part for his buoyancy, his navigating nearly painfree the transition into middle age, and his spending many weeks of many years, and nearly all of 1965, his sabbatical year, in places like Jersey City, Kansas City, and the Bronx. It changed the rhythm of their lives. The two little ones had a traveling salesman of a father, and he'd come home from being on the road loaded with presents to a big dinner, and later he would make love to Angela quickly, and roll over and be fast asleep in a minute. He loved her, was grateful to her, and once in a while when he was tasting the sharpness of his own success he would acknowledge that the credit went to Angela—who kept expecting him to progress like Pilgrim or watch out!—who never tired of pointing to those men who were done at forty, who had quit, were finished. "You can always tell who they are by their being so cheerful and having such a good time!" "It's like living in a house with a sibyl on the ceiling," he was also fond of saying.

Angela was spinning off, and Charlie was letting her. The shift in their marital relationship was remarkable for the absence of tension, of conflict—a peaceful *de*-consummation devoutly to be wished in the generality of aging marriages. Angela was becoming her own person, her own woman, and was alternately exhilarated and complacent, or—as it was otherwise put—smug.

Two "smugs," the double puncture: that was quite a deflationary coincidence. She was limp for a long time after, perhaps six months. She left off congratulating herself for having become a somebody independent of her roles, her formal associations. Feeling hurt and vulnerable and dependent, she had the tremendous reawakened need to rush back to Charlie, to re-attach herself to him mind and soul, to tell him the whole story of her writing, this larger surprise about the third-floor room, a surprise for *him*, that she'd made something more substantial of herself, she who was his. It would be his gift. There were times through that winter of her post-smugness when the yearning to re-embrace that shared life with Charlie was painful.

But when she would have reached out to him, he wasn't there: he was in the Bronx. She would have reached back to him, canceled her autonomy, beetled in retreat to the mutuality of their past, to hear again that close, caring companionable chord they sometimes struck—when she was in labor with Angelica, no Josie, and they played Scrabble and he kept two scores, the one for the game and the other for timing the pains. When she was really sick, or really frightened by a sick child, he encircled her with comfort, with love. Now when she was feeling hurt and a fool, she was ready to drop the whole autonomy business for that dear encirclement.

For a long stretch of that winter she would climb up to the

third floor and sit down and not write: smug but not smug enough to stay untouched and indifferent to an assessment that there wasn't an original thought or a graceful sentence in the single piece she had submitted for an outside opinion. Intending to begin a full-length novel, she was unable to put down a full-length sentence.

Instead and finally, she took up the unfinished business of Theo's manuscripts. Her cousin Will, that strange man, had in effect prodded her about them. He had slipped into the room so quietly during his wife's blast at Angela, that she neither knew he was there nor knew how he'd gotten her back down to her car. She was about to drive off when he said, "Why don't you push over?" and he took her off in her own car northwest through the warm haze, his red head hailing the brotherhood of high color that Indian summer afternoon.

"Yes, you are smug, but you are entitled to be smug," Will had said mildly, and then they didn't talk for a while.

"I was meant to be a bachelor, my dear, and in fact manage to lead something of a bachelor's life. You must never waste any pity on me—I should never have married her. It was a great disservice to her—which somebody else, I do regret, hadn't got there first to perform."

"Well, you know Will, she isn't the first woman with a sick child who——"

"She was like that when I met her. Every day there she'd be over the sink in the filthiest lab coat, eaten with acid holes, great hunks of the hem burnt away—I saw how that happened!—and in some curious way it amused and touched me. She had come to hate biology, physics, the whole business; felt she was trapped in it by the available scholarship funds, wanted to retire from the scientific world forever, become a woman! I saw that I was elected to be the man to make the woman—she was just using the materials at hand—and I let her do it." Will told Angela all this in a mild tone. "I don't need women. I don't need people." He'd taken a dirt road, and they bumped slowly along for perhaps a quarter of a mile through tall thick brush, when the brimming river appeared steamy in the hazy sunset just in front of them. Following his lead, she got out and walked through trampled grass to an ordinary, entirely overlookable cabin. It was built on pilings, and they climbed wooden steps, walked through an unlocked door and were inside a large most strikingly shipshape room, the front half of which was covered with a handsome thick woolen rug of a beige base with geometric designs in greens, blacks, and browns. Will said he had been after Braque's colors. The fireplace with its chimney ran up the center of the room. There was a bench before it with a long needlepoint cover, two dark easy chairs, a cot, and behind the chimney in the rear a small loom, a cedar chest, things on shelves, the whole of it as clean and trim as geometry itself.

"Actually it isn't really true, my dear, that I don't need *any* people. My father comes here often. Theo used to bed down here for weeks at a time: only the cold would drive him off. When Theo died I brought Sally. She loves it. We roast potatoes and steak. Would you like to come sometime?"

"My goodness, Will. I believe we are a queer family for having secret lives. You and Theo and our grandmother . . . and me" (she didn't tell, he didn't ask how she was queer) "—there's a sly strain coming strong through some of us."

"It's in Sally."

"It's in Tina"—where Angela did not like it at all. It frightened her to think of Tina's private world. "You know, Will, I find lately that I am very absorbed by the story of our grandmother. Do you ever think about her?"

"No, I don't, but Theo never let her alone."

"What do you mean?"

"I thought you'd had his papers? You haven't read through them? Well, my dear, he let me understand he'd finally seen her. He didn't want to talk about it, but it was my understanding that he'd written something."

"What do you mean he saw her, when did he see her?"

"Well, let's see, she died in the winter of '57. I think it was something like the spring before."

"Really I am incredulous before such secrecy. I think it is so astonishing, you know, that if he really did find her, he wouldn't tell anybody. That doesn't seem odd to you?"

"Of course, I'm odd that way too, you see."

"I guess I'm getting odd that way myself."

Theo's papers were still neatly boxed in a closet of the cottage in Moriches, and Angela couldn't get them mailed out to her until spring. It was not a simple matter to locate an old grandmother in the manuscript copies of two novels, several long critical pieces, correspondence going back to 1928, and dozens of short stories. She was angry and frustrated at first when she realized that the revelation amounted to no more than a little sketch of an old Provençal woman who has just learned that she has cancer. The son is the narrator, a prodigal son who has by chance in his lift-drift about the world paid her his call after an absence of twenty years. It reminded Angela of Camus and the opening of *l'Etranger*, the short-reined sentences, the emotion held in short rein: "I took the bus from Marseilles to Aix. It was an old bus that rattled and wheezed and finally broke down halfway. I walked the remaining six kilometers. The mistral blew without pause and made my head light as though it had been thoroughly aired. . . ."

The son comes upon his mother stooping in the kitchen garden, picking some early greens. She straightens up, and he is shocked to see how small and lean and old she is: the structure of her face had lost its soft flesh, is outlined now, is distinguished actually, and intelligent. When she recognizes her son she doesn't seem very surprised, nor very glad, but on the other hand not distressed—as if it were an ordinary event. Neither asks much about the other, not "What have you been doing these twenty years?" She makes a supper for them both in the little kitchen or her apartment and in a matter-of-fact way allows him to know what she has lately discovered from the doctor, and that she has pills for pain. After two hours, which has been like an interview between casual associates, he tells her that his business might keep him in Marseilles for a while and that he would in that event return. They both know he will not. The next morning in Marseilles the son secures passage on a freighter bound for Buenos Aires. About his mother he concludes that with her widowhood and the estrangement of her one son she had assumed complete charge of her own life, had long since cut ties of sentiment, and that she was now further narrowing her forces to take charge of her own death.

Angela read the story twice through on a night when the rain pounded loud on the slate roof of her aerie. Little Ange woke and called her, and she went down to keep her child company on the long walk through the dark hall to the bathroom. There she sat, her tubby sweet-natured last little girl with her round legs shooting out from the toilet seat, her arms folded in her lap, her head rolled backwards, eyes closed, one-tenth awake. Then trot-trot-trot back through the dark hall, into her own bed, already fast asleep. Angela could not go back upstairs to the third floor to so much estrangement, so much alienation.

She took off her clothes and bathed, brushed out her long thick hair and tied it back for the night with a ribbon, and went down to wait for Charlie. By the dim kind light of the reading lamp she looked very young, quite lovely. She passed the time amassing the data of her emotional experiences of the last three years, putting it all in some quiet order. She yearned to return to a shared life with Charlie. All those cold crazy isolated *selfish* Porters—how she had romanticized them! So many unfeeling people. She was repelled by them, in revulsion against the remorseless way they each of them looked after themselves, pruned themselves of unnecessary attachments, made cold unfeeling wives—look at Caroline, look at Louise, and even Jo who wouldn't even deign to be a wife, who was essentially unpossessable—and men like Theo and Will who cultivated and cherished the distance between themselves and any other living human being, ever alert to make that distance wider—and that weirdly secretive old woman being herself the very source of five children and seven grandchildren, of first spawning them and then *snip!*— spurning them, cutting herself off clean once and for all and no regrets.

It was nearly midnight when Charlie came home and Angela greeted him, ready to slip herself into his arms, but he was drenched. "Don't come near me, baby, unless you want to be soaked through. What's the matter? Is something the matter with one of the kids?"

On the shelf of Angela's mind, all this evening there had sat a story she remembered very dimly, by Katherine Anne Porter (Porter-Porter, Lewes-Lewes) about a woman who had for a long time been withdrawn into herself out of reach from her husband. And then on this night she had unaccountably a tremendous welling up of love for him, and desire, and it filled her with joy to anticipate, when their guests were gone—they had guests—to anticipate offering herself to him willingly, delightedly. All evening she sails high along to the end of their party when by the chance angle of a mirror she catches sight of her husband with another woman in his arms. A person who has been thrust out might not just hang around waiting until he can thrust himself back in, was the moral of that, she thought.

"Nothing really is the matter," Angela began, "only I've come across the most bizarre thing." She trailed Charlie into the kitchen where he began poking into the refrigerator. He turned his head encouragingly towards her and said, "I'm listening. Go on."

"Well, you know all that stuff Theo left that I've been putting off reading?" Yes he knew it. "Well there's a short story dated the spring before Grandma died. It's about a son who visits his mother after twenty years, and it takes place in Aix-en-Provence! Charlie, I haven't one doubt that Theo did go over there and find her. Isn't that wild?"

"Theo was a damn spook, I always thought. And so for that matter was his old lady." Charlie moved through the kitchen leaving his marks, ham, cheese, tomatoes, mustard, relish, milk on the counters, and sat down to listen and eat. Angela faltered.

"It's a really good story," she commented lamely, and then determined to go on. "You know, there's something I've been trying to do myself. I've been writing. Up there in the third floor room. Isn't that surprising?"

"I think it's terrific. Barbara Goldman writes those children's stories. It's the perfect sort of solution for a woman. I always thought you ought to do something like that. Why don't you take up your drawing again?"

This was being the most perfunctory, the most blanched confession, greeted with no surprise, but simply with a kindly nod of encouragement, and it was having the effect of cauterizing Angela's open heart. "I've done four short stories, quite well finished," she went on gamely.

"Speaking of Barbara Goldman, I'll tell you who's a

spook, that Elliot Goldman. He's got these two tape recorders in his office and he's got them talking to each other!"

"You know who put me on to Theo's story about Grandma? It was Will Drinkwater. Do you remember that time when I—"

"And that's *another* spook!"

"Charlie, listen to me, I'm very serious about writing."

"Well, I really think you should be!"

"I haven't told you about it because you've been busy with your bosses——"

"Speaking of that, I think I'm going to cut out graduation and take those three weeks I'll have before summer school and go down and spend them in the Bronx County Court House."

And so Charlie, who thought what Angela was doing was swell, did not confuse her own sense of being terribly pregnant with things, with her actually having another baby, and therefore did not know that he was to respond to her momentous revelation with commensurate interest. "I'm not talking about hobbies, Charlie, for crying out loud. I'm talking about—Epiphany!" was what Angela was on the verge of crying out loud. But she abruptly did not. Then *ping*. Another *ping*, and she saw herself a pea in a peashooter being stretched heart and soul as far as she could go in one direction. *Ping!* and she is released, and shooting all the way in the other, up to that private third-floor soul the secret existence of which she now shared with Charlie, who would never think to mention it.

✐✐✐✐✐✐ CHAPTER NINETEEN ✐✐✐✐✐✐

*C*HARLIE came back from his sojourn in the Bronx at the end of June bringing the surprise of Edmund Hardie with him. Angela, in the interval since her abortive attempt to be re-embraced by her husband and the past, resumed her writing with a kind of grim excitement generated, probably, by adrenalin released from what was essentially treatment her children would now call a Giant Put-Down. The new better gifted Angela was spurned. One thing you don't do with new better gifted autonomous selves is pat them encouragingly. But in the irrational way that the spirit works, her pride was restored somehow by her husband's resolute underappreciation of herself as an unprecedented phenomenon. He went on about his own affairs, checking in lightly to patronize her, and she on her part broadened her own affairs, remembering lightly to matronize him. That was his Angela, his baby, his old girl.

She led two lives easily. If one were taken away she would wither and die; either one. Upstairs on the third floor she had fallen unilaterally in love with the fantasy of her third-floor lodger, so much so that when Edmund Hardie was actually holding the front door open for Charlie she had a jump in the heart at his opacity, this hunking ill-remembered grizzle-headed actual man. He stood there a little stooped— all the tall men she knew stooped, except her father, who tilted—he ducked his head in a mock shy way, his expression affectionate, secret, amused, and she gasped something memorable like "Oh Edmund!" after which Charlie boomed past him saying, "Hi baby, Guess who I brought home!"

In respect to forks for *women*, two paths, a choice, and Angela's encounter with a moral dilemma, the wonder to her was not that the image was apt, but that it wasn't. Unless you used rivers. Because if you are taking a path and come to a fork, you must make a deliberate choice, exercise your will. With a river-fork on the other hand, one can be, and she was, swept downstream on the side of the swiftest current. Edmund Hardie involved Angela in no decisions, no tussle with old loyalties and old moralities. The only predeterminate feature in her relationship with him was to be unmoored, to have become unmoored first. And it was thinking about it this way, the very willessness with which she had come to make rapid ricochets out of her Mainstream, her own named and designated Mainstream, that made her wonder the more about her grandmother. She reaffirmed her passionate alliance with her grandmother. All her grandmother really probably ever did was unloose herself from her moorings, and off she was swept by the current of events. Somehow each woman in her time imperceptibly rocking in the gentlest quietest way rocked herself out of her berth, although in the case of her grandmother Angela could more readily perceive how it happened: that there was the deep well of an old Victorian woman who as a young girl was transplanted into a land of English-speaking people, her soul silenced by their language. Then afterwards, when she has done everything assigned to her, been everything asked of her, and all her purposes are wound up and disposed of, along comes a Mrs. Brundage speaking Czech to her and the sound drops into the well of her, all the way down, and she hears the *chink, chink*. The vibrations of her one true language are what start the rocking. Of the last dozen years of her grandmother's life they knew the barest minimum, little more than what was on the official form apprising her father of his mother's death January 3, 1957, with the shipment of her ashes by boat mail to New York COD. The form began:

> nom: Mme Angele Čapek
> née: inconnu
> occupation: concierge

And the letter was from the American consul in Marseilles, who wrote her father in the briefest way that the widow who had been concierge for twelve years at the Pension de Repos, Aix-en-Provence, was discovered upon her demise to carry an American passport under the name of Angelina Porter, that this name had been on their Missing Persons list since September of 1939, and they were glad to have it off. Something like that. And equally cool was the family response. Nobody dashed off to the South of France to find out who their mother was and what she did and whether it had been bad for her or good.

Angela talked to Edmund about her grandmother, about the Porters and their secret lives, and finally about her own secret life. After all, he was the court psychiatrist, Charlie having sought him out purposely to consult about his bosses. Charlie was full of bonhommie, but his friendships were functional. You had to bring something to them like a willingness to play on his softball team, to be fascinated by the personality of Ed Flynn or Mayor Hague, to be fascinated by him, Charlie, into which category fell the many Smith girls (they represented, these girls, the female sex as far as his warm associations went). He couldn't make a friend of a mature woman. This kind of man cannot, because he needs in his social intercourse, and in his sexual intercourse, to enjoy some kind of a triumph, and a mature woman won't let him. (Did Angela let him? It would have been hard for either of them to say at that point, had they been inclined to ask themselves the question, which they were not, whether Charlie's physical interest in his wife was suffering the normal suspension of a man past forty, or whether he sensed then, what he said later, that "she was not herself.")

For the three days of Edmund's visit Angela engaged in a mocking dead-serious flirtation with him in which she knew her judgment about her own behavior was impaired, but this was the consequence of her experiencing an intense physical excitement that altered her chemistry, and she was helpless, and she wasn't the first woman of forty to have this happen to her. Edmund participated in the flirtation, but with circumspection. She kissed him when she handed him a drink in the kitchen, and laughed and was uncharacteristically flighty for her, she thought, but not for that category of premenopausal women who exhibit a desperate flightiness in their sexuality. She did not like to be placed in any category, did Angela, and this one of foolish, aging, sagging women very eager to become cheating wives, was as degrading a category as could be thought up. She took all those women out of this category and gave them her sympathy. Edmund never lent himself to her mockery. He looked at her seriously, and treated her with a consideration, a courtliness, with which indeed he approached everybody, but in his manner towards Angela it was more warm and deliberate, she thought.

Edmund listened to Angela. She opened her mind to him, asked him to believe in her astonishing metamorphosis, how

her insight about women and people expanded with a geometric progression that left her short of breath, that her senses
were losing sheaves and sheaves of casing, sloughing them off,
that her ear and taste and eye were responding ever more
acutely, raining messages down on her nearly-passive self,
and that she had nobody to tell this to. And he wanted to
hear. It is a miraculous coincidence to a woman in whom the
need to talk was welled up with explosive pressure, to do
just that: to talk, unstopped, unflinching, straight, and passionately to a man who listens attentive, untiring, unflinching,
whose long large self sits on one haunch in a wicker chair on
the porch in Northampton, and later on the porch in the
cottage in Moriches. All talk was their affair, all talk. Sometimes she would pick at a stitch in Edmund's quiet interior
self and a seam of thought would open in him, and he would
talk. Gradually, very gradually she began to yield to his wel-
coming love for her. Jo had said to her one day, "Well, you
know, he struggles with an underlying depression," and she
was shocked at how things fell into place about him then,
how in his quiet responsible way he looked after an old
mother and an odd sister; how he stood by a most tempera-
mental mistress in a manner that suited *her* temperament
with its staccato shifts of needing him instantly, and leaving
two planes later for Istanbul on a three-month concert tour
of the eastern Mediterranean, how even his profession was
lopsided in its requirement that he *give* patiently, that he
take pain. He plied a singularly isolated course in psychiatry:
he worked with criminally insane children. In the beginning
Edmund seemed to Angela enormously urbane, incredibly
free, able to arrange everything to suit his tastes. But he had
never arranged to have someone like her in his life; and he
wouldn't have arranged it, she thought. She did. Angela
was more the aggressor in this liaison, which was still all talk.

Thus together they accreted; they were building, through

intermittent visits, on deposits of excitement and caring and amusement already laid down. It had nothing to do with Charlie, who said: "Ed's fantastic. Really, for a guy who says hardly anything at all, he's terrifically articulate in his field— what he knows! My God, you know his judgment is so subtle. He restrains *me*. If this book amounts to anything I'll owe him a lot."

"For somebody you think so highly of, I just don't understand why you always make him sound like Your Friend the Fairy. As if he were the Company Homosexual! As if you needed a homosexual to prove how deeply unprejudiced you are! Really Charlie, it looks ridiculous. There isn't a man around who looks more certifiably male than Edmund Hardie." Angela unpenned her fury.

"Homosexual! Homosexual! My God, Angela you always sound like a case worker. You've got a case on him, have you? Ha! you going to make a man of him? Well, go ahead," he said with derision.

But Angela could not bear his anger, and she turned placatory and said she just thought it was queer he would call Ed queer when there wasn't one sign.

"My God, Angela," said her husband, more provoked by the pleading in her voice than the anger, "He doesn't drive a car!"

"Well, for crying out loud, of all the dopey things to say! He doesn't drive a car! That ties up your argument, I suppose? You had to buy yourself that powder-blue convertible —does that prove you're impotent and you wished you had the guts to have a mistress—the *capacity?*"

Charlie would have liked to sock her about then, but as he noticed suddenly that she had tears brimming in her eyes, he was quieted and touched and slipped his arm around her shoulders instead and said he really didn't think Ed was a homo, and she said, "Well, I love Ed, I love to be with him and he asked me whether I would have dinner with him next week when I'm in New York." And Charlie said, "Go ahead, baby," in the most affectionate way. "It would take one hell of a woman to rouse him. You can count yourself perfectly safe." He didn't intend to be cruel to either of them when he said that.

Jo persuaded Angela to let her arrange an interview with JSM Lowood, literary agent. In advance he had been sent two short stories and the first draft of a novel about the effect upon her grown children of the abrupt and silent escape of their old mother to a life of her own. Percolating beneath her as she wrote was Angela's growing determination to pursue the wraith of her grandmother in actual fact, her actual flight to the South of France.

Charlie was all for the trip to France but not for the trip to the agent. He was shadow-boxing with her on both issues, showing tokens of his sober interest in her craft. And as to an agent, "He just picks up his ten percent. There isn't a damn thing he does for you but pass on your rejection slips. I'll tell you what I think, I think when you're ready you ought to send it straight out to a publisher and then see what he thinks. Try a few. Then if nothing comes of it, then you can think about an agent. But I promise you he's worse than useless."

Angela was as forthright with her husband as she was with Edmund about her reasons for wanting an agent, her need to find an ally in her writing life, somebody who had a professional interest in what she did, an interest she *elicited*. Charlie replied cynically about the prime likelihood of *that*, and she fenced with him so that there would continue to be a record in their lives of interchange, of dialogue, of mutuality. But it was all gesture. On those issues between them that had their source at the third floor she never in the end yielded.

It was towards the end of the next August, August of

1964, that Angela was down at the Moriches cottage with the two youngest girls and her mother and father. Charlie was off in a Kansas City heat wave, working in a fever in the city archives, plunging straight and early into his program for his sabbatical year, and Angela acknowledged silently relief at having him gone, having it so. She was herself suspended nervously, awaiting comment from JSM Lowood, literary agent. Edmund, through everything, occupied one lobe of her brain. As for the ghost of her grandmother, that ghost had become insistent about being put to rest. To that end Angela had quite made up her mind to fly to Marseilles in October for two weeks when the children would be settled in school, but Charlie said that the fall would be a bad time to go for seventeen reasons but he guaranteed March, that he promised to be home in March, that one of them should be home with Mrs. Hamsun and the children, and of course she concurred. March gave her time to think what she must do. Think French, that was what she must do, and she read three Simenon paperbacks de l'Inspecteur Maigret.

Then one morning there was the letter forwarded from Northampton:

Dear Mrs. Lewes:
I have now read the two short stories and first draft of your novel and would be interested to talk to you about them. If you should find it convenient to come to New York I would be happy to see you.
Yours,
JSM Lowood

She called. It would be lunch on Friday. Thursday afternoon she left the two children to their grandparents and drove into the city, which was jammed full with a Shriner's convention; crossed it to a room on the tenth floor of a new motel high above the Hudson River, overlooking the Drive and the piers, in which were berthed the *France* and the *Leonardo da Vinci*. The situation of this mo-hotel was marvelously convenient if you were sailing for Europe, but she was not. It was only three o'clock on that Thursday afternoon and the center of the city was shimmering with heat— you could look across to it and see the buildings shimmer— and she had been sticky and dirty two minutes ago and now frozen by the most relentlessly efficient air-conditioning system, and was even sterilized by the peculiarly sterile motel muchness that offered her two supersized beds bridged by a longish water-colorish view of the Ponte Vecchio. The decor was Italian Modern but the bathroom was patriotically American with two sinks and a wall mirror filled with a surgical light that pierced the pores and gave the clearest possible view of the toes. So much mirror, so much sight of herself from which she couldn't flee in that fine bathroom, brought her to a dead stop before her reflection. She stared in deadly earnest. "I'm not fooling!" she said out loud. She wore a deep orange cotton dress but it looked pink in the surgical light.

It was marvelous, she thought, the way this scientific light brought out the lines in your face, and lots of blotches only some of which she'd previously known she'd had. A great graceless mass of unlovely gray hair sent her into a trance. She let it loose and brushed it and tied it up again. "Frankly," she asked the mirror-mirror, "Do I look like a woman who's had four children?" "Frankly, closer to eight."

Finally and determinedly she left the bathroom, picked up her pocketbook, and went off eastward on Forty-second Street, pushing into the heavy heat passing "one-night cheap hotels and . . . restaurants with oyster shells," and skin flicks and army-navy stores until she found a cutlery shop, its windows silver-slivered with knives and even swords, and corkscrews and scissors. She put down $7.50 and walked back with scissors to her fascinating bathroom. In it she peeled off all her clothes, and was further unsteadied by a most unkind sight of her naked self, a sight she nearly never saw, not regularly living in a motel. She grabbed a hank of her loosened thick hair and cut it off, stared at the fistful in her hand and dropped it into the wastepaper can. She was immediately delighted. She was a great hair-cutter, cut all the girls' hair, and their friends' hair, and proceeded to shear off her own, and thinned and razored the edges and made it very short and wispy around her face, and then she went into the shower and washed it and came out and combed it, turned out the light firmly, walked into the much dimmer bedroom, slipped into her Little Black Dress and waited lightheaded until Edmund would return her call.

CHAPTER TWENTY

FINALLY these two middle-aged people came together in a liaison characteristically short of traditional moral and esthetic qualities, it is true, but having other properties instead, compensatory properties. Humor, for instance. About twenty years after the fresh blush of taut pink skin had finished blushing they discovered beneath the aging and frankly rolling surface of themselves a love of elemental generosity. And, besides, in Angela there were called into service emotions and a language and even muscles that she had not heretofore in her whole life employed. From the first she was extremely enthusiastic about having a love affair.

It tested her mettle. She had, after all, the temerity to make another unprotected, unsponsored, unapproved demurrer to the assumptions her world held concerning her, and this one it would not look upon so breezily. She ventured her brand-new autonomous self, the self about which such a fuss has been made—not Charles Porter's daughter, not Charlie Lewes's wife, not Christina's mother, anybody's mother, anybody's anything. Not Edmund's mistress.

"I know it is a courtesy title, but I'd just like to have my name stand on its own, all by itself, without attaching helpful reminders like "Charlie's wife" or "Edmund's mistress." I mean, I want to see whether if I am just Angela Lewes people would really be at a loss to account for me. Edmund? . . . Could you be my dear friend?"

"Your comrade-in-arms, how about?"

As she had so tardily become an independent entity, it was only natural she should wish to preserve the independence, but not to the very letter.

"Edmund, am I 'B?' "

"What do you mean?"

"I have some no doubt unworthy compunction about being 'C,' is all. . . . Don't you remember when we were on the porch in Moriches and you said you could, you know, readily make love to 'A' and 'B?' "

"Angela! Oh, you're 'A!' 'A' for Angela." And as it turned out she really was, chronologically 'A,' the first mature love that he had known. His memory was all damp and salty with those bicycle rides out from New Haven to walk barefooted in the sand, little Tina holding hands between them. He saw Angela's face and hair covered with tiny beads of mist and he watched her as she talked passionately about politics, Citizen Angela, and piously about "mature" relationships, matronly asexual Angela, and he thought, "I would like to ravish her. She would really love that," but he didn't have the cool to suggest it, much less to do it. It was after that he met Rosa Benson who was 'B.' And there had been other women whom he had cared about very much but for the present he had come full circle: A and B.

"I am not really a very sexual person," Angela was at pains to explain fairly often. "What I mean, Edmund, is that sexuality is not the . . . theme . . . of our love, for me. . . . It is the proof of intimacy. I love the intimacy. I love the nakedness. Always before I associated nakedness with shame and now I associate it with trust. . . . I am shameless. Yes, I am shameless!" she said as she wrung the two meanings out. "I love this warts-and-all love, the timelessness of it, the irresponsibility, the illicitness. My father once explained to me that the exquisite quality of a love affair was prolonged by its being clandestine."

"You are lucky to have a father to tell you useful things like that."

"My mother," she said on another occasion, ". . . I've been thinking about this. When I was a child I was very obedient and my mother seemed mildly amused by my being so good. She wasn't delighted by it. She didn't reward it. So I would be even more obedient—typical of human ineptitude, to give more of the same of what was not successful in the first place. But I was so practiced in obedience that I have been tidy and useful and accomplished every waking hour since and through the whole of my marriage. I've tried so hard. I've been the greatest trier. Then sometimes I'd fail. I'd have lost my temper with a child or overroasted the beef or interrupted Charlie, and I would go to bed at night suffering with the most disproportionate sense of guilt. And part of this petty, but short-lived misery, was always, I believe, a half-conscious annoyance over how *little* my sins were, how meager and undignified.

"And so I anticipated a guilt, a walloping guilt worthy of such an obedient woman who has become unfaithful, but I have no guilt whatsoever. It is among the curious psychological phenomena I monitor in myself these recent years."

Once in the spring they were going off together when he said, "Why don't we drive with this weather so nice? I'll pick you up at your mother's."

"Drive?"

"Sure."

"Do you drive a car?"

"Sure I drive a car."

"Why then you're not a homosexual after all!" She said to herself with a private grin.

ƚƚƚƚ CHAPTER TWENTY-ONE *ƚƚƚƚ*

*H*ER love affair seemed to Angela a most star-favored benignant immoral act, for she met the very next noon JSM Lowood, literary agent, when she was in a state of mind about herself that was nearly beatific—irreverent, immodest as the admission was—and in a state of mind about the rest of the world's population that was very loving. Mr. Lowood was a tall slim man in his fifties, she guessed (he was sixty), very handsome with the unaffected poise of a New England airstocrat (he was born in Newark) reflected in the loose way his clothes hung from his bones and muscles. She saw him first being led by Jo through the lobby of the Barclay, and Angela loved him instantly. She already loved Jo, as noted. And was JSM Lowood one of the men Jo loved? (Not entirely.) If it is remembered that not twenty-four hours earlier Angela's spirits and confidence were brought very low by her having asked that bathroom mirror-mirror for the surgical truth, and gotten it, then she seemed indeed metamorphosed into a woman of the supremest self-delight, which made her laugh, which laughing became her, she knew. She gave her love to Mr. Lowood not in vain, since he proved on

202

his part to be exceptionally lovable for his thinking that although her short stories were . . . in effect not good, the novel, as far as it went, was quite fascinating.

When one is depressed there are other little things that feed the depression and make you heavier, but it sometimes happens contrarywise, which is only fair, that one is feeling in unaccustomed and joyful command of things and then somebody will say an enhancing thing, and in this instance Jo said, "Why Angela, you've cut your hair all off. It's wonderful! It makes you look ten years younger!" And Angela came a hair's breadth of telling her that well, she was compelled to repeat the rite of passage of her grandmother (Jo's own mother), and that there must be an enormous human heritage of hairy significance (which the young were about to rediscover), and that she had borne in mind as she sawed grimly into her scalp in that motel bathroom that orthodox Jewish brides had their heads shaved on the eve of their marriage, but that on the other hand unbelievers before they became mistresses didn't have to be so drastic, their change in status not so singular.

Mr. Lowood was plain John, and Angela asked boldly if it was "John Stuart Mill," and it was.

"Have you liked that name? Have you felt odd about it?"

"I've felt lucky I wasn't my brother. He's G. S. Lowood, and we call him GS. That's what he goes by."

"But I can't guess."

"My father was a student in philosophy at Harvard when Santayana was there."

"My goodness. Do you have a sister?"

"The truth is that what caught my attention about you from the very first was this name business and your Marian Evans. My sister who's a sunburnt blond sailing nut ten years my junior—but she admits to being twenty years my junior— is Charlie Buckminster (which he said as though Angela would have known who Charlie Buckminster was, but she didn't). But she was christened Charlotte Brontë Lowood, the farthest cry. She's our greatest misnomer. She's barely literate. She knows who Charlotte Brontë is, but it is doubtful she could place George Eliot. In any event, all three of us dismayed our father from the beginning."

"You are none of you philosophers or . . ."

"GS does live in Italy, in Milan, but he's in the oil business."

"Well, how did you go about naming your own children?"

"I've found it depends upon your wives. My first wife's name was Mary, so we were John and Mary, and she cherished a great belief in simple Christian names, so the girls were Susan and Ann and Ellen. But Vicky picked Vanessa and then Nicholas. So we have both sorts, plain and fancy."

Jo had left them to lunch by themselves, and at one point Angela asked John how he'd met her.

"Oh it must be fifteen years ago. Bill introduced us."

"You knew Bill first? Isn't that curious, I always assume that one meets people through Jo, she seems so catalytic."

"No, no. Bill's an old friend. I've known him forever. I ran into him first at University Hospital when we were living in Forest Hills. He cured me of a nervous disorder."

"What was that?"

"My first wife."

"Why, you should have said 'Physician, heal thyself.' "

"One would suppose so, perhaps, but in the end the wise thing might be to make a sort of accommodation with life. Not attempt to start fresh."

"I have a tremendous stake in starting fresh. I don't want to believe that 'anatomy is destiny' or that you can just—of course, things have to be fortuitous, but I *know* that one can diverge, don't you know, defy the *insistence* that you are what you are from the cradle to the grave."

"And the book you've written is a parable."

"Well, you know, I really did have a grandmother who

bolted. I rather scooped her out of my memory and made her something she undoubtedly never was. Nobody knows what happened to her except that she died in the south of France. My family—they were whipped into a frenzy of pursuit in the beginning, but their interest has frittered away."

"The grandmother draws me on. Were she mine, I would have had to track her down."

"I *have* to, I——"

"She was my age when she made her break. An old lady makes an improbable siren. But I'm an old man."

JSM Lowood moved into Angela's third-floor fantasy world with Edmund and the grandmother, a world which was not gaining in credibility so much as substantiality, ghost included, upon the actual world in which she cooked and worried over children and talked on the phone for half an hour to Charlie in Kansas City at night after the rates changed. John had initiated what rapidly became a passionate correspondence in which the old grandmother was an obsessive theme, as were the plans Angela could make to trace her in Aix-en-Provence. They met frequently in Boston: he would come down from a second home in Rockport. It was in Charlie to disappoint her hope to take two weeks in March, and then he was uncertain and did not want to be harried, and in the end she would not land in Paris until the first of June, and then fly down to Marseilles on the second.

At the last moment she almost couldn't go at all, for her marriage suddenly reasserted its centrality in the real life of what was distinguishing itself as a family of escapists. Adam came home from his junior year at Exeter, whereupon it developed that he had flirted with the idea of, if indeed he had not already tried, drugs—which in 1965 meant marijuana and/or LSD—and his mother, rational, angry, irrational, adamant, and above all badly frightened, assaulted *tout court* this outrageous "tampering of the mind," but his father, ever ready

to outyouth the youth, she thought, had the viciously irresponsible notion that it would be grand to take off on a
dad 'n' son weekend, go off on a "trip" together. And she said
that was a damn matey thing to do and was so distraught
about Charlie's judgment, about his *ethics* on the subject of
drugs, that it became clear she couldn't go to France or anywhere unless he promised he would not offer Adam this "trip."
He promised. He looked across the furlong of change between
them and saw her puffed and lined with anger, a heavy matron, and *he* thought, "My God, it's like she's my mother!"

So that until then, on the very eve of her questing, except
for her shift from a unitary to a dichotomous system of moral
bookkeeping—the kind of double entry that would account
for her pursuing relentlessly her own true honest self on the
one hand, and selflessly, nobly espousing duplicity on the
other (so as not to do what she liked to do and make Charlie
pay for it)—except for that shift, the normal daily life of this
worn autumnal heroine had not been affected by her regularly
ducking out of it. Classical Angela was a classical heroine of
the old school—unusual, egregious. As superintendent of her
own life story she could only find it worth unfolding if it were
predicated upon this albeit overlooked fact—that she was a
heroine.

Her relationship to Charlie was not directly affected by her
infidelity, but by indirection it underwrote and sealed critical
differences between them in respect to the older children. She
left for France thoroughly rattled by the threat of drugs and
the threat of Charlie as "a for crying out loud fatherly
pusher," and she landed at Logan Airport, Boston, two weeks
later in the middle of the threat of sex, of Link Two in a
concatenation of circumstances the last links of which she is
not freed of yet. Her father, most unexpectedly, was waiting
for her at the airport all by himself. He was standing, so un-
alterable a man, with his weight on the one leg, the one hand

in its pocket with the suggestion lingering from her childhood of his contemplating becoming an egret. At the sight of this most distinguished of fathers, with his hair not much greyer than hers but the crown of his head bare and browned by the sun, and his warm eyes set in rays of creases, Angela felt her heart contract, and saw how like him JSM looked, and thought "Good grief, I love too many and too well, and that's the truth."

"What a beautiful sight you are," she said, pressing her cheek against his. "Is everybody all right?"

"Everybody of your immediate concern, whose numbers run to three figures, is fine, and the one who isn't fine will be."

"Who?"

"Sally Drinkwater."

It was odd to hear the very name that had been in her mind these last days, although not so much Sally Drinkwater's as Louise's. This was because Angela had wondered about guilt, that guilt had never attended her initial departure from orthodoxy, nor had it been activated by subsequent departures from her departure. Did this absence of guilt, her shamelessness indict her sanity? Was she incapable of guilt? She was fresh from an episode that allowed her the somewhat morbid pleasure of realizing she was still capable of guilt.

There was a road that wound up the hillside from Aix-en-Provence through the summer colors Cézanne had painted to the villa he had lived in, and across from it was a small house that invited you to knock there for permission to visit the studio. This was Monday in Boston, and it had been the previous Saturday in Aix that a woman of about thirty with a strong, composed face answered the door. Clutching at her skirts there peeked out at them the round blue face of a cyanotic boy of perhaps four. Blue, swollen, his eyes crossed, his tongue bulging out of his mouth, he turned his head about vaguely while his mother transacted her business. He wore a washed blue schoolchild's smock. Since then Angela's mind's eye had rolled up again and again from the bloated blue face to the mother's, set hard around the mouth that didn't do much chatting, but might cut off any suggestion of sympathy with the cool statement, "Mine's a most ordinary fate." "Mine is extraordinary," Angela thought. "I'm dogged by good luck. Suppose we had had a defective child, a spastic child like Louise's Suzie, what would it have done to me?" There was no question in her mind that had she given birth to a defective child she would irrationally have assumed the guilt of having done so. That unreasonable foolish riddling guilt she would still have. When she thought of Louise in this wise, all her guilt muscles came into play. The miracle of these last years was that guilt, amorphous and adaptable, that she'd always known, which she had borne like a hump on her back, seemed to have slid off, the way an ocean cliff, because of an unsuspected geological fault, one day slips into the sea. She was reassured to see that a piece of the hump was still attached, still operative.

What emerged about Sally Drinkwater, that nice responsible caring child, eighteen now, was that she didn't take care of herself. She was in Boston having an abortion, which information somehow or other became the property of a lot of people. The reason Charles had met his daughter's plane was that he was going to be in Boston anyway, as he told Charlie, because, as he did not tell Charlie, the person co-responsible for Sally's situation was, of all people, Cybele O'Brien's son.

"Well, that's really very incestuous, isn't it, my father?"

"I must say everybody's being very civilized. The O'Brien boy has been straightforward with Will, and Will isn't one to scold and draw morals, and Bill always comes through for everybody . . ."

"But why would Bill have to know?"

"Well, of course, he's our man in abortions. They're very

difficult to manage, and we don't know offhand any abortionists socially. It's your husband who's blown up about this. Tina seems to have detonated him."

"Tina! Well, why does Tina know?"

"Oh well, Tina was in on it from the beginning, more or less. After all, they're all there in Cambridge together. Sally talked it over with her and they divided the problem. Sally was allocated the worry what to do about her own personal predicament, while Tina, who doesn't Think Small, having discovered another outrage perpetrated upon another repressed minority, women—has embarked on a national campaign to make abortions legal."

"And Charlie?"

"Well now, Sally's end of the problem is in the process of being aborted, so to speak, but it looks like Tina and her crusade, if she doesn't watch it, are going to be packed off to an Irish convent. You know, Angela, I'll tell you something rather nice. Your mother and Tina are becoming very thick over this. Evidently the legal abortion issue is very much alive down at the Civil Liberties Union—something I should have guessed. Anyway, Mother came up with me and is being both legal and loving to your girl. I laugh, but I must say it touches me to see them with their heads together."

"But what about Charlie?"

"And another funny thing is that Cybele's reaction is very much of a woman's right one too. She's agitated about Bud's irresponsibility. She says the students—the boys—are all very righteous about liberating the girls so they can be slept with, and it doesn't occur to them that there are any precautions left for them to think about. You know how it is said a man's mistress will have a temperament very like his wife's? A nagging wife, a nagging mistress? I sometimes think if Cybele and Margaret got together they'd ride off into the sunset leaving me to . . . slump in my porch rocker back at the ranch."

"Come on Pa, what about Charlie?" Irritation, just the feathery breeze of it, touched her nerve endings. Did it work, husband and lover, the same way? Were the men she loved all alike? Absolutely *not* like each other. Which reminded her of Jo's belief that a pattern is laid down in a woman when she is a very little girl, which makes her always finally only really want a man who is like her father. Edmund was like her father. And so in his way was JSM.

"Charlie seems to belong to the old school. He isn't evidently on the barricades of the *sexual* revolution, however much he is with it about politics and civil rights. He's got men still being wolves, I believe."

They had driven over to the hospital and were waiting for Bill to come down. When he did, there was a young man with him who slid off in another direction, young O'Brien, no doubt, and Angela left the car to duck into this great bear of an uncle's arms.

"And I love you, too," she said, laughing, looking at the one man who was friend to all her principals.

"I hear you tracked down your ghost."

"My ghost, my goodness, my father didn't even *ask* about my ghost, his own mother! Is Sally all right?"

"Sally's fine."

CHAPTER TWENTY-TWO

*S*ALLY was all right, but Charlie was not all right. Angela had given a first bowdlerized rendition of her French adventure to her father and Bill on the way home from Boston, and a second once home, enlarged by Charlie and her mother and the children. They were all attentive, of course, indeed fascinated by her untoward success, but she was talking, she knew, into a controlled tension. She charged into this tension with her story, and caught sight of her own arms spread wide folding the air as though to coax her listeners to yield to her entirely, let go the other thing. She could see herself lightly folding beaten egg whites into a heavy batter.

She had taken the very long taxi ride from the airport in Marseilles to the university town of Aix-en-Provence and was quite undone by the color of this Mediterranean world with its own tree-green, its own sky-blue, tile-red, orange; and the smells of Aix, of old stone and unAmerican tobacco and un-American exhaust fumes from hundreds of fiercely aggressive little cars that played a mean dodg'em through the wide avenues and right onto the sidewalks when balked. At least half of the cars, she believed, bore large "Auto-Ecole" signs, with the insane promise of car-breeding, of fumey fecundity, of engine-explosion, but it was only June of 1965. It was still, to Angela, funny, a wild disaster-in-the-making, in the future.

She settled into her hotel and then walked down the lovely broad Cours Mirabeau under the trees, passing the old stone façades, the cafés, the fountains, their cool mossy smell still holding its own against the acrid petrol smell, but not for long, probably. Just beyond the end of the Cours Mirabeau, through a wriggle of conjoining narrow streets on any one of which one could be more easily killed by an impatient driver than not, there was the Pension de Repos. The vestibule had a white marble floor, and the stairs running up from it were white marble, but nonetheless there was nothing handsome about the Pension de Repos. In fact it would reveal itself to be less a pension, more a sort of three-purpose hotel, still the lodging of a few old people left over from an old war, and these supplemented by university students. But there also appeared to have been available some room for a brisk night trade, and Angela was never to be sure whether the women who plied it were in actual residence too, whether the Repos was part House, or whether it was open to transients. The concierge she had asked to see referred to herself as the pa-tronne, and might have worn more than one hat and been a madam nights. She looked like a madam to Angela, who had never seen a madam. She was a businesslike but sympathetic woman of no ascribable age. As Angela described her mission, Madame's strong family feeling heaved in her black blouse and her bright-red mouth drooped a pout of pity. In the South of France when you're looking for news of a grand-mother eight years dead, you don't have to account for your-self, for an undue interest. With family, interest is always *due*.

Alas, Madame regretted never having heard a word of her supposed predecessor, though this would be not unusual, since the ownership of the Repos had changed twice in recent years and as a matter of fact the last concierge was an old woman who had died too, about three years ago. Angela left the Repos, restless, with nothing, absolutely nothing, on the first day of the quest.

She was depressed, naturally. She was deflated, she explained. She could not think what to do next.

"Well it's quite obvious," Charlie commented tautly. "You had to talk to one of those old lodgers." She had such a plodding mind, sometimes, he thought. She'd get there, but no short cuts, always inside the speed limit, inside the law.

"I was in a trance, Charlie. I was never in a for crying out loud foreign country before by myself, you know. I had to take all the French in—which was very hard, it's not Parisian, sometimes not even French. So well, anyhow, two days later I leapt instantly to the conclusion that I had to talk to one of those old lodgers."

She was carefully folding the lightly beaten truth into the batter, a French omelette of a story she was cooking.

It was true that she had been in a trance. This truth was preceded by her uncanny meeting with John Lowood in Paris the day before, and followed by her call to him two days later to join her in the questing. Once he was with her things firmed up immediately. They walked together to the end of the Cours Mirabeau, saluted the mossy statue of the Good King René, proceeded ten paces up to the left, then ten to the right, and there they were at the densest and smallest center of honking horns, screeching brakes, and motorcycle racket in the town, if not the world. They looked up at the four shuttered stories of the Pension de Repos, many of the shutters opened, and strung across with drying laundry, and potted plants and old people, and at a window just above the entrance there was sitting a wide-eyed frizzy-haired old woman with a fixed mad smile, nodding mildly at the noise beneath her, or the people or the cars, none of which nodded back. Angela nodded. "A sign," John said.

The patronne knew that particular old lady was crazy, and besides they were not on speaking terms, which was altogether agreeable since Madame's French was execrable, but they had had some words over Madame's cats—the smell— "She had as many as twelve, but I have set the limit at five, it's down in the terms of the agreement." There had been a rapprochement effected between the patronne and Madame, an informal committee of old boarders having appointed themselves to intercede—"This Ancient is their mascot!" she explained, half laughing, half annoyed still. She shrugged and said Mme Corbeau, No. 14.

"Everything was beads!" said Angela to her family. "Beads hung like curtains from the doorways of her rooms. Beads hung from her neck. She had two beady eyes. You know, she reminded me of an aged Elsa Lancaster playing a mad Slav, with a wild brush of kinky orange hair needing to be redyed. There was a part in the center of it with a two-inch pathway of dark hair. It looked like Halloween on her head."

What wasn't beads was cats, doilies, photographs, bric-a-brac, plants. The chairs and sofa were tucked with shawls of a dead maroon, the color of old theater seats, but they were merely base upon which crowded the live cats and memorabilia of the dead.

Madame opened the door to them and, nodding and smiling, welcomed them in. "I was expecting you," she said, in execrable French. Angela, anxious to explain they were the wrong people, told her as simply as possible that she was trying to find somebody who might have known her old grandmother, the concierge here at the Pension de Repos those dozen years, and Madame smiled and nodded and said, "I was expecting you." Angela counted seven cats, an evident breach of contract. The shutters were wide open to a sunny wall opposite, and to the furious traffic noise. John, languid, a cat on his lap, a glass of wine in his hand, asked her casually where she had come from originally.

And she nodded and smiled encouragingly at him as if he were among those who had trouble understanding anybody, and said, "Why, I was born in Czechoslovakia, just like your grandmother," in execrable English.

"So you know who it was now, don't you! Mrs. Brundage! Mrs. Brundage that was." Angela was triumphant with Charlie and her mother.

Madame was really quite out of her mind, but in her own way. Selected sections of her past ran concurrently with the present, so that in the case of tracking down the grandmother, she was now dead, now alive, but alive for the purpose of throwing Mme Corbeau-Brundage into high relief. In a moment there was a knock. Entered Bibi.

Bibi, as her name might not suggest, was a tiny aged black-dressed widow, her severe face marked by two verticals, a long lean nose and, hanging parallel to the nose, a black cord from a pince-nez. She might have been eighty, but she had jet-black hair, red lipstick, white powdered face, red rouged cheeks. Whom did it please that she should be so beautiful but herself? She never smiled. A smile would have cracked the veneer of her face and flaked off. Bibi was a go-between for Madame employed by the outside world. She was liaison to those forces—like the Bank of Zurich and the French Internal Revenue System—which persisted in their attempts to storm the private preserves of Madame's madness in order simply to count her money and take some. The mad mind has its reasons too. There must be people like Madame that they're loath to lock up but can't bear to let remain totally unassessed. So they adapt, those outside forces. In this case, through Bibi, they circumvent the computer and work out a mutual accommodation, and if they learn nothing else, it is that a fool and her money are not necessarily soon parted.

Bibi spoke Czech with Madame and French with Angela and John.

"It was a story that had to have nine tellings, like a portrait that needed nine sittings," Angela said to her family. "Every afternoon at five I left the Cours Mirabeau and just off it was the Pension, coming down like a prow between two narrow streets that shot off up the hill. Madame at the window nodding. She'd open the door. 'I was expecting you,' she'd say. Really what that amounted to was never anything in the way of clairvoyance. It was one of her Englishisms. And temperamentally she was always expecting something— out of her confusion of past and present she had a wide range of expectations, wider than one normally has. I think she was so regularly disappointed by the nonarrivals in her life that she'd become quite low these last years. My turning up, why you know, I believe it reinvigorated her—that she'll live off the activation of so many old memories—maybe to her end.

"Bibi. Well, I have to tell you right here that I was a long time in catching on to Bibi. It was one of the last afternoons, when it became clear to me that Bibi—you know, she seemed at first to have no capacity for emotion, Bibi. But I begin to see now that the old conserve their resources. I mean even physically she kept herself so still, immobile. She stood every day in the same place before the armoire, unmoving. If you didn't want her there you might pick her up by the shoulders and set her out of the way. She wouldn't weigh very much. All her stuffing must have dried. Well, there was nobody who was in closer association with grandma through the whole of her life in Provence than Bibi, and that's what I didn't really see until almost the last day. And that's what I meant when I said this story, Grandma's story, seemed to have to have nine tellings."

"Well, now baby, we're not going to have to hear it that way, are we?" Charlie asked nudging along his earnest story-telling child-wife.

Angela flicked the boy-man a mature and subtle, she believed, look of rebuke, and thought to herself, "What the hell have you done, Charlie, to the grown-up grey of your temples?" but said out loud, "It was only my second visit when Madame answered the door, her hair like a burning bush, all newly dyed a fresh-fruit orange. Little black-lacquered Bibi was standing at her station prepared, with no change of expression, to convert into a brisk condensed French a lot of voluble Czech. Bibi's head was connected to her body by the ribbon of her glasses. That's the way it was every day—Bibi standing quite still, Madame rising, fluttering, resettling. *She* didn't conserve *her* energies. Madame had such a high-colored temperament, I don't know how much of what she had to say was lost in translation. I mean, if I hadn't gone back again and again I don't think I would have gotten such a rich story. That's what I mean about nine sittings."

"Angela!" Charlie said impatiently. She was about to boom back a defense of her story when her eye caught his no-longer-grey temples, and she tilted her head in a shift of gears and ignored the naughty child.

◂ CHAPTER TWENTY-THREE ◂

*F*ROM the spring of 1940 until Mrs.
Porter's death in 1957, the lives of the two women, of the
old grandmother and Mrs. Brundage, crossed the years the
way two wavering lines cross a graph, occasionally kissing,
for a long time weaving together. They left Strasbourg inde-
pendently. They were poured south by the flow of events,
and it was not a great coincidence that they should both land
eventually in Provence, since it was a center for the sorting
and aiding of refugees, and among others Czech nationals. It
was not a haven, however, and Mrs. Brundage, who in some
way or another became detached from the perfume manufacturer, Corbeau, was put into an internment camp, established to take care of those people who were jobless and
indigent. It is believed that she spent four years there under
conditions nearly as miserably degrading as those striven for
under the more efficient direction of the German government.
The terrible overcrowding, the collapse of sanitary arrangements, inadequate food, the absence of medical treatment
were the consequence of the inefficiency, the helplessness, the
indifference, the petty venality, but not the *policy* of the

French. Madame emerged from that long black night into the sun of Provence a near skeleton, wild and blinking and smiling.

Mrs. Porter with Čapek had slipped off by stealth with their press and the minimum of equipment in a band of printers and their families. Soon, however, they split up and dissolved into the hills, seeped into the underground. There is a full year unaccounted for by Mrs. Brundage, that first year of flight from Strasbourg, in this saga of the grandmother. In about the spring or summer of 1941, Mrs. Brundage said, Mrs. Porter had found hiding near a little village tucked deep into the remote countryside northeast of Aix, into the Vaucluse, the foothills of the Alps. An unused farmhouse had been requisitioned by relief workers as a refuge for orphaned or abandoned Czech children, and it was with them that Mrs. Porter passed the war years. She was a tutor. She taught them their letters.

Bibi made the acquaintance of Mrs. Porter during this period. Bibi was a nurse who had not practiced her profession for some time but must have sought and found a refuge and safe disguise in it when German pressure tightened on the French to weed out alien elements of the population besides Jews and Gypsies, to include Poles, Czechs, the Slavic races, in the pulling up. This was not done with Germanic efficiency, and some people in the category of weed were overlooked if they were attached to a service like medical relief. So for Bibi. She was assigned to an itinerant and, of course, understaffed and under-supplied medical team that threaded its way through the network of old farmhouses and outlying village hostels in which were hidden alien children and alien old. This "team" was often only one doctor and Bibi. They made their rounds through the windy spring of '41, and while they were looking over the inhabitants of the farmhouse to which Mrs. Porter had been assigned, a message was sent from their headquarters in Nîmes to lie low, to keep their heads down and out of sight. It was this chance, therefore, that brought Bibi and Mrs. Porter into close quarters for several weeks. They were drawn to each other by their shared language and age, and the fact that in a society of victims something like an extra portion of toughness or adaptability had them both administrating; they were not among the administrated. At some time in the distant past Bibi had been wrenched from her roots in Prague and through the long second span of her life she lived and worked in Nîmes, alien, speaking a terse French, acquainted with few people, close to no one. Her capacity for closeness, however, had not altogether shriveled. Her relationship to Mrs. Porter became intimate. It was a friendship. She knew what had transpired in the heart and mind and calculations of the other woman in that first year of the trek south from Strasbourg. It was only a question whether this American granddaughter was worth the telling of it.

In the end she yielded. There was even a snapshot, strange as it may seem that in the gaunt existence of hunted and hiding people there could be a camera and film and the will to take the picture and two women to pose smiling. The women had stood too far away from the lens. Angela again and again had looked close at them under a good light but could not connect the seeming tall (compared to Bibi) handsome smiling woman, the hair close-cropped and becoming, wearing a belted military raincoat, with the little round amorphous old lady who had been her grandmother the year or two previously.

Well before they had fled Strasbourg Mrs. Porter had grasped how critical was the situation in Europe, and her own situation. She knew the significance of a United States passport, and in fact, for the first time in her life, she knew everything that was going on in the world and her precise

position in it. The experience of comprehending, of seeing
clearly after a life of blurred vision, was the consequence of
her reading Czech proof for the newspaper day after day all
day long, and of listening to Czech talk down at the press,
with Čapek and Svoboda at the café. All the talk, all the copy
she read contained reason for despair, unabated, unrelieved.
She was nonetheless exhilarated, revitalized, by being in a
constant condition of *understanding;* and the possibility that
existed for her almost alone among refugees, of escape
through her American citizenship from the impending disas-
ter she foresaw clearly, the vicious war she *understood* to be
ineluctable, that possibility she never seriously entertained.

However much her understanding burgeoned, she could
not articulate too well in Czech, much less in English. She
had always drawn upon a mélange of simple words in the
two languages to think with: they were too simple words and
too few, and the limitations they imposed upon her capacity
to explore her feelings oppressed her often through her
American years. Now in Strasbourg she was able finally to
talk a little to Čapek about her past life, about the safe haven
America would be to her, that is to say Moriches, and the
farmhouse, and how once returned she would be disconnected, defused, impotent; she would lose charge of her life
there. She spoke of her children and grandchildren, of
Charles and Theodore mostly, and a great tenderness for them
all, almost all, welled in her. It was a welling that subsided,
never changing to a longing that inclined her to go back
while there was still time. Charles had been her fragile lonely
child and seemed so still.

The editor of the press was a sardonic old Czech Jew whom
they all called Papa K. It was he who laid their plans for
escape, but he was prey to terrible fears verging on hysteria,
and the plans were not sane, and their troop ended by criss-
crossing the country, leaving Strasbourg for Normandy in

a small caravan consisting of a truck that carried the press and supplies and three automobiles, altogether making eighteen people and their sparest belongings. They moved only at night and on obscure lanes and back roads, directed by Papa K, whose panic increased with his certainty that they were being pursued, and ten days along, in a little village near the mouth of the Seine he lost his wits entirely. It was a morning in early spring and the river was nearly flooding. On the far bank there were rows and rows of bare pollarded trees. There was a blush of pink in the sky, in the river, in the fields, a Sisley painting. Mrs. Porter and Čapek and two children of their group came out of the narrow street into the wide beautiful riverscape carrying several long loaves of bread and were in time to see Papa K, fierce and quick, climb into the truck and drive it over the embankment into the Seine.

Seventeen people now, nine of them children, and bereft of their mad leader as well as a reason for staying together. They were of one mind about Normandy. To get out of it. They were of many minds where to go and agreed to separate. Čapek with Mrs. Porter and another old man with his two grandsons of ten and fourteen years retraversed the country south of the Loire. France fell. They hid uneasily in a village in the Cevenne. The men were determined to join the Resistance and the boys were determined too, but the boys were ill with congestion. It was suggested they all get somehow to Nîmes.

"She took Čapek's name for safety. At that time it was more dangerous to be an American than a Czech," Mrs Brundage said. "Everybody had to be as clever as possible. Ah," she sighed, nodding slowly, "I wasn't clever. I was beautiful, but I wasn't clever in *that way*."

But Bibi said that Čapek and Mrs. Porter were married at the *mairie* in Nîmes, that they cared very much for one another, that "Angele" wished to commemorate, you might say, and on the eve of their separation, their friendship and the renewal of her inner life at the very moment that all outer life was marked for the holocaust. The marriage was a public seal and a private joy to her and, furthermore, it facilitated her eventual placement at the farm hostel with the two boys who had come under her care. She spoke no French, it had to be remembered. She never learned it. She was carried in an eddy of Czechs to the end of her life.

The farm in the Vaucluse was no more than the hollow hulks of an old stone building and its outhouses, and at the height of its occupancy nearly sixty people were living in them, most of them children. Existence there was delineated by privation and the fear of being finally hunted down by the Germans. They never were. There was a painful attrition in their numbers from death, due mostly to tuberculosis, with which both Edward and Anton, the two grandsons of the old printer from Strasbourg, were afflicted.

"Anton was a poor little fellow, weak, and marked for death. I saw it the first time I laid my eyes on him," said Bibi. "He died the spring of the following year, and then they got word his grandfather had been killed, and after a while that Čapek was shot. It was very hard times. You got tough."

Mrs. Porter had the will to be toughened as well as the physical stamina. It would have to be so for someone who so short a time before was accustomed to retire to her room with the vapors and a cool cloth for the forehead. She became lean and sinewy working out of doors through the long growing season when every advantage had to be coaxed from the earth to make their hostel self-sufficient. It was never sufficient, but while recognizing the hardship of their situation and the regular visitation of sorrow and loss, they managed to live on (those who didn't die), and to enjoy often

a spirit of camaraderie and of satisfaction over some accomplishments. Mrs. Porter tended cabbages, she tended Anton,
would wrap him up and settle him against the south wall by
the garden, in the full sun protected from the wind. She
tended the minds of an assortment of little children, teaching
them their letters (in Czech, of course) and could be quite
imperious in commanding Bibi or the doctor or any other
visiting functionary to supply her with paper and pencils.
She was deeply grieved to see Anton slowly slip away, and
after he was dead she turned to Edward and tended him the
more assiduously. He was a scholarly boy, bilingual in French
and Czech, and she scavenged through the nearby village
for books for him. She'd see him propped against the stone
wall in the sunshine reading intently, and the sight gratified
her. She kept him alive, Bibi said. He was eighteen when the
war was over. The old grandmother was sixty-five and
looking younger.

Through the confusion of peace and the sorting of people,
Mrs. Porter cut her route directly to Aix-en-Provence because she shared with Edward his hope to enter the university there. In the meanwhile Bibi, the now deep and true
friend who knew the whole of her story, was on the lookout
for Mrs. Brundage and came upon her in a relocation center
needing to be released in the custody of somebody or other.

"I looked at her, poor wild thing she was, all bones. She
couldn't even talk, and I said to myself, there stands two
Swiss bank accounts. I used my head. Not very sentimental,
am I? There wasn't a sou among us. I was of course entitled
to wages with the Relief people, but they had nothing to
dispense, except, thank God, a little sinecure, the place of
concierge at the Pension de Repos. It was, this place, anyway,
in the days after the war, filled to the brim with people who
had no place to go. They said some wealthy benefactor lent
it to Czech relief. Well he was a godsend, I tell you, for all

of us. In those days we had friends in the right places; we were lucky."

Mrs. Brundage was delivered to the care of Mrs. Porter and was installed along with Edward in the small apartment of the concierge that had a front entrance leading to the white marble foyer and a back door opening upon a court-yard that was flooded with the morning sun. Bibi, whose interest in the Swiss banks never wavered, divided her time between work at the emergency health stations and the Credit Lyonnais, where her niece's husband was employed as a clerk. She never trusted this fellow, so she pried care-fully for information. It was nearly two years before any good came of it, and then it was the Bank of Zurich that had succeeded in tracing Mrs. Brundage.

It seems to have been the case that when the war was over the old grandmother was quite determined to inform her family in America of her whereabouts and well-being. This was something that preyed on her mind, Bibi thought. Six years had passed in which she had lost the fear that she would somehow be forced to yield her freedom to her children and return to America, to the farmhouse in Moriches. She was a confirmed expatriate, literally in a world within a world, in a small colony of Czechs in southern France. But the transla-tion from the hard simplicity of the farm to bustling city life took more strength than she had expected. Mrs. Brundage was a constant care. And finally, there was the fate of Ed-ward. He had worked very hard to pass his entrance examina-tions to the university, he was successful and accepted, and then one morning he came home blanched and wet with perspiration not only having failed his physical examination but with an order requiring him to enter the provincial sani-tarium twelve kilometers north-west of Aix. That the infec-tion in his lungs had not been arrested was crushing news to Edward as well as to Mrs. Porter. His prognosis was not very good. For twenty-two months on Thursdays and Sundays Mrs. Porter took the noon bus to the sanitarium, and she watched the life slip from Edward as she had from his little brother. That is what she did instead of turning attention to her American family. Afterwards, her emotional energy exhausted, she knew herself to be an old woman for certain, and no mistake.

She lived quietly alone for nine more years as concierge, Mrs. Brundage having removed to an apartment above. She looked after the little Czech world that remained at the pension, and it looked after her. She kept a small garden in the courtyard and grew cabbages, beans, tomatoes, lettuce, eggplant. She had pain in her stomach which persisted, and finally she consulted a doctor who allowed her to understand that it was cancer and gave her pills for the pain. She saved them. One night she took them all.

✐ CHAPTER TWENTY-FOUR ✐

*A*NGELA had not slept for twenty-two hours. Through the last six of these she had talked steadily and evidently could not stop. Charlie, who from time to time became fed to his ears with the Porters, their numbers, their complacency, was experiencing an acute sense of surfeit over them which had begun before his wife's return and which was exacerbated beyond his endurance by her extra-long extra-heartfelt delivery of the story of yet another Porter whom none of them had so much as laid eyes on for quarter of a century. His father-in-law and mother-in-law had been spending the last few days with him. He liked them. More than that he felt a respect, and in fact awe, for their seeming inborn civility which, faultlessly, they extended in their liberal egalitarian way toward lesser breeds. He bridled now when he felt that they were stretching their tolerance for him. What entitled them to their aristocratic airs he couldn't say. They weren't one generation out of the lumpenproletariat. And Angela. She could be the most ingenuous snob of them all.

She was propped up in bed waiting for him, flushed and

THE SEA CHANGE OF ANGELA LEWES

overstimulated, and in a voice high-pitched, she asked him with unabated enthusiasm, "Don't you think it's an incredible story?"

He turned on her. "No I don't think it's an incredible story. You exaggerate everything, Angela. You've got to make everything a melodrama."

"Well for goodness' sakes, Charlie, she's a bona fide heroine!"

"What are you talking about! She was a *nobody* here and she was a nobody *there*. And I want to tell you about heroines. Now that you've got that old woman out of your system I hope you will pay attention to the three heroines in this house. They are in need of a goddam firm maternal hand!"

"What the hell are you so upset about Charlie? It wasn't Tina who had to have an abortion."

"Tina! Do you know what she says about Sally? She says Sally is the victim of an irresponsible social system which is the product of male chauvinism! So I said to her, 'Now wait a minute, baby. Just let's take up this question of responsibility. Who is responsible for her getting knocked up?' And she said, 'The Commonwealth of Massachusetts is responsible because of its primitive anti-birth-control laws which are manifestly an intrusion upon the private . . .' . . . And do you know where she gets all this stuff? She gets it from you. So I said, 'Listen my friend, let's cut through all this baloney. Sally is responsible and this O'Brien kid is responsible, and don't for one minute get confused about who's responsible.'"

"What she means, Charlie, is that the state denies the individual the responsibility for the consequences of her own private acts when it doesn't let a woman forestall a pregnancy."

"What *I* mean, *Mother*, is that all unwitting you have perverted, if you'll excuse the expression, the teaching of sexual morality to your children. Modesty, self-restraint, virginity,

228

fidelity, none of these eternal values seems to have been brought to their notice. They never heard of them. I mean," he said softening suddenly, and running his hand over her hair, "that's what you represent so regally. They are the essence of the fine person you are." Angela's head tingled, her ears buzzed, she could say nothing. Charlie went on quietly and reasonably, "You know a lot about being a lady. My God, I look up to you there. But, baby, you don't know anything about being a man. Nothing. You talk about sexual equality as if sex were a political act. You know what Tina's ready to do? She's ready to charge out to the barricades and get screwed for the cause.

"You, your mother, your daughter, you think by fiat you can abolish the double standard——"

"There's no more double standard, Charlie——"

"And with that splendid doctrine you leave that child vulnerable to abuse and contempt from any guy who's looking for a piece of tail. And I want to tell you something, every guy, Angie, every male undergraduate that ever was and ever will be is looking for just one thing, and all the rhetoric in the world isn't going to change that. And when he gets it, it's his victory, his boast, his triumph, and he has no use for the girl, no respect for her, no interest in her political morality."

"I think things are changing very rapidly with the young. A lot of these boys Tina and Adam bring around, they really don't——"

"I'm not talking about social change, I'm talking about biology, physiological evolution. That'll take a million years, and until then the double standard stays as an ugly little piece of realism."

A few more words and they turned amicably back to back to sleep. The two minds could not have been farther apart in their reflections over what had been said. Charlie never examined his inherited assumptions about sexual modesty, fidelity, motherhood, virginity, and the double standard. He was a true believer in the purity of the female. He doubted nearly everything else he was asked to doubt through that decade of exploding social myths, and even in the matter of sexual practices he was a sincere champion of private choice. There was no question but he would defend the right of a man to sleep with a willing whomever he wished—another man, another race. It was at a willing *girl* that he balked. Contrary to his wife's assumptions, he had himself been unfaithful to her six—he thought it had been seven but he could only count six—times since their marriage, always, of course, with a willing girl. In fact it was out of fidelity and respect for Angela that he could have these quick affairs with women he would assuredly never wish to be the mother of his children, and indeed with women who quickly bored him. He thought Angela was not sexually excitable. He thought this was appropriate and seemly in mothers. He could not and would not entertain the proposal that she might have a love affair. It was too far-fetched. It would bore him were he asked to do so.

To be accurate, not all of his conquests were demoted to matters of indifference to him. The first was not a conquest. Betsy Burger was a law student when Charlie was in the graduate school in New Haven, a dark-haired good-looking girl she was then, with thick eyebrows and a mole she kept blackened on her upper lip. She had long slim fingers and was given to poking one into her opponent's chest to emphasize her point. She was always with men, and she was always arguing with them. Charlie met her when occasionally she floated along with the drift of late-evening beer-drinkers. It happened one night that they were the only two cruising and she asked him, with what was clearly a single intention in mind, to come up to her apartment with her. This he did, and made love to her, and recalled not the act itself, but *her* indifference upon their later social encounters, as though she had no record of their having shared anything more intimate than a pint of beer, as though an evening of doing anything, let alone what, with him, Charlie Lewes, was so unmemorable that she might honestly bite her lip if asked to place him.

Through the years she would not subside. He always knew something or other about Betsy Burger. That she married a career diplomat, he read in the *Times*, and also that they'd postponed their honeymoon because of a jammed docket *she* had. Inevitably his mother-in-law was to know and admire her. Once Margaret asked Charlie whether he had run into her when he was at Yale, and he said Yes, and from then on she would courteously pass along news about her from time to time. She had left the diplomat and married Bolkonsky, the director of the Metropolitan Symphony Orchestra.

This experience of the bed would not lie still for Charlie because of something else he knew about Betsy Burger which was that she was very thick with one girl, a student at the Conservatory of Music, and that this student, a kind of intense unnerving woman, was secretly (but he, Charlie, knew it) Ed Hardie's mistress when they were all in New Haven together, and continued to be so, and that he, Charlie, managed to cut down that Betsy Burger in absentia by his perverse tilting at Ed, and through Ed at Angela, and it was a private joke upon himself and all of them. Did he know he was engaged in some interesting psychological shenanigans? Sure.

Meanwhile he never saw Betsy after New Haven, and if he were to meet her would not be interested in a woman who must be nearly fifty. She would bore him.

Charlie felt no more unfaithful on his side of the double standard, male couchant, than Angela couchante considered herself on hers. If she asked herself how far in these last years she had departed from an unquestioning acceptance of what has been classically understood as marital fidelity she would have acknowledged that she had felt it entirely; and not only in deed but more significantly in mind. She was sometimes overwhelmed by the exaggerated absorption societies gave to sex. For herself she now thought of the sexual part of a relationship as immensely small. And altogether a private matter. And how could she convey this to Christina and the girls as they grew up without putting in jeopardy their safety and even their sanity? Did one have to be forty to know? Tina had already announced she doubted she would marry, that marriage was a contract for a woman's body too debasing to be party to. "Oh my Tina, Tina, your father is right," she thought. "Sex isn't a political act. The caring, the tenderness, the mutual respect with which two free and independent people can come to each other, that's a glad marriage, Tina." Angela, the mother, could still think in favor of a glad marriage, but her own experience with caring and tenderness and mutual respect, in fact with love, occurred with a man she wasn't married to, and in fact with two men.

One morning the summer before, she was sitting squeezed in the kitchen of the farmhouse with Annie while Caroline put up her countless jars of green beans, that were healthy and economical and disagreeable to the taste. "I can tell you one thing," Caroline assured them with great satisfaction. "I hate this job." They were talking about a very absorbing sexual matter themselves. There was a large brown paper bag with beans spilling onto the white-enamel kitchen table, and Annie and Angela were cutting bean ends off with paring knives. "You might as well do something besides warm the seat of a chair, ha-ha," Caroline the wit said to Angela, handing her the knife when she had sat down. It was sometimes difficult, Angela found, to face Caroline with a knife and not thrust it into her.

"You probably won't be very surprised to hear we're talking about Louise," Annie said to Angela.

"Now what's she done?"

"She doesn't sleep with Will."

"Annie! What kind of talk is that?" Caroline said in an angry voice.

"Well, I'm just making a long story short, Mother. After all, that's what we've really been talking about."

"I just don't understand," Angela exclaimed with visible bewilderment, "how other people's intimate private relationships become common knowledge."

"Because they tell," Annie said reasonably. "Didn't you know about Will and Louise?" Angela grunted assent, and Annie continued, "So I said to Mother he ought to have taken a mistress a long time ago."

"How do you know he hasn't?"

"And I said, 'I may be old-fashioned, but I don't believe in adultery, and I call a spade a spade,'" Caroline announced yet again.

"But if they can't stand each other, Caroline?"

"There's always the divorce courts," she announced severely.

"Will won't leave Louise with poor Suzie. You know he won't, Mama. It's really an impossible situation."

"Nobody can tell me anything about impossible situations," Caroline boomed. "I myself have had to put up with a man who's been chased by women and flattered and had his head turned, and it turns very easily, I can assure you——"

"Why did you put up with it, Caroline?"

"Listen, Angela, he saddled me with all those children. Why should I stand for his taking off and leaving me to all the work of bringing them up and keeping the house? It's his family, and he belongs in it, and that's where I've kept him."

"You shock me, Caroline. You sound as though you have the right to own another person body and soul."

"Don't be too shocked," Annie said lightly. "She hasn't been all that successful." Her mother ignored this.

"You're just asking for trouble, Angela, if you take that attitude. Before you know it Charlie will be off with the next pretty young thing who wrinkles her nose at him. And you're no spring chicken any more, you know."

Angela shuddered as her mother had shuddered before her.

"Every marriage has its ups and downs," Caroline said heartily as she clapped the lid down on the blue-enamel cooking pot that Angela remembered to have been her grandmother's. "I love my husband and he loves me. We're just the average American couple" (escaped from a soap opera in about 1936, Angela believed).

In the days that followed her return from Provence, Angela struggled with a revulsion against marriage, although not her own marriage, she thought. Caroline interposed her gaunt formidable body and sinewy soul to act as spearhead to Angela's passionate assault upon this institution. She checked off all the Porters, opened the door to the lives of her neighbors, threw a fierce look at the friends she and Charlie had, and concluded that marriage was not a good place for women. They did poorly in it. It was hard to think of a married woman at the top of her form. And they weren't good for the men, and they were terrible for the children. Nobody was making it. When she thought of a stringent, delicious, refreshing lasting love between two people, she thought of Jo and Bill, beautifully illicit.

111 CHAPTER TWENTY-FIVE *111*

*I*F you read about somebody, a diarist, for instance, or an essayist, that "he is looking for the man beneath the man," you know what is meant. Now, with the times what they are, it is what is happening to woman. She is after the woman beneath the woman. Angela's pursuit of her grandmother merged with the pursuit of herself. To pursue yourself is an interesting and absorbing thing to do. Once you have caught the scent of a hidden being, your own hidden being, you won't readily be deflected from the tracking down of it. There are consequences. Angela was aware upon her return from Europe that the ballast in her, the center of her gravity, had shifted once and for all away from the orderly compliant wife and mother who trimmed and tacked not only to keep them all afloat, but to show the world what a damned proud little fleet could sail out under the Lewes ensign. She realized, and it was like cold salt spray in her face, that the meaning of that game, that play, had vanished.

And what was fiction and what was fact? The very fictive quality of her semi-secret third-floor life was rooted in her belief that she was now a writer, which was romantic. Her writing nourished her absorption in her grandmother—that there was One who went before her and marked the way— which was certainly romantic. Upstairs in that fictive life she undid, knot by knot, the strings attached to the use of her woman's mind and woman's will, and shaken free she moved into the most intimate relationship with not one but two men: surely the most romantic aspect of it all.

But in fact it was downstairs rather than up where her life with Charlie called most insistently upon her powers of imagination and invention. That was where the fiction really was. For the first time she acknowledged a division between herself and her husband so serious as to make her falter in her determination to hold that plot together, that plot, their marriage. What was upheaved by the issues of drugs and sex which came to the surface on either side of her trip to France was the tiger mother in Angela, the fierceness of her maternal reaction to what she saw threatening her children. Charlie and she were split on these visceral issues which made a bad fissure in their mutuality. She could treat with Charlie and win on the drug business, because, after all, he would not insist that Adam's or anybody's inalienable right was being violated over LSD. He would yield to what he would call her emotionalism in the matter. It would not be the first time he'd yielded on that score. On the other hand, the matter of a woman's sexuality for Angela had become indivisible from a woman's autonomy. This is what she now thought to be entirely true, and she could not unthink it. The implications of that truth resonated like soundwaves into infinity, is what she had begun to believe. She could disguise them from Charlie, but she would not from Tina and the girls, nor even from Adam. And where that truth would lead her own self she couldn't say.

From her classic familial responsibilities she would dart out to Edmund. A most *un*utilitarian melding their love was: a most openly arrived-at, a most frank, most freely exchanged love with an underside private and illicit. Angela wanted to make love out of caring, she said to Edmund. Not really out of passion. Call it what she would, he said.

This love was unutilitarian, and it wheeled along kaleidoscopically, as did everything every day now for her, with the exception of that singular suspension in midair that she had felt on the flight from Boston to Paris en route to Marseilles, the maiden transoceanic flight of the newly autonomous Angela. Up in the sky, disconnected from all her assignments, she felt herself off on a chase that seemed scarcely creditable, that seemed fraudulent, contrived, that was tax deductible and floated by a rich husband. She sat anonymous between two meaningless people, their heads banded with earplugs, eyes locked to a television screen, drinking mechanically. It was too painful to take them in. Down plunged her soul. She was now singularly accountable to herself, and herself was insufficiently surprising. A life with that self in charge would be tediously predictable. She needed people, if not roles. She dozed. They kept waking her to feed her. It was like a hospital, that same brand of uncaring care.

But then came the light. The depression, the boredom of the flight gave way as its trajectory had them run to meet the sunrise and they landed in an almost empty airport on a glorious early summer morning.

Orly is a vast, tiered hangar for the sorting and processing of people, but there was hardly anybody in it this dawn, and each exchange Angela had with customs, with flight checks and baggage was quick and personal. And meanwhile the sun was up, and it was a French sun, and Angela's spirits plunged up, cross-Atlantic and counterclockwise. She caught sight of herself in a huge mirror and was shocked at how handsome she was. Why was she handsome *now?* Why wasn't she when she was young, when it was appropriate?

Because, was the answer, now the moulding of her face showed, the good bones. She had finally lost her babyfat was what it was. At forty-two. And she must have laughed to herself, because she heard the most unexpected, "What are you grinning about, Angela?" and it was John Lowood, who greeted her with a great warm hug and kiss, in Paris, which he did not do in Boston.

"Well, my goodness! What are you doing here?" Angela asked, but Angela knew. "I thought you were in Cannes!"

"I was in Cannes, but now I'm here meeting your plane."

Angela understood that the Lowoods were having a kind of annual gathering of the clan in Cannes or Monaco or wherever there was the regatta, because of Charlotte Brontë the sailing sister, and the convenience of the Santayana branch, coming up from Milan. Vickie who was a *young* wife, was very suited to this International Set stuff, but old John didn't seem to have a place in that world. He didn't seem to have a place anywhere. Angela had never met Vickie, but Jo and Bill knew her, and Jo said she was very attractive, angular, small-breasted, and disarming, that her hair was sunbleached actually by the sun and she wore it chopped short and uncombed and her skin was brown summer and winter and she smelled rich and she didn't wear any underclothes. It wasn't a criticism. "I like Vickie," Jo said, "but it's no great mystery why he's at loose ends with her. He ambles along the edges of her life like a good-natured, somewhat bored patron of a prodigy, like somebody who couldn't actually be expected to sustain an interest in a child, however clever."

Had he ambled along the edges of life itself? Who was he? What had he done? Angela looked at his dear familiar face across the taxi seat from hers, but knew very little of him, only one small sunny patch of a large expansive unknown stretch of inner self. Lowood had cultivated sixty years of inner self, which may have been sixty bitter years, and she knew only a patch, but on the face of him there was nothing telltale. He was tall, lean, a little *fané*, with a high bare brown crown to a narrow skull, and where his hair was gone she could watch the pulsebeat at his temple. His nose was long and pointed, a genus-anteater of a nose, a delicate probing nose, and his manner was easy and elegant. It was hard to have him come from Newark. He wore with seeming indifference a dark-grey suit and an oxford-cloth pale-blue shirt, clothes that exactly suited the handsome man he was: he wore them as if he didn't know what he had pulled out of his closet. Angela said her reservation was on the Rue de Rivoli, and John said he was staying near the Luxembourg Gardens. "I've come to bring you back there with me, if you will," he told her, and his eyes wrinkled suddenly with old age and pain and passion and need. She had never never seen that need in him. He took her hand and watched the concern and uncertainty in her face. The mobility of Angela's expression was notable and seemed to record all her feelings as efficiently and relentlessly as an electrocardiograph does the rhythms of the heart, but in effect the mobility dissembled and protected her as much as control and impassivity did somebody of less volatility, like Lowood, usually, in fact.

"Well," she said, a little breathless, "perhaps we should go someplace and talk about it."

"We have a long ride into Paris. Let's talk about it, of course." The radio was booming the Beatles' "I want to hold your ha-an-and." Angela was aware of the intense physicality of this holding of hands.

"Holding hands is a very intimate thing to do," she found herself whispering. "Even to hold a child's hand. It's very touching."

"I know you so well and love all that I know and now I want to touch you, touch all of you. So the question is, dear, do you not want to be touched by me?"

"No, John, I can't say that. That wouldn't be true."

"And I suppose the second question is whether you have a . . . moral thing about . . . being unfaithful."

"Not initially!" She laughed quietly, wondering about herself, her situation. It was all wondering, no assessing. She seemed to be floating easily into a second pair of arms and caught herself thinking vaguely, "How will it look? What will people say?" She was laughing at the absurdity of herself and he didn't ask her what she meant by "Not initially." He was diffident, had always been careful about intrusion. She loved that in him. For that matter she loved it in Edmund. This made her laugh some more. And then she asked him, "Has your wife— Do you think Vickie has been unfaithful to you?"

"I don't know," he said thoughtfully. "I don't know her that well." It was a curiously funny answer, she thought.

"What about Charlie?" he asked.

"I had the idea that he never— But I don't know him that well either, I guess. But," she continued with hesitation, "it isn't Charlie——"

"It doesn't matter. Only if you want to come all the way to the core of a man, of me. If you *want* to do that."

"That means that I would have to be quite free of 'a decent respect to the opinions of mankind?' . . . The *wisdom* of institutionalized values . . ."

"Quite free of what is quite dead, at least."

"Loyalty isn't dead."

"No, no, but who is to define *disloyalty* for you, or for me, or for anybody? You already have experienced a kind of new consciousness, Angela, in which *you* will evaluate, *you* will judge what is right for you. You have slipped out from the hold. You can't slip back under again, not as a true believer, in any case."

"So that if I go back with you, it's a higher morality I obey?"

"You laugh and laugh. Will you be laughing all the time that I am making love to you?"

"Oh no," she said, and her eyes unexpectedly teared for a moment. Then it was settled, she thought. Actually it was settled at the first sight she had of him that morning.

The morning *after* they were sitting in their bedroom at a table set for breakfast at the open-shuttered open window just at the height of the trees in the summery Jardin de Luxembourg. John had asked, "How are you the morning-after?" Angela smiled assent but couldn't think of anything to say. He was confident and began to scan *l'Express*, and she thought of the answer she wouldn't give him; "I've discovered that I have a proclivity, a natural bent, one might say, for being loved and wanted and needed by a man—by a man or two. In an affair like this I am being put to optimal use."

He looked up and asked, "Why are you laughing *now?*"

"I'm happy."

tttt CHAPTER TWENTY-SIX *tttt*

*J*OSIE came down to the library in the house in Northampton and said to her mother, "I have something very sad to tell you, Mama. I heard on the radio that E. M. Forster died today." It was the seventh of June 1970.

"How tender of one's child to accept that his death—somebody so remote as an author—would be a personal loss," Angela said to Jo. Josie was fourteen now, a tall intellectual girl who kept her long fair hair parted in the center and pulled back to a bun the way Jo did, because Jo did, for whom she was named. Sometimes the effect was of a big wise blond madonna with hexagonal horn-rimmed eye-glasses. She and Angelica, who was now twelve, were the only ones left in that large house. About an hour after the two older women learned that Forster died they learned that Bill died. They had been waiting to hear it.

The burial took place two days later in the cemetery in Moriches. If there is some sort of ideal funeral, Bill's was ideal. People cried and cried with real grief. The ones who were close to him and watched the wasting and the pain of the last six months were relieved. It was those final six months that Caroline, who had always claimed Bill, actually took possession of him. He was never sent to the hospital: she nursed him all the way. Angela was concerned that he might chafe under her constant superintendence. "We are both quite contented, as far as the circumstances allow," he assured her. Jo relinquished him. She was a nearly constant visitor to the apartment in Springfield, but she was content to sit with her sister in the kitchen drinking coffee.

The cemetery lay green and sunny at the bottom of the wall of black pines. The gravestones were flanked by geraniums and little American flags left from Memorial Day. Drawing around Adam Porter's plinth the oldest live generation was flanked by grown children and grandchildren. Charles stood at the foot of the freshdug grave in which the coffin had already been lowered. He was holding the Xeroxed sheets of a Forster essay, waiting for the large number of people to settle before he pulled out his reading glasses. Angela was on the one side of him, Jo on the other, and they had decided, those three together, that they wouldn't read Frost any more, that Frost had betrayed them by being a great poet but a small man, too small. At Margaret's funeral two years before it was Bill who spoke, but he used his own words, not being a literary person, and was very touching. Her headstone was just a few feet beyond him. Angela remembered how put out the family was when her grandfather came home all those years before with his title to a cemetery plot, how they thought he had been flattered and gulled, what a folly it was, and how expensive. But there is a necessity to deposit human remains somewhere, an emotional necessity as well as a logistical, and Angela reflected that if she herself died now they would probably put her by her mother, whereas if there were no plot, if her bullheaded grandfather hadn't such a patriarchical regard for himself, every living Porter since would be a potential waste-disposal problem.

Angela cared very much to be in the line of a lineage, to come from a past, have a personal history that linked to her grandmother, to have held her grandfather's hand when she was not more than five on a Memorial Day, as sunny and mild a day as this, when she watched an open touring car lead the parade with three shriveled old Civil War Veterans bunched side by side in it, wearing the caps of the Union Army. The next year there was only one of those veterans.

She looked around for Angelica and Josie. She wanted to tell them about the Civil War veterans. They were standing, all three girls, with their father. Charlie had called her the day before.

"Angie, Tina told me about Bill's death. Listen Angie, I loved that guy. I'd like to go down to the funeral if it's all right with you."

"Oh, I think that would be very nice, Charlie."

"Angie, are you sure? Are you all right?"

"I'm very all right, Charlie."

When they'd hung up she folded into the armchair in the library and cried as she could not remember crying for a long time. And for what and for whom? For Bill and for E. M. Forster and for her finished life with Charlie.

That life finished most unexpectedly.

The winter that followed Angela's return from France was a long season of discontent for her. She finished the first draft of her novel, but it failed, she felt, as fact as well as fantasy. She reworked the whole of it at fever heat: it seemed to curdle. JSM foundered as an adviser.

"You can't sleep with people and keep your detachment," she said to him severely.

"Yes. In time. It's a matter of getting your sealegs."

"Has it happened to you before?" She was surprised.

"Once in a while. Not often." He laughed at her surprise.

So that upstairs she wrote to no avail and downstairs she

plunged into a determination to reconstitute the good working relationships of all of them, to no avail. The children were
difficult. That is to say, they were going their own ways.
Tina had shared an apartment with the now-tainted Sally in
Cambridge that summer in spite of her father's irritation.
("Abortions aren't catching, Daddy." "Don't be so fresh-
mouthed, friend!" was the way their irresolute exchanges
went.) Charlie told Angela that he was sure the O'Brien boy
was there too, and Angela was sure, and temporized and was
politic. Adam rather slouched through that summer with the
job of assistant park attendant, did very little work, detested
what he did do, was moody, and Angela was certain he was
smoking marijuana. She felt he was not open with her about
anything and she drove him back to school with a sense of
foreboding. In February he was suspended for having drugs
in his possession, but he won, thank God for herself she felt,
an appeal. Charlie was in Kansas City for ten days, and she
called him and for the first time in their marriage asked him
to come home. It took him three days to do that. Inevitably,
with so many children, there were other undercurrents of
concern, the one coming to the surface that winter being
Josie and her eyes. Josie was very nearsighted and the question
was whether there was something more serious besides. She
was about ten then. Every morning Angela went from room
to room to wake the children for school. When she leaned
to kiss Josie her sleepy head would pop up and her eyes would
open wide, then crease nearly shut as she smiled and tried to
make out her mother's face and reached out an arm to grope
for her glasses. Every morning. Finally it was determined
there was nothing the matter with her eyes, "Except she
can't see through them, is all," her mother would say in great
relief.

Angela felt the strain of that winter as a principal partici-
pator, of course, but also as spectator. She questioned the

sanity of her situation. That is to say she didn't really wonder whether she was going out of her mind, but she knew that she was *going;* had become the opposite of that stolid woman rooted in tradition, stilled and soothed by it. She was uprooted, radicalized, and had moved from a static to an evolving condition. So the question was not whether she was going out of her mind, but whether she was going mind and soul so far beyond, or at least wide of, the self that had played Charlie's wife, the self he had picked and kept, that it would remain sane to uphold his illusions.

But things settled. There followed several seasons of muffled calm. Angela set on a shelf in her aerie, a speckled-cardboard lawyer's box containing the exhausted body of the story of her grandmother. Thereafter regularly she spent four hours at her typewriter, and countless hours stolen from her orthodox life sometimes with Edmund, often with Lowood. In 1966 the *Altantic* bought a story, and she was released from the spell of being unsellable. She had begun another novel, this time drawing upon little from her own life. Meanwhile Charlie's finished manuscript was an uncannily long time in reaching print. Nineteen sixty-eight was the year of his distinction. He had finally managed to clamber up to the topmost tier of his profession where the air was rare: two prestigious institutions made firm bids for him. It was in that astonishing and cataclysmic year, 1968, that all the Porters worked for Gene, then all the Leweses switched to Bobby, and then Margaret Porter flew back to New York from the Democratic National Convention in Chicago, and fell asleep on the plane and never woke up.

Angela was struck by her loss. Many people cared for Margaret. Charles mourned her, and she had loved Charles. It was really the truth. There were simultaneous conflicting truths in their life, and they got through them, all told, summed up, pretty well.

On the following raw autumn Election Day Angela walked home with Angelica after marking her ballot with a pencil, to see a workman marking her street with two broken lines of red paint ("I betchoo I could hop across those lines Mama, without touching!"). Death marks for the two giant elms, it was—the city's elms—at the bottom of their lawn. ("Just be sure you wait till that paint dries, old girl.")

"Oh Charlie," she said to her husband when he came home for dinner that night, "they've marked our two elms!"

Charlie blinked and shook his head as if to clear it from another matter that absorbed him. "Well," he smiled, patted her, was affectionate but fidgety, "We knew it was only a matter of time. We'll put in a double row of maples. How about that?"

She smiled and said, "How about that? How about that? About that it can be said that the Dutch Elm Disease will not kill the maples. DDT will do that. American know-how will do that. Elms, maples, beech trees, earthworms and people. It's all over."

"The voting get you down?"

"I'm up."

"You look funny. Was there a letter from Adam?"

"That is my philosophical look. We did get a letter and he sounds pretty much in command of things." Adam had entered Harvard the previous fall and did not drop out until the following spring and was lately situated in Saskatchewan on a communal farm with two other Harvard men and a Radcliffe girl who would not sew but would reap. "And," said Angela, "I spoke to Tina this morning. She refused to vote of course."

"She's right. She shouldn't vote."

"She isn't. She should."

"She shouldn't vote and she shouldn't shack up with that derelict . . ."

Charlie flicked his eyes uneasily at Angela and went into the kitchen to pour them both a drink.

"What's the matter with *you?*" she asked.

"I think you know."

"No, I don't."

"Listen, Angela, we've been playing cat and mouse with each other for a long time now. Let's stop."

"What do you mean?" Her mouth went dry.

"I mean it's time to be honest with each other. I think we better lift the lid."

"Lift the lid? You mean and let hope out?" She had intended nothing by this remark about hope, a silly mechanical response she bought time with, time to scan the scripts she had prepared against this day.

"Hope, yes. It is my hope that you'll tell me what they've been saying to you about me, what you've seen . . . what you think."

"I think you're a damn queer Pandora."

"Angela! For God's sake! I'm pleading with you to face this issue between us. I know you saw us last night!"

"Saw who?"

"Come on, Ange, I caught your eye when you passed us getting out of the car."

"For goodness' sakes, Charlie, I didn't see anybody!"

"My God, you're so wrapped up in yourself you don't even know what you're seeing! You're so *removed!*" Charlie was unexpectedly fortified by this evidence of his wife's growing inattentiveness, his wife's *dereliction.* "It's been impossible to talk to you about anything. About Adam, for one thing," said Charlie, ready himself not to face the issue between them. "I would have given him an ultimatum: you leave Harvard, then that's it with us. We're finished."

"We would have been finished."

"And what you've let Tina do to herself!"

"Charlie, who the hell was that girl I didn't see you with getting out of the car last night when you caught my eye!" She was angry.

"Don't you really know who it was?" He was angry.

"Barbara Goldman?" Angela asked vaguely, knowing Charlie liked her. Angela was in fact groping a bit wildly, so entirely surprised was she to be performing in Charlie's playlet, while not knowing Charlie's plaything.

"Are you out of your mind? It's Cathy Compton! My God, I didn't want to tell you this way." He sincerely regretted his sincere fury.

"Little Cathy? Why don't you have an affair with her?" Angela smiled, dazed and bemused over its being this pretty little senior, a friendly, helpful, and thinking upon it, *regular* visitor toward whom Angela felt part fond, part bored.

"I *have* been having an affair with her," Charlie barked, his fury now unregretted. "I neglected to ask your permission, I know. If I realized how generous——"

"You want to *marry* her?" Angela's voice was high and quiet with disbelief. And then she said in a gentle affectionate way, "She's just a baby," and by this unforgivable remark Angela extended Charlie's permission: he *could* marry Cathy Compton. It was not her finest hour, she knew. It had never dawned on her to wonder about Cathy or anybody else. She had indeed been classically inattentive. She was bowled over by his announcement, bouleversé.

There ensued a most agreeable, civilized separation and divorce. They were both extremely considerate. There was no problem about money. She was to have the houses, of course. He had been offered a job at Princeton: he and Cathy would live there. Whether they reduced or heightened the anguish of the children by their appearing to be never-before so in harmony, they couldn't say. Everybody claimed to be shocked, but not very shocked; except for Angela who was truly stunned for a week or two.

Two years later the second Mrs. Lewes did not of course come to Bill's funeral. Charlie took the full morning sun of that sad solemn day and absorbed it handsomely. He had a beard running from his sideburns to a goatee, all very brown and very trimmed, and he looked like a young nineteenth-century poet, his former wife thought; just what he meant to look like, she thought. Angela appeared older than he by several years in the same full sun. She liked to see her daughters with their father; although it hurt her that Tina would show up at a funeral dressed for a strike, her skirt so short, and with sandals on her bare feet. ("I don't *own* shoes and stockings, mother!" "I would have floated you!") Just next to Tina was a groomed daughter of Bob Drinkwater from Atlanta, whose skirt was provocatively short but not *politically* short. Did Angela want her daughter to look so safe and square? At Bill's funeral, yes.

"It's as well she's renounced marriage," Angela had said to Jo about Christina, "because otherwise there would come down the aisle our beautiful white-satin bride with a red fist painted on her back."

"But you could have the bridesmaids wear pink fists and pale-green fists and matching knapsacks. Lovely."

As it turned out about the Atlanta girl, she was head of Women's Liberation in the Medical School of Emory. Will's Sally was in it as well. The most interesting looking of all their young was Sally, with her carrothead and rather aquiline nose and her crisp bearing. She would go into psychiatry. She stood between her mother and her father. Little Suzie had died three years before, but her father had not therefore left her mother. People were wrong guessing he would. People said the Atlanta son and heir wouldn't cut his hair to come north for this family affair so he was left behind, but he couldn't have made a mark against Annie's boys, who looked like twin Allen Ginsbergs. They were young to produce such beards, Angela thought. Precocious. Perhaps they were false. Annie wore a bouffante wig and held her stoical mother's arm and looked very calm. Her elusive husband, whose own long hair was done by a Stylist evidently, twitched a bit at her rear. Ted Drinkwater, who was a doctor in the air force and in uniform, sported sandy-colored earlocks and little curls at his neck, and his wife wore a mini-skirt. Were they making a statement too? What statement? Everybody was doing his own thing in the costume business. There was a Mardi Gras quality even to funerals these days.

Angela would have had to say frankly about her son Adam who was at her other elbow that he was the most attractive of the young men there, and was after a couple of years on his farm in Canada bewilderingly matured. Ursula was with him, the young woman. She was a tall angular girl with brown hair that she wore to the shoulder. Angela had never met her until the day before and wished that Adam would cement the thing and marry her, and wondered immediately, why she would wish that? The old ways of wishing die hard, catch you out.

She searched for Edmund's head above the crowd. She loved that head. John Lowood was At Home on the Riviera again, regatta time. She loved that head too. People wondered whether she would marry again, but she had carefully made an emotional arrangement with herself that precluded marriage. She saw that.

Her father was bereaved by this death, and his voice broke as he read his essay and placed Bill in "the aristocracy of the sensitive, the considerate and the plucky." Angela and Jo wept for the broken voice.

To conclude from all this emotion that Angela grieved at

the turn her life had taken would be to misconstrue the meaning of her spate of weeping. Whether a person is born with a sense of autonomy or painfully and joyously achieves the sense of self that has hitherto eluded him, he will not thereby be freed from contradictory emotions, from wistfulness, longing, loneliness. By far the larger portion of Angela's tears were shed in gratitude for her release.